Alice-Miranda
Keeps the Beat

Books by Jacqueline Harvey

Kensy and Max: Breaking News
Kensy and Max: Disappearing Act
Kensy and Max: Undercover

Alice-Miranda at School
Alice-Miranda on Holiday
Alice-Miranda Takes the Lead
Alice-Miranda at Sea
Alice-Miranda in New York
Alice-Miranda Shows the Way
Alice-Miranda in Paris
Alice-Miranda Shines Bright
Alice-Miranda in Japan
Alice-Miranda at Camp
Alice-Miranda at the Palace
Alice-Miranda in the Alps
Alice-Miranda to the Rescue
Alice-Miranda in China
Alice-Miranda Holds the Key
Alice-Miranda in Hollywood
Alice-Miranda in Scotland
Alice-Miranda Keeps the Beat

Clementine Rose and the Surprise Visitor
Clementine Rose and the Pet Day Disaster
Clementine Rose and the Perfect Present
Clementine Rose and the Farm Fiasco
Clementine Rose and the Seaside Escape
Clementine Rose and the Treasure Box
Clementine Rose and the Famous Friend
Clementine Rose and the Ballet Break-In
Clementine Rose and the Movie Magic
Clementine Rose and the Birthday Emergency
Clementine Rose and the Special Promise
Clementine Rose and the Paris Puzzle
Clementine Rose and the Wedding Wobbles
Clementine Rose and the Bake-Off Dilemma

Alice-Miranda Keeps the Beat

Jacqueline Harvey

PUFFIN BOOKS

PUFFIN BOOKS

UK | USA | Canada | Ireland | Australia
India | New Zealand | South Africa | China

Penguin
Random House
Australia

Penguin Random House Australia is part of the Penguin Random House group of
companies whose addresses can be found at global.penguinrandomhouse.com.

First published by Puffin Books, an imprint of Penguin Random House Australia
Pty Ltd, in 2019

Cover and internal illustrations by J.Yi
Cover image of musical notes © Martial Red/Shutterstock.com
Cover design by Mathematics xy-1.com © Penguin Random House Australia Pty Ltd
Typeset in 13/18 pt Adobe Garamond by Midland Typesetters, Australia

Printed and bound in Australia by Griffin Press, part of Ovato, an accredited
ISO AS/NZS 14001 Environmental Management Systems printer

A catalogue record for this
book is available from the
National Library of Australia

NATIONAL
LIBRARY
OF AUSTRALIA

ISBN 978 0 14 378603 0 (Paperback)

Penguin Random House Australia uses papers that are natural and recyclable products,
made from wood grown in sustainable forests. The logging and manufacture processes
are expected to conform to the environmental regulations of the country of origin.

penguin.com.au

For Ian and Sandy

Chapter 1

Alice-Miranda's fingers tapped rhythmically on the desktop as the song played over and over in her head.

Caroline Clinch glowered beneath her blunt fringe. 'Enough!' the woman barked, causing the entire class to jump in their seats. 'That is terribly distracting.'

'And *that* wasn't,' Jacinta whispered, garnering several giggles from her classmates.

Alice-Miranda looked up. 'Oh, sorry, Mrs Clinch. I hadn't realised.'

'I don't know what's going on with you lately,' the woman replied, shaking her head. 'You're always tapping your foot or drumming your fingers. I would suggest you take up a percussion instrument, but music teachers are a bit thin on the ground around here ... Mr Trout might be able to point you in the right direction.'

'Thank you, Mrs Clinch – that's a marvellous suggestion. I'll look into it,' Alice-Miranda replied with a winning smile.

Cornelius Trout was the Music teacher at Winchesterfield-Downsfordvale and also accompanied the Winchester-Fayle Singers, who had recently lost their conductor, Harold Lipp, the Drama and English teacher at Fayle School for Boys. Mr Lipp had moved to Los Angeles to be with the love of his life, Frau Grizelda Furtwangler, a talented and highly strung musical director. They had met on the set of *The Life and Times of Nellie Williams*, a film which starred a number of the students from both schools, though it was Caprice Radford who had won the biggest child role. Since then Professor Winterbottom hadn't been able to find a suitable replacement for the man and Mr Trout didn't feel up to taking the group on his own, so the Winchester-Fayle Singers had been on an extended hiatus.

Alice-Miranda grinned to herself. She wasn't about to say so, but she'd already found a teacher. The whole thing had come about quite serendipitously and she was enjoying herself more than she could ever have imagined, but had decided to keep it a secret until she had something worth sharing. It wasn't easy to get away two afternoons a week without anyone noticing, although it helped that Millie was at tennis lessons on the same days and Jacinta had picked up gymnastics again. Despite no longer competing, Jacinta reasoned that it was a good way to stay fit and had also enrolled at an acrobatics school in Downsfordvale on Saturday mornings.

Mrs Clinch stalked to the whiteboard at the front of the classroom. 'So, what number to the power of three will give us a solution of 512?' she said with her marker poised in the air. Her eyes narrowed as she spotted the tiny girl with chocolate curls gazing out the window. 'Alice-Miranda, do you know the answer?' the woman asked with an arched eyebrow. While she liked the child well enough, she thought it wouldn't hurt for her to be caught out just once.

Alice-Miranda looked at her and smiled. 'Yes, I think so, Mrs Clinch. I believe that it's eight. Eight to the power of three is 512?'

Caroline paused, her lips quivering. 'Yes . . . yes, it is,' she said before turning back to the board and rolling her eyes. 'Well done.'

Chapter 2

'Wow, look at the sky!' Alice-Miranda exclaimed as she and her friends reached the end of Rosebud Lane. It was a wash of pinks and blues.

'It's so pretty,' Chessie gushed. She raised her right hand in the air and fanned it about as if she was trying to capture the scene on an invisible canvas. 'Like a painting by Turner or Constable.'

The girls had recently attended an exhibition featuring works by both artists. The excursion had proved particularly inspiring for Chessie, who had been sketching almost non-stop since. Her work had caught their Art teacher Miss Tweedle's eye, prompting the woman to suggest that Chessie develop something for the village art show.

Jacinta twisted her long ponytail around her finger. 'I like to think of this time of year as Goldilocks weather – not too hot, not too cold, but just right.'

'That's very literary of you, Jacinta,' Millie said, pushing her glasses up the bridge of her nose. 'And I must say I'd much rather be reading fairytales than that awful book Mrs Reeves set before she left.'

'I prefer summertime, when I can spend all day by the pool,' Sloane said. 'Except that when we're at home, in Barcelona, Mother orders me to fetch her drinks and snacks and rub her shoulders with sunscreen. She treats me like a slave. Although I do love to tease her about all those giant poisonous skinks.'

'Skinks aren't poisonous, are they?' Chessie said, wrinkling her nose.

'Of course not, but my mother doesn't know that,' Sloane replied with a cheeky grin. 'Whenever one appears, she hotfoots it inside and I get a break.'

'Poor September,' Jacinta said, shaking her head. 'Don't you think that's a bit mean?'

Sloane raised an eyebrow. 'You have met my mother, haven't you? For a long time, "mean" was her middle name, closely followed by "vain", "selfish" and "stupid", but I suppose she has her good traits too . . .' Sloane paused for a moment then shrugged. 'It's hard to remember what they are sometimes.'

'Nonsense,' Alice-Miranda chided. 'It's true your mother has made some interesting choices, but you and Sep have helped her on the straight and narrow. She was a wonderful chaperone on our trip to China.'

Chessie sighed wistfully. 'I wish I'd been there with you all. You've had the most amazing adventures together.'

'Trust me, you've come at the best time.' Jacinta nudged the girl playfully. 'You wouldn't have wanted to know my mother or Sloane's back then.'

'She's right.' Sloane nodded. 'We have plenty of time yet for our own escapades.'

'Well, I think September and Ambrosia are fabulous,' Alice-Miranda said.

Sloane and Jacinta looked at each other and rolled their eyes.

'The small one is completely delusional,' Sloane said.

'As always,' Jacinta agreed.

'Which is exactly why we love you,' the pair said in unison. They each wrapped an arm around Alice-Miranda's shoulders and gave her a squeeze.

The five girls were on their way back to the boarding house after enjoying a long barbecue at Wisteria Cottage with Jacinta's mother, Ambrosia. The woman had also invited Lucas and Sep to join them, but the lads had a cricket match against their archrivals, Shedstone College, miles away in the village of Upshed. Jacinta had been terribly disappointed as she'd barely spent any time with Lucas this term. Now that she was in year eight, school was always so busy and weekends were just as tricky. Jacinta wondered if Miss Grimm and Professor Winterbottom had planned it that way. She and Lucas got to speak on the phone every Thursday evening, but it wasn't the same. Then again, she was a little worried that she wouldn't be able to resist kissing him if they spent time together in person, and that would likely land them both in big trouble. After their trip to Scotland, where they'd shared their very first sneaky smooch, they'd agreed to cool it for a while – at least until they were a bit older.

'Your mother is a great cook,' Chessie said. 'That pear and walnut salad was delicious and her chocolate cake was perfection.'

'It still surprises me every time,' Jacinta confessed. 'When I was younger, Mummy couldn't even make toast – well, maybe she could, but she never did. She was too busy going to parties and getting herself photographed for *Gloss and Goss* and worrying about whether her look was "right now" or "last week".'

The girls giggled. Chessie couldn't imagine Ambrosia being like that at all. While there was no denying the woman had an uncanny knack for putting things together – from her clothing to the house decor – she clearly adored Jacinta and was a devoted mother.

Alice-Miranda rested her head on Jacinta's shoulder. 'That was a lifetime ago and look at her now – your mother is an award-winning fashion journalist. She helps Mrs Parker with the village show committee and she's also become an expert gardener. I don't think she buys into any of that other nonsense these days.'

'Your mother and Aunt Charlotte have had a lot to do with bringing her around,' Jacinta said, looping arms with Alice-Miranda. 'And you're right – I have to stop dwelling on the past. For so long I thought Mummy hated me, but I think, really, she hated herself. Now she's become the woman she was always meant to be, she's *much* happier.'

The group walked on in companionable silence for a minute or so before Chessie asked a question that drew a collective gasp from her friends. 'Do you ever hear from your father, Jacinta?' she asked innocently. Little did she know that the man was never mentioned because he was something of a sore point.

Jacinta pulled a face. 'No, and I don't care if I never do again – not after the way he left me and Mummy. He's a scoundrel who doesn't deserve us.'

'I'm so sorry. I didn't realise,' Chessie said, biting her lip.

'That's the spirit, Jacinta,' Millie said, nodding her approval. 'Although I do think it's sad that you've lost your title these days, seeing as you've become such a reasonable human being and all.'

Jacinta frowned. 'What are you talking about?'

Millie grinned with a cheeky glint in her eye. 'The school's second-best tantrum thrower.'

'Was I really?' Jacinta asked.

'Absolutely!' Millie laughed.

'But you weren't scared of me, Alice-Miranda,' Jacinta said, shooting the girl a quizzical look. 'I remember you marched into that gymnasium on your very first day and I bellowed at you, but you just stood there and asked me what the matter was. I have to say I thought you were the strangest person I'd ever met.'

'You didn't bother me at all.' Alice-Miranda smiled. 'But your tantrums were legendary and that one, as I recall, was quite impressive.'

Chessie sighed. 'I wish I could have seen it.'

'I'd say Caprice is now the frontrunner for best *and* second-best tantrum thrower these days,' Jacinta said.

Millie rolled her eyes. 'Thank goodness she's gone to the National Eisteddfod this weekend or she'd have insisted on coming to the barbecue despite the fact she seems to hate all of us.'

'She definitely hates you,' Jacinta quipped. 'That's not even up for debate.'

'I suspect Caprice finds it awfully hard not to be jealous that we're such good friends,' said Alice-Miranda. 'I'm sure she wants to be part of the group, but she doesn't always know the best way to go about it. We shouldn't give up on her.'

The girls walked arm in arm in a wide line before Jacinta, who was in the centre, charged forward, propelling the rest of them ahead of her. They laughed and stumbled as Jacinta turned them in a circle, spinning like a top. The girls' cries echoed through the air, then ceased unexpectedly. The perfectly painted spring sky was now pierced through the middle by a plume of smoke.

Alice-Miranda gasped as the black smudge grew darker and thicker. Jacinta began running towards the village. 'Come on!' she cried over her shoulder.

Without a moment's hesitation, the others raced after her, hoping against hope that the reality wasn't as they feared.

Chapter 3

Tabitha Crowley hung the last of her blouses in the wardrobe and turned her attention to the small pile of sweaters that were going into the bottom drawer of the chest under the window. In comparison to her previous school, this studio flat was huge. It fit a double bed, a wardrobe and chest of drawers, a small kitchenette, study area and bathroom. A two-seater couch sat against the far wall, opposite a small television set. Tastefully decorated, the flat was a world apart from her accommodation at Marchant's Academy. She still couldn't believe she was here. Winchesterfield-Downsfordvale was the sort of place teachers stayed for life, and why wouldn't they? With the gorgeous grounds and superb facilities, not to mention students who had a reputation for hard work and good manners, it was simply irresistible.

Tabitha finished putting away her clothes and opened a box containing her folders. Everything was colour-coded and had a strict order and she soon filled the bookshelves before sitting down to memorise her timetable. She was about to make some notes for her first day of classes when a loud knock on the door caused her to jump.

'Who is it?' she called.

'Caroline Clinch,' a clipped voice replied.

Tabitha quickly checked her hair in the mirror, took a deep breath and opened the door to a stern-looking woman with a blunt fringe. She wore navy pants and a crisp white shirt with smart navy loafers.

'Hello,' she said. 'I'm one of the teachers – Mathematics. I thought you might like to join us downstairs for an early supper. The Fayle sisters are renowned for their Sunday spreads and it's a good opportunity for you to meet some of the other staff.'

Tabitha sighed inwardly. She really wanted to get on with her planning for the week, but even with her somewhat limited experience, she knew that faculties could be tricky and it was always best to have a good understanding of the lay of the land to work out your allies and potential foes. She smiled broadly. 'Thank you – Miss Clinch, is it?'

'Caroline is fine, and I'm Mrs Clinch to the children,' the woman replied.

'Does your husband teach here too?' Tabitha asked. She'd often found that to be the case in boarding schools.

'No,' the woman replied abruptly.

Tabitha decided to leave that alone. It was none of her business and she didn't like people asking about her situation either, although she did harbour high hopes that Winchesterfield-Downsfordvale would provide the kind of family environment she'd been deprived of for so long. 'I'll fetch a cardigan and be right out,' she said, and closed the door before returning a few seconds later.

Tabitha walked alongside the woman down the hallway that housed several staff flats. She hadn't yet met any of her neighbours and wondered if Caroline was one of them.

'That's me across there,' Caroline said, pointing to a door, 'and Mr Pratt, who teaches Science, is next along. The largest quarters at the end are vacant. That's where Mrs Reeves and her husband, Gerard, lived before he took ill. It's a two-bedroom apartment – they often had their son, who's at university, come to visit them.'

Tabitha recognised the name as belonging to the woman she was taking over from. She had no idea of Mrs Reeves's circumstances and hoped the woman's husband was on the mend. 'Do all of the staff live on site?' Tabitha asked.

'Not everyone, but most,' Caroline replied. 'Caledonia Manor was originally refurbished with the intent of turning it into a teacher training college, but the red tape was horrendous. So Miss Grimm decided that she would extend the prep school into secondary instead. It was a very popular decision, particularly after the scandal with Mildred Jelly and Professor Crookston over at Sainsbury Palace School. The woman was a tyrant – I can tell you from personal experience, as I used to work there and was ever so grateful to gain a position here. The girls are lovely for the most part. There are a couple you might find tricky, but when are there not? Anyway, the manor was a right wreck – or at least half of it was for years until the restoration. There are some photographs in the foyer, if you're interested to see the evolution of the place. It's quite extraordinary.'

Tabitha could only agree as they wandered past antique side tables and impressive artworks. There was a whole floor of classrooms below and rooms on the ground floor, which must have played host to grand dinner parties and balls in days gone by. The original owners, the Fayle sisters, lived in an apartment that opened out onto the garden at the rear of the building. Tabitha was yet to meet them.

Caroline ushered her through the foyer and down another long passageway to a door marked 'PRIVATE'. She gave a gentle knock, then pushed it open into a shorter hallway, which led to a large kitchen where two elderly ladies were preparing dinner. One pulled what smelt like lasagne from the cooker and the other was pouring tumblers of soda water. Caroline introduced them and Tabitha immediately noticed the dreadful scar on Miss Hephzibah's face. She tried not to stare but her gaze must have lingered too long.

'It's all right, dear,' Hephzibah Fayle said with a kind smile. 'It happened when I was a young woman. I know it's confronting, but it's just a scar and it doesn't hurt.'

Tabitha was mortified at being caught gawping. 'I-I'm sorry – I didn't mean to upset you,' she said, fiddling with the buttons on her cardigan.

'Oh no, you didn't. I was far more sensitive about the children in the village calling me "the witch in the woods" on account of my burns and the fact that for a long while I had rather a lot of cats.' Hephzibah shook her head and chuckled. 'When I think back now, it was utterly deserved and, if I were a small child, I'd have been quite scared of me too.'

'Nonsense. No one ever had reason to be alarmed by you, dear sister,' Henrietta said, placing a hand on Hephzibah's shoulder.

Tabitha spied a large tabby asleep in a basket by the range and a black kitten preening itself on a chair in the corner. She wondered how many cats there still were. Henrietta Fayle set the deep dish of pasta onto the table, then fetched a pair of silver salt and pepper shakers from the pantry.

'I'd hidden myself away here for decades, but it was only after I met Alice-Miranda that I realised exactly what I'd become,' Hephzibah explained. 'She helped reunite me with Henrietta and it was Alice-Miranda's father who organised for the manor to be rebuilt and made useful again. It's as if we've both been given a second chance at life.'

'Alice-Miranda?' Tabitha asked.

Hephzibah smiled. 'You'll meet her soon enough.'

'And you will never have met anyone like her before, I can assure you of that,' Henrietta chimed in as she added a generous drizzle of balsamic vinegar to the garden salad.

Tabitha nodded, surmising they were talking of a relative.

'Anyway, come and sit down. We're expecting Miss Reedy and Mr Plumpton too. That poor lady works so hard that I cornered her husband and made him promise she would take some time off over the weekend,' Hephzibah tutted.

Minutes later, a tall, thin woman entered the room, trailed by a short, round man in a waistcoat. They were followed by a fellow with wild silver hair and a moustache that looked as if a furry caterpillar had crawled onto his top lip and set up camp there. He was wearing a lab coat, which seemed unusual attire for a Sunday afternoon.

Tabitha was swiftly introduced to her colleagues, who took their seats at the table.

'Please make a start, everyone,' Hephzibah said, nodding at the delicious spread of lasagne and garlic bread, crispy chat potatoes and salad.

'Have you been working this afternoon, Mr Pratt?' Henrietta asked.

Percy Pratt broke off two slices of garlic bread and placed them on his plate. 'Yes, it's important to ensure the experiments are going to be successful. The girls need to see competence along with enthusiasm.' He glanced in Mr Plumpton's direction. 'Wouldn't you agree, Josiah?'

The short, round man grinned. 'Oh indeed. When you love science as much as we do, there's no room for error.'

Percy coughed into his handkerchief. Josiah Plumpton was a walking catalogue of errors.

Never in his life had he witnessed such bumbling yet no one else seemed to notice – not the girls, not the headmistress and especially not Josiah's besotted wife. It was as if a jolly demeanour was enough to plaster over all of the cracks – no, *craters* – in the man's teaching. One day he'd take a step too far and people would finally be awake to his ineptitude.

'How wonderful that you were able to start so soon, Miss Crowley.' Josiah Plumpton smiled at the woman as he passed the salad to his wife. 'Livinia wasn't looking forward to picking up all those extra classes.'

'Don't be so silly, Josiah. I would have managed,' the woman said, batting a hand in his direction. 'I'm only sorry I was away for your interview. You see, Miss Grimm is technically still on maternity leave and I've been running the school since her daughter, Aggie, was born. Tell me, what are some of your favourite texts to teach?'

Given Livinia was currently acting headmistress, she'd been miffed that Ophelia Grimm had arranged the interviews for Philomena Reeves's replacement while she was at a conference. It had caused some tension between the pair, particularly

21

as Livinia had always thought of herself as the head of English. The fact there were only two members of the faculty was beside the point. While she agreed that Tabitha Crowley seemed suitable, if a little inexperienced on paper, Livinia would have preferred to have met the woman before she'd been offered the job.

Come to think of it, Ophelia had undermined three of her recent decisions – by letting Caprice off her detention to attend the National Eisteddfod when the girl had been horrid to several staff members, lightening Percy's extracurricular load because he'd complained of teaching more classes than Josiah, and promoting Benitha Wall to the position of acting deputy head after the children's trip to Scotland even though no such position had existed before. If that was the case, Livinia was going to demand it was hers when Ophelia returned to work full-time.

Tabitha bit her lip and a long silence ensued.

'Darling, you mustn't put poor Miss Crowley on the spot like that,' Josiah said cheerfully. 'She's only just settling in.'

'Nonsense. It's not a trick question,' Livinia replied. She'd had two bites of supper and could already feel her hackles rising. If the woman couldn't conjure a single book to mind, how was she going to keep up with the children?

The group stopped speaking and all eyes fell upon Tabitha.

'Well,' she began, 'there's *To Kill a Mockingbird* – a classic for the ages – as well as Shakespeare and Dickens, but I'm also rather fond of newer texts, which the children find more relatable. I think it's important we support contemporary authors and don't get stuck in a time warp of nostalgia for the books we experienced as children.'

'Is that so?' Livinia pursed her lips. 'Would you care to enlighten us?'

Tabitha rattled off a list of at least ten titles, none of which Livinia was familiar with. She went on about the awards some had won, waxing lyrical to an appreciative audience.

'Goodness me, you've made them sound so thrilling that I'm going to seek them out on my next visit to the library,' Hephzibah said, and was joined by enthusiastic nods from the other diners.

Livinia set down her knife and fork on her plate. 'I'm sure you understand that the texts are set for this term. You'll have to keep those other books in mind for next year, assuming you make it through your probationary period and become a permanent member of staff, of course.' She offered the woman a pinched smile.

Tabitha felt her stomach twinge. 'Yes, of course. I'm looking forward to making a start with the Winchester-Fayle singers next week too,' she said, eagerly changing the topic.

Livinia's brow furrowed. 'What do you mean? You were appointed to teach English.'

Percy flinched inwardly. The woman's passion was admirable, but she'd soon learn that putting one's hand up for extracurricular activities wasn't very sensible.

'And that's absolutely my first responsibility, but Miss Grimm noted my musical accomplishments and said that she would talk to Professor Winterbottom about having me take over the group,' Tabitha explained. 'Music has always been a passion of mine, so when Miss Grimm mentioned that the Winchester-Fayle Singers were in need of a director, I leapt at the opportunity.'

'Oh, how thoughtful,' Caroline enthused. She hoped the woman leapt at every co-curricular opportunity so the rest of them could get on with the jobs at hand.

'Marvellous!' Josiah exclaimed, waving his fork in the air. 'The children have been adrift since Mr Lipp found love with Frau Furtwangler. Livinia worked with them for a little while, but she doesn't have the time nor the training. Isn't that right, dear? They'll be thrilled to have someone with your skills at the helm again, Tabitha.'

Livinia stared at her husband, willing him to close his mouth. 'Frankly, Miss Crowley, I doubt you're going to have the time. Mrs Reeves had a very full load and the sheer amount of marking alone is enough to send any teacher reaching for the aspirin.'

Tabitha Crowley plastered a smile across her face. 'Thank you for the warning, Miss Reedy, but I'm a stickler for routine and I've never had a problem with workload before. I can promise you that.'

'Well,' Livinia said with a raised eyebrow, 'let's just make sure that the English classes always come first and the Winchester-Fayle singers fit in around your schedule.'

'Of course.' Tabitha swallowed a large gulp of soda water and hoped it would settle her churning stomach.

Hephzibah met her sister's eye across the table, prompting the woman to speak.

'Tell us, dear, where do you come from?' Henrietta asked, trying to shift the mood.

'North,' Tabitha said, and left it at that. If Caroline Clinch could get away with a one-word response, then she could do the same.

Chapter 4

As the girls sprinted towards the smoke, it became apparent that it was coming from a building in the high street. Being late Sunday afternoon, the road was all but deserted with just one lonely car parked outside Herman and Marta Munz's general store.

'It's Fattoush!' Millie yelled.

Flames shot out from under the restaurant awning and thick grey gusts billowed in an endless, rolling wave.

'Has anyone got a phone?' Alice-Miranda puffed, and was answered with a cacophony of noes.

'I'll go to the Munzes' to call the brigade,' Jacinta said, and raced away.

'Don't the Abbouds live upstairs?' Sloane said.

'Yes, they do.' Alice-Miranda looked up at the second storey and that's when the true horror of the situation hit her. Pressed against the window was a child's face. Her tiny hands were banging on the glass and she was screaming. 'Oh no, one of the little girls is inside!'

A narrow alleyway separated the building from the hairdressing salon next door. On the other side, the shop was attached to the bakery. If the brigade didn't get there soon, the entire street could go up. Alice-Miranda used her jacket to cover her mouth and nose, then tore through the thick haze to the back of the building, hoping there was a way to get to the second floor. Chessie, Millie and Sloane followed, shielding their faces too.

Millie pointed to a small balcony accessed by a staircase leading from the garden. 'Up there!'

'Shouldn't we wait for the brigade?' Chessie shouted.

'There's no time.' Alice-Miranda scampered up the stairs and used her jacket to grab the doorhandle. It wasn't hot but it was locked.

Millie picked up a flowerpot and hurled it at the adjacent window, shattering the glass, then carefully reached inside and unlatched the door. The air was black and choking, but with their jackets providing makeshift filters, Alice-Miranda and Millie plunged into the haze. Outside, Chessie grabbed a hose and turned the tap as far as it would go. With Sloane's help, the pair sprayed the flames that were escaping from the restaurant and licking at the back of the building. But it was a losing battle. Despite their best attempts, the fire was intensifying.

Meanwhile, inside the flat, Millie and Alice-Miranda charged through from the small kitchen and into the living room, where they found the little girl slumped on the floor by the window. She couldn't have been more than three or four years old. Millie scooped her up and retraced her steps to the landing, where she passed the girl to Sloane and Chessie.

Sirens wailed in the distance. Around the front of the shop, a crowd had begun to gather.

Jacinta searched the group for her friends, her stomach in knots. The fire truck roared into the street and pulled up with a whoosh of air brakes. As the crew of six leapt out and rapidly set to work, Jacinta jiggled on the spot. After a few more seconds, she couldn't stand it any longer. She dashed into the wall of smoke and down the alley.

'Stop!' one of the firemen yelled, but she was already gone.

She rounded the corner into the back garden and found Chessie bent over a tiny girl, who was coughing and sputtering. 'Where are the others?' Jacinta asked. Her eyes widened when Chessie pointed to the flat.

Jacinta met Millie and Sloane at the door. They were supporting a woman who was sobbing while cradling a bigger child in her arms. She let out a cry of relief when she saw another of her daughters was with Chessie.

Two firemen wearing breathing apparatus with oxygen tanks strapped to their backs ran to her.

'Is everyone out?' the tallest of the officers yelled.

The woman shook her head. 'My husband is downstairs and my babies are sleeping in the attic,' she said, her voice shaking with fear. 'My oldest . . . I do not know where she is.'

Another two firemen raced into the garden, pulling a long hose behind them.

'Cover us,' the taller officer ordered as he used an axe to break down the back door of the restaurant. Tendrils of fire shot out like a dragon's tongue, but the other men held tight to the hose and released a torrent of water at the flames. It wasn't long before the firemen emerged with Mr Abboud. They laid him down on the small patch of lawn just as Constable Derby arrived on the scene.

'I'll take it from here,' the constable said, and used the radio on his vest to find out how far away the ambulance was. He was surprised to see Sloane, Chessie and Millie there with the Abboud children and their mother. 'Is anyone still inside?' he asked.

'Yes!' Millie said frantically. 'Alice-Miranda's up in the attic with Jacinta.'

'Good heavens,' the man rasped.

Two paramedics ran up from the rear lane.

'Over here!' Constable Derby shouted. 'It's Mr Abboud. He's breathing but it's shallow and he's suffered burns.'

The paramedics quickly realised they needed back-up. One called for help while the other tended to Mr Abboud, who had slipped into unconsciousness. By now half the village was standing on the other side of the building, in the high street, watching the events unfold.

Myrtle Parker was beside her husband, clutching his arm. 'I hope they got them all out. You know they have five children including the babies. Mrs Abboud has been pregnant for years.'

'The brigade's doing everything they can, dear,' Reg said, patting his wife's hand. Alerted to the unfolding drama by the Parkers, Ambrosia Headlington-Bear had hurried down to the high street and was standing beside her elderly neighbours, staring helplessly at the scene.

Herman Munz was there too, his mouth set in a grim line. 'If it vosn't for the children, the place vould have burned to the ground before ve knew it.'

'What children?' Myrtle turned to look at the man. 'You mean the Abbouds?'

'No, Jacinta and her friends,' he said.

Ambrosia's face drained of colour. 'But the girls are at school,' she said. 'They left Rosebud Cottage half an hour ago.'

Herman slowly shook his head. 'I'm sorry, Mrs Ambrosia, they are at the restaurant. I saw Jacinta run down the lane vith my own eyes. The fireman vos yelling for her to come back but she did not stop.'

'Dear God in heaven.' Myrtle's legs folded from the shock of it all. Reg only just managed to keep the woman upright.

'Look!' someone yelled. A face momentarily appeared at the attic window, causing a collective gasp from the crowd.

'Alice-Miranda, you get yourself out of there!' Myrtle Parker screamed.

'Alice-Miranda, where are you?' Jacinta cried out, then coughed fitfully. The air was hot and thick and scratched at her throat.

'Up here,' Alice-Miranda called. She felt her way through the gloom until her hands found the timber slats of a cot. She passed Jacinta the first infant, relieved to find the baby squirming and objecting loudly to being disturbed.

'There, there,' Jacinta cooed between sputters.

'Go!' Alice-Miranda ordered. She picked up the other child and pressed its face against her own. It was cold. For a second Alice-Miranda feared the worst until the child let out a startling scream. 'Oh, thank goodness! Cry as loudly as you like, little one,' she said. Holding the baby as tightly as she dared, Alice-Miranda scrambled down the stairs after Jacinta. They were met by Constable Derby and another officer who had arrived from Downsfordvale.

Not a minute later, the girls and babies were being checked by a second team of paramedics. Apart from looking like they'd been through a war zone, Alice-Miranda and her friends appeared to be fine. The Abboud children, on the other hand, would need to go to hospital for a thorough check-up and monitoring.

Their mother was hovering over the twins when she realised that her eldest daughter wasn't with them. 'Zahra!' the woman screamed, turning circles in the yard. 'Where is she?'

Flames shot up from the restaurant and had forced their way inside the flat. The curtains in the kitchen window were now well alight.

'Oh no.' Alice-Miranda raced over to one of the firemen. She shouted above the hissing and crackling to tell him that there was another child still missing.

'Are you sure she's in there?' the fireman called to Mrs Abboud.

'Of course!' But the woman wasn't certain at all. She had put the twins in their cot and gone downstairs to fold a mountain of washing. She remembered sitting on the edge of her bed and feeling overwhelmed with tiredness. She must have fallen asleep because the next thing she knew she was choking in a room full of smoke and her six-year-old, Esma, was tugging on her sleeve. The last time she'd seen her eldest daughter she'd been in the sitting room playing with Hatice. 'Hatice, where is Zahra?' she asked, but the child simply shrugged and laid her head on her mother's shoulder. Ada Abboud's eyes darted around the yard and back to the house. 'Please, you must find her!' she wailed.

The firemen pulled down their masks and charged up the stairs again. Alice-Miranda and her friends looked at the house expectantly. Chessie held her breath while Sloane whispered the only prayer she knew. All eyes were glued to the building. It seemed an age before the firemen reappeared, empty-handed.

'Zahra!' Mrs Abboud screamed, collapsing to the ground.

'She can't be in there,' Millie mumbled as fat tears streamed down her face. She wiped them away, leaving a smear of black.

There was an almighty roar as the roof caved in. The five girls huddled together, unable to tear their eyes away from the devastation.

The Abbouds had moved to the village and opened their restaurant around the same time Alice-Miranda had started school. At first people were wary. Myrtle Parker had been spotted several times with her nose against the glass, trying to peek between the pasted-up newspapers on the front windows. Two weeks later, a sign had gone up announcing the arrival of Fattoush, a Lebanese-Syrian restaurant with a modern flair. Fortunately, curiosity prevailed and it didn't take long for word to spread about Mr Abboud's delicious cooking.

The interior decor was like nothing the village had seen, with a huge mural of the ancient ruins of Palmyra on three walls and faux stone columns dotted throughout. While the food was far more exotic than most of the locals were used to, Fattoush soon became a favourite for all occasions. It was a true family affair with Mehmet in the kitchen while Ada and Zahra worked the floor with a staff of four.

'No one could survive that,' Sloane whispered.

The first ambulance sped off with Mr Abboud inside, its sirens blaring. Paramedics had loaded the twins and the two younger girls in the back of the second ambulance with Mrs Abboud, who was now sedated. There was nothing more to be done. If Zahra was inside, the operation had tragically gone from a rescue mission to one of recovery.

Constable Derby took a deep breath. He stared at the smouldering building. It was a miracle that the firemen had been able to contain the blaze, but it was hard to comprehend the family's loss. 'We need to get you back to school,' he said to the girls. 'Everyone will be worried sick.'

'But what about Zahra?' Chessie asked.

The man shook his head. 'I'm sorry.'

In her short life, Alice-Miranda had experienced quite a deal of drama and many adventures, but this was something so awful she couldn't believe it was true. Alice-Miranda had met Zahra a number of times when her parents had come to visit and taken her to eat at Fattoush. It was hard to imagine that, in the blink of an eye, the girl was gone.

Alice-Miranda clutched Millie's hand as they followed Constable Derby down the alley to the high street, where they were met by a rousing cheer. Ambrosia flew out of the crowd and enveloped her daughter. Myrtle Parker just about suffocated Alice-Miranda against her chest. Chessie burst into tears, as did Jacinta and Sloane. Alice-Miranda stared at the mass of blurred figures. It was as if the world was moving in slow motion ... until she spotted Zahra Abboud, walking around the corner as if it was any other Sunday.

Alice-Miranda ran as fast as her jelly legs could carry her. 'Zahra!'

The crowd gasped and turned to see Alice-Miranda grab the girl with both hands.

'What's happened?' Terror and confusion clouded Zahra's face. Her bottom lip trembled as she took in the charred remains of her home. 'Mama, Papa?' she screamed, trying to get away.

But Alice-Miranda held on to her tightly. 'They're alive – and your sisters and brother too. They've gone to the hospital in Downsfordvale.'

Tears sprang to Zahra's eyes. 'I'm sorry,' she sobbed. 'I'm so sorry. I shouldn't have been . . . It's my fault. I should have been watching the girls.'

'You have nothing to be sorry for,' Alice-Miranda said gently. 'Thank heavens you weren't home.' She gave Zahra one final hug before the police officer guided the girl across the road and into a car.

The street was quiet save for the hissing and crackling of the doused fire. It was Mr Munz who broke the silence. He began to clap and was soon joined by the rest of the village.

A single tear ran down Jacinta's left cheek. 'Well, that was a good surprise.'

'Absolutely,' Millie said. 'What a relief.'

But Alice-Miranda couldn't help wondering where Zahra had been. Her mother had seemed so certain she had been inside. The tiny girl shook the thought from her mind. It didn't matter – the important thing was that Zahra was alive.

Chapter 5

Myrtle and Reg Parker helped Ambrosia Headlington-Bear ferry the girls back to school, where they were greeted at the boarding house by a very anxious Miss Grimm and Miss Reedy. Ophelia, who had been alerted to the drama by Constable Derby, had arranged for Livinia to meet her at the Caledonia Manor Stables. She had then telephoned the children's parents to let them know what had happened – all except for Hugh Kennington-Jones and Cecelia Highton-Smith, who were trekking in the Andes for a month. Instead she'd notified Mrs Oliver, the family's cook, who said that she would pass on the message when she heard from the pair.

'Good grief, look at you all,' Ophelia Grimm gasped as she surveyed the soot-stained group. The rest of the girls in the boarding house were safely tucked away in the dining room, having their evening meal, and their housemistress, Petunia Clarkson, was under strict instructions to keep them there.

'It's nothing a shower won't fix,' Millie said. She licked her finger and wiped the back of her hand, smearing the black to prove her point.

'Come along, Myrtle,' Reg said, steering his wife by the elbow. 'We should head home.'

The woman looked at him as if he were mad. 'We're not going anywhere until we know the girls are all in perfect health,' she said, wrestling her arm away. 'Besides, I can make tea while Joan gives them the once-over.'

Sister Joan Guthrie had been a nurse for more than forty years and had taken care of the boys at Fayle for the past ten. She was beloved by all and not just because she had the best stash of lollies in the school. With her short crop of grey hair, stylish red glasses and practical trouser-and-shirt combinations, she was everyone's favourite surrogate grandmother. In the absence of their own school nurse, Livinia had called the woman to give the girls a thorough check-up.

'That's awfully kind, Mrs Parker,' Ophelia said, 'but we don't want to keep you.'

'Nonsense. I'm very useful in a crisis,' Myrtle insisted.

Reg sighed, knowing full well there was no point arguing with his wife once she had made up her mind. Ambrosia leaned down to whisper in Jacinta's ear. She hadn't let go of her daughter's hand since they'd alighted from the car.

'I'm *fine*! I've told you that ten times already,' the girl snapped, then promptly burst into tears.

Ambrosia pulled her in for a hug. 'Oh, darling.'

'Right, that's it. Tea and honey sandwiches for everyone.' Myrtle Parker marched inside and set to work in the kitchenette by the sitting room. Reg hurried to help her.

Ophelia and Livinia could see more tears were building. The ordeal had clearly been a shock for the girls, and no doubt a hearty cry would do them the world of good. Livinia took Sister Guthrie to set up in the infirmary across the hallway while the girls, clearly struggling to comprehend the full extent of what had happened, were ushered into the sitting room by Ophelia and Ambrosia. Millie sat on the sofa beside Sloane and surprised the girl by reaching across to hold her hand. Sloane didn't object. Instead she held on tightly and brushed stubborn tears from her face. Alice-Miranda stood beside Chessie, their arms entwined, while Jacinta clung to her mother.

Reg Parker walked over with a tray of sandwiches and Myrtle followed with the tea.

'Has there been any news on the Abbouds?' Alice-Miranda asked, passing a mug to Chessie before taking another for herself.

Miss Grimm shook her head. 'Not since Constable Derby phoned earlier to tell us the news. I suspect he'll give us an update as soon as he can.'

Miss Reedy called Millie over first to see Sister Guthrie. Thankfully, everyone was given the all clear. Jacinta had a cough, which probably hadn't been helped by working herself into such a state.

Physically, they were all in good health, but Sister suggested that it would be wise for each of the girls to pencil in a chat with a counsellor.

Petunia Clarkson appeared in the doorway. 'Excuse me,' she said with a tentative smile. 'Jacinta, there's a phone call for you.'

A sheepish look crept over the girl's face.

'It's probably your boyfriend making sure that you're okay,' Millie whispered, loud enough for everyone to hear.

'Jacinta is far too young for all that nonsense,' Myrtle tsked. Reg caught Millie's eye and gave the girl a wink. 'Besides, I've heard the boy's mother is getting married and is taking him to live with her and her new husband in New York. I wouldn't get too attached if I were you, Jacinta.'

The girl's jaw dropped. 'That's not true,' she said. 'Lucas hasn't said anything to me.'

Alice-Miranda was as surprised as her friend. She couldn't imagine her cousin keeping that to himself, but Myrtle Parker's knowledge of village gossip was notoriously reliable.

'It's not Lucas on the telephone,' Petunia said. She pushed a strand of brown hair behind her ear. 'It's . . . your father.'

The woman was met with a room full of wide eyes and open mouths. Myrtle's lips quivered. She was even more pleased that she'd insisted on staying.

'Daddy?' Jacinta wrinkled her nose. 'I can't imagine what *he* wants.' Without so much as a backwards glance, she was out the door and heading for the telephone booth in the hallway.

Ambrosia felt sick to her stomach. As far as she knew, Neville hadn't been in contact with Jacinta for ages. Actually, not since the night he had unceremoniously declared their marriage was over and told her she could go and live in the cottage in Winchesterfield permanently. Neville was a scoundrel through and through and had never been much of a father to the girl, but maybe he'd heard about the fire and wanted to make sure that his only child was okay. Perhaps the man was human after all.

Chapter 6

Alice-Miranda woke with a start, her brow peppered with tiny beads of perspiration. She pushed off the covers and tried to calm her breathing as the rain drummed a steady beat against the windowpane.

Millie looked up from her book. 'Morning,' she said, dog-earring the page she was on. She placed the copy of *Lord of the Flies* on her bedside table. 'I think you were having a nightmare. I gave you a shake earlier but got thumped on the head for my trouble.'

Alice-Miranda sat up against her pillows. 'Oh, Millie, I'm so sorry.'

Millie hopped out of her bed and padded over to sit beside her friend. 'I had a bad dream too,' she said. 'I hope the other girls are okay.'

'We'll be fine,' Alice-Miranda said, giving Millie a hug, 'but I'm pretty sure the Abbouds have lost everything. It's times like these that remind us to treasure each moment with those we love and not take life for granted.'

'Trust you to find that silver lining.' Millie grinned, then a pained look came across her face and she threw herself on the mattress as if she'd been dealt a heavy blow. 'Urgh!' she groaned. 'I just remembered Caprice will be back from the eisteddfod. I can't wait to hear how amazing she was,' she added sarcastically.

'Please try to be patient with her, Millie. You can't deny she's very talented.' Alice-Miranda glanced at the clock. 'We'd better get a move on. I still smell of smoke even though I practically scrubbed myself raw under the shower last night.'

There was a knock on the door and Mrs Clarkson poked her head around. 'Good morning, girls. How did you sleep?'

'Okay except for some bad dreams,' Millie said.

'Well, I suppose we might expect that for a little while.' The woman walked into the room and picked up Millie's uniform from where it had fallen off the back of her chair.

'I love that top, Mrs Clarkson,' Alice-Miranda said. 'Those flamingos always make me happy.'

The housemistress smiled, as that was exactly the effect she was hoping it might have – for her and the girls. She had taken an extra few minutes to get dressed this morning, locating her favourite blouse and navy trousers and adding a strand of pearls to the ensemble. 'You'll be pleased to know that Mrs Abboud and the children have been discharged from hospital. Unfortunately, the news is not so good for her husband. The poor man has suffered third-degree burns and has a very serious case of smoke inhalation. He's in intensive care. I'm sorry, girls, but I knew you'd want to be kept updated.'

'Oh, that's awful,' Alice-Miranda said. While she was relieved to hear that Mrs Abboud and the children were in good health, the thought of Mr Abboud in such a precarious state made her feel quite sad and helpless. Surely there was something she and her friends could do. She spotted a card on her desk and picked it up. It was from her Granny Valentina sending her love and best wishes for a happy school term. 'We should make Mr Abboud a get-well card from all of us,' Alice-Miranda suggested. 'Chessie could do one of her drawings for the front and we can create a collage or something on the back.'

Mrs Clarkson nodded. 'That's a lovely idea. I'll arrange for art supplies to be sent over from school. Now, you two had better make a move. I'll see you at breakfast.' Petunia wished she could bottle Alice-Miranda's thoughtfulness and share it among a few of the other girls. She'd already had a run-in with Caprice, who point-blank refused to take off the nail polish she'd worn for the eisteddfod. Petunia had resorted to threatening to remove it herself if it wasn't gone by lunchtime.

Alice-Miranda and Millie followed the woman into the hall, with their bathroom bags and towels in tow, chattering about what they could put on the card – perhaps not a picture of the restaurant but maybe a village scene would be nice.

★

Caroline Clinch looked up from the staff table to see Alice-Miranda and Millie enter the dining room. They were followed by Jacinta, Sloane, Chessie and Caprice. She'd spoken to the rest of the girls about not making a fuss, but her words had fallen on deaf ears. Upon seeing the group, Susannah Dare and Ivory Hicks stood up and clinked their spoons against their glasses.

'Three cheers for the heroes of the day!' Susannah called loudly, and the room erupted in overwhelming response. Even the teachers joined in.

Millie felt a lump in her throat and her eyes began to prickle. She brushed away the tears and took a deep breath.

'Really, girls, that wasn't necessary,' Caprice sighed, with her hand on her chest. 'It was a gruelling weekend and utterly exhausting, but I did it – National Eisteddfod Junior Champion once again.'

There was a collective groan.

Ashima Divall rolled her eyes. 'We're not cheering for *you*, Caprice. We're cheering for the others – they rescued the Abbouds from a fire yesterday in the village. The family would have died if it hadn't been for Alice-Miranda and the girls.'

'What?' Caprice snarled. No one had mentioned anything to her about a fire – not even her room mate, Sloane. 'That's hardly the biggest deal around. I just won the National Eisteddfod and I'm going to be on a new television show – surely that counts for something.'

'That's fantastic news, Caprice,' Alice-Miranda said kindly. 'Well done – we're all very pleased for you. Girls, I think Caprice deserves three cheers of her own.' The tiny child jumped up onto a chair and threw her hands into the air. 'Three cheers for Caprice!'

There were some grumbles but the majority of the students repeated their earlier effort, although with noticeably less enthusiasm.

'You could at least sound as if you mean it,' Caprice spat, and stalked off to the servery with her chin in the air.

'Seriously, I could punch her in the nose,' Millie said, clenching her fists.

'You won't, of course,' Alice-Miranda said. 'It doesn't hurt for us to give Caprice a bit of positive reinforcement every now and then – she works hard.'

Sloane rolled her eyes and picked up a tray. 'If only someone could teach her about humility, we'd all like her a lot better.'

'Good morning, Mrs Jennings.' Alice-Miranda smiled at the stout woman behind the counter. Rachel Jennings had been the cook at the senior school for a while now. She was quite a bit younger than Mrs Smith, with dark curls scraped into a messy bun. Her uniform was the same as always: a starchy white shirt with the sleeves rolled up, an A-line navy skirt paired with thick stockings and sensible brown shoes, and a navy apron over the top.

'Hello, dear, I've made scrambled eggs this morning. I thought it might be easier on your throats in case they're still sore from the smoke,' the woman said, giving the watery yellow blobs a swirl in the tray.

It was unfortunate that Mrs Jennings's skills didn't exactly match her enthusiasm. Despite undertaking bouts of intensive training with Mrs Smith and her assistant, Ginny, there were still a few dishes the woman had not yet mastered – scrambled eggs being one of them.

'Thank you,' Alice-Miranda said warmly, spooning the smallest amount she felt she could get away with.

'Oh, sweetheart, you'll need more than that to keep you going all day,' the woman said. She heaped a full serve onto the child's plate with a wink. 'Eat up.'

Luckily, Mrs Jennings did a much better job with the bacon and it was pretty difficult to ruin baked beans, so Alice-Miranda made sure she had plenty of both to mask the tasteless eggs.

'Did you all sleep okay?' Millie asked as the girls sat down.

'Like a baby,' Caprice sighed. 'I was so tired. Honestly, it was such a long three days – the waiting around was diabolical – but that was because there were so many competitors in my section. If only they'd known it would be a total waste of their time.'

'I wasn't talking to you,' Millie said to the girl, who immediately retaliated by poking out her tongue.

'Forgive me for thinking you might be interested in someone other than yourself,' Caprice retorted. She took a bite of her eggs and spat them out all over the table. 'Oh, that's disgusting.'

Alice-Miranda passed her a napkin.

'I talked to Mummy for a while before bed,' Chessie said, cutting herself a piece of bacon. 'I think that helped a lot. She said to tell you all how proud she is of what we did, although I got the feeling she was a bit mortified too.'

'And what about you, Jacinta?' Alice-Miranda asked. After the phone call with her father, the girl had whispered a few words to her mother then headed off to bed.

'Pardon?' Jacinta said, looking up from her plate.

'Are you okay?' Sloane asked. She'd noticed Jacinta hadn't said a thing all morning and had barely touched her toast.

'I don't know,' Jacinta replied. To say she was feeling mixed up would have been the understatement of the year. Right after talking to her dad, she'd telephoned the boarding house at Fayle and was surprised that the housemaster put her straight on to Lucas. Having heard about the fire, the boy spent the first five minutes telling Jacinta how brave she and the other girls had been. But it was

Myrtle Parker's gossip that was really on her mind. She didn't want to come straight out and ask if it was true, so instead she had told him about the call from her father. Her heart sank when Lucas revealed that he'd been speaking to his mother quite a bit lately too, and given their relationship had been strained for a while, he was feeling optimistic that things were on the up and up. Jacinta was sure that, if Lucas was planning to move to America, he would have said something. When he didn't, Jacinta failed to mention it either. And now she was kicking herself because, between thinking about her father, the fire and Lucas, she'd hardly slept a wink.

'What happened with your dad?' Millie asked. She exiled her eggs to one corner of her plate and popped a button mushroom into her mouth.

Jacinta took a bite of her toast and chewed slowly. 'He's, um, coming to see me.'

'When?' Sloane and Millie crowed in unison.

'This weekend,' Jacinta replied. 'He said that he has a lot of explaining to do and he wants to make things up to me.'

'And how do you feel about that?' Alice-Miranda asked. The thought of Neville Headlington-Bear being back on the scene worried her enormously, given the man's track record, but there was always a chance he'd undergone some positive personal transformation. And who was she to judge?

'Part of me doesn't want to get my hopes up,' Jacinta confessed, 'but part of me can't help thinking that maybe he's changed for the better. I mean, Mummy's a completely different person to what she used to be like. Why couldn't Daddy do the same?'

Alice-Miranda smiled at the girl. 'You can only take people as you find them.'

'Are you kidding me?' Caprice baulked. 'He's a deadbeat dad and, believe me, no one goes from foul to fabulous with a snap of their fingers – it doesn't happen.'

'You'd know,' Millie muttered.

Caprice narrowed her eyes at the girl. 'What did you say?'

Millie looked at her evenly. 'I'm just saying that all your promises to try to be a better human being after what happened in Scotland clearly meant nothing.'

Caprice stood up and slammed her hand on the table so hard that the room was immediately silenced. 'They did so!' she screeched. 'It's *you*. You're always mocking me no matter what I do. You don't even care that I beat everyone in the whole country to win the eisteddfod, which is a seriously amazing achievement – not that you'd know, seeing as you have *no* talent whatsoever!'

'Calm down,' Alice-Miranda implored the pair of them. 'You're both going to say something you regre–'

'How dare you!' Millie lunged towards Caprice, grabbing a handful of the girl's hair and yanking hard.

Caprice squealed, clutching her ponytail. She clambered over the table, knocking plates and glasses sideways before throttling Millie. Sloane and Jacinta leapt from their seats and were doing their best to loosen Caprice's grip.

'Girls! Stop that at once!' Miss Reedy boomed from the doorway. 'What a dreadful display. I will see both of you at Winchesterfield Manor straight after breakfast – and you will walk there in the rain!' Livinia turned to the young woman beside her. 'I am sorry about that, Miss Crowley. Millie and Caprice tend to push each other's buttons,' she whispered out of the corner of her mouth.

'Actually, Caprice pushes nearly everyone's buttons. Something to look forward to.' She cast another glare at the duelling redheads before proceeding to the front of the room.

Millie sat with her arms folded tightly in front of her while Caprice had conjured fat tears. Chessie passed her a tissue, but she slapped the girl's hand away, determined to stew in her misery.

The woman beside Miss Reedy did nothing to betray how she felt about the scene in front her. Alice-Miranda thought she must be mid-twenties at most, though she dressed with a style and elegance befitting someone far more mature. Her blonde fringe was swept back by two mother-of-pearl barrettes that complemented her navy pants suit and white silk blouse. A beautiful dragonfly brooch was pinned to her blazer lapel.

'She must be the new English teacher,' Chessie said. 'She's pretty, isn't she?'

Sloane had just been thinking the same thing.

'Good morning, girls,' Miss Reedy said. 'I'd like to introduce Miss Crowley, who will be taking over Mrs Reeves's classes. I'm sure that you will all make her feel very welcome.'

The girls burst into a round of applause, which Miss Reedy silenced with a querulous glare. She then looked at Millie and Caprice. 'You two had better hurry up and finish your breakfast. I will see you both at nine o'clock sharp.'

Livinia began to walk away when Miss Crowley gently touched her arm.

'I wondered if I might say something,' Tabitha said, earning herself an arched eyebrow. 'I'll be quick.'

'Be sure you are. I have to get over to the junior school,' Livinia replied, taking a step back to give the woman the floor.

Tabitha turned to face the group. 'Hello girls,' she said brightly. 'I am so delighted to be here and I can't wait to make your acquaintance. For those of you who are in my classes, I have lots of fun in store. I hope you enjoy drama and art and singing as I have been known to incorporate all of those elements into my lessons, and I am thrilled to announce that I will be resurrecting the Winchester-Fayle Singers as well.'

The hall burst into another round of applause. Jacinta was particularly pleased to hear it as that guaranteed at least an hour a week with Lucas.

Livinia frowned. The woman had been here all of five minutes. This was not the time to go making promises she might not be able to keep. Livinia could almost guarantee Miss Crowley's commitment to the singers would fall by the wayside as soon as she realised she'd bitten off far more than she could chew. 'Thank you, Miss Crowley. It sounds like you have many talents and we will look forward to seeing them in due time,' she said, and marched off towards the door. Livinia turned to discover that Tabitha had stopped to talk to Millie and Caprice. 'Miss Crowley, we need to go now!' she barked.

Alice-Miranda glanced over in surprise. Miss Reedy once had a reputation for being meaner than a dragon with a toothache, but she had mellowed considerably over the past few years. Ever since she'd found true love with Mr Plumpton, she was fun and cheerful and one might have called her breezy on occasion, but none of that was evident this morning. Miss Reedy hadn't even asked how the girls were feeling after what had happened yesterday and that was most unlike her. Alice-Miranda wondered what could possibly be the cause of such ill humour.

Miss Crowley whispered in Millie's ear, causing a smile to sweep across the girl's face. Unfortunately, it had the opposite effect on Miss Reedy and Caprice, who both looked as if they'd swallowed something particularly unpleasant.

Chapter 7

Ada Abboud cradled a twin in each arm as she gazed through the window into the hospital room where her husband was attached to a multitude of tubes and monitors. He had been in a coma since the fire and the doctors had explained that for now it was best that way.

'Hello dear,' said a lady with curly grey hair. She was wearing a pink pinafore over a white uniform and was pushing a tea trolley towards Ada. She manoeuvred her way past and stopped on the other side of the corridor. 'Would you like something to eat?'

Ada shook her head. 'No. Thank you, I am fine.'

'You must be hungry. At least have a biscuit.' The woman placed a couple of packets into Ada's pocket. 'I've left some for the children, and juice too,' she added, her blue eyes twinkling.

Hamza squirmed in Ada's arms and his sister, Miray, began to whimper. They were both hungry and Ada had been having trouble with her milk since the fire.

'I'll fetch someone to help you,' the tea lady said. 'I'm Sue, by the way.'

Ada's eyes filled with tears. The thought of starting over – again – was almost as overwhelming as the journey that had brought them to Winchesterfield in the first place. When she, Mehmet, Zahra and baby Esma had fled the bombs that had rained down on their city, Ada had wondered where they would end up. Anywhere safe was all she had prayed for. At first the villagers were wary of them – suspicious, almost – but Mehmet had such a bright smile and an infectious personality that it wasn't long before the residents embraced them. How could they resist? He was the happiest person she knew. Ada had fallen in love with Mehmet the day they had met, when he'd made her laugh at his silly jokes. Only Myrtle Parker had taken a while longer to win over. In the end it was Mehmet's falafels that did the trick. The woman couldn't resist them.

'Here, let me help you,' Sue said, taking Hamza in her arms. 'Don't you worry. I'll speak to someone. I'm surprised the social worker hasn't been to see you to sort out your accommodation.'

Ada reached into her pocket for a tissue as Miray's screaming grew louder. She had to feed her or else the matron would come. 'Please, give me my baby,' she said.

'I'll take him to the room for you,' Sue said, abandoning her trolley for the moment.

She followed Ada down the hall to the room and halted at the door. Feather down from the inside of two pillows was falling like snow and the two little girls were jumping on the bed as if it was a trampoline.

'Stop!' Ada yelled, startling them. She then spoke harshly in Arabic, causing Esma and Hatice to burst into tears. 'Enough! Or they will ask us to leave and then where will we go?'

The simple fact of the matter was that there was nowhere *to* go. Their home was destroyed and they had no family in the country. The nurses had been terribly kind, setting them up in an empty room with two beds and a large chair, but Ada knew they couldn't stay there forever.

'Clean up this mess, Zahra. You are the oldest and you should know better,' the woman scolded. 'But then what do I know about you? Always coming and going and not telling anyone where you are.'

Zahra's eyes hit the floor. She'd just run to the toilet for a couple of minutes and returned to find her sisters misbehaving. She'd told them to stop, but they wouldn't listen, and now it looked as though she was being irresponsible yet again.

Sue waited for Ada to settle on the bed with the twins before piping up. 'Would you like me to organise some formula and bottles?' she asked. 'I can get them from the nursery. The staff here are very appreciative of us tea ladies and I'm sure it won't be a problem.'

'Thank you,' Ada said gratefully. She hadn't wanted to ask for another thing.

As Sue stepped into the hallway, an idea came to her in a flash. She would call her friend Myrtle. Yes, that's exactly what she would do. There was nothing that woman couldn't fix.

Chapter 8

Millie and Alice-Miranda huddled under an umbrella as they dodged puddles on the path that linked Winchesterfield-Downsfordvale and Caledonia Manor. Caprice stomped along behind them, avoiding the cracks as she recited an old rhyme in her head. Alice-Miranda had thought it best that someone chaperone the two hotheads and had sought permission from Mrs Clinch, who agreed it was a very sensible idea. It was only a short detour — ten minutes at a clip — so she wouldn't be too late for her first lesson. Before the renovations, most of the girls had never realised how close Grimthorpe House was to the old stables and derelict manor, which had been separated by a thick patch of scrubby woodland. That was probably a good thing, given the stories that did the rounds, scaring the life out of many a new student at their midnight feasts (which always took place at nine o'clock because no one could stay awake until twelve).

'You'd better tell Miss Reedy this was all your fault,' Caprice yelled over the thrumming rain. 'If you weren't so awful to *me*, I wouldn't need to be mean to you.'

Millie held up her free hand. 'Speak to this because I don't care to hear your whining.'

Caprice screeched in frustration and kicked at a clump of mud, which flew into the air and splattered the backs of Millie's legs.

Millie turned to examine the brown flecks. 'Are you kidding me?' she exploded. Against her better instincts, she picked up a handful of dirt and threw it at the willowy girl. It splodged on the front of Caprice's tunic, spraying the girl's face and hair as well.

Alice-Miranda quickly wedged herself between the pair. 'Stop it,' she ordered.

'Or what?' Caprice sneered. 'You'll tattle to Miss Reedy and say it's all my fault because Millie is your bestie?'

'I asked you both to stop,' Alice-Miranda replied. 'Millie may be my dearest friend in the world, but you're my friend too.'

Caprice's eyelashes fluttered in surprise. 'I am?'

'Yes, and I'm sure everyone would be a lot kinder to you if you refrained from showing off and stirring trouble,' Alice-Miranda added. Millie twisted her lips to stop a smug smile from forming. 'Come on, we'd better hurry,' Alice-Miranda said as the rain began to beat down harder. 'And you shouldn't take every bit of bait she dangles in front of you,' she whispered to Millie.

The girls had been so distracted that they hadn't realised they'd reached the main school until Millie very nearly tripped over Charlie Weatherly. The man was bent down in his grey raincoat and hat, planting clumps of petunias along the edge of the path.

'Morning, girls,' he said, tipping his hat and creating a mini waterfall. He noticed that Millie and Caprice were spattered in mud but, judging from their miserable expressions, thought it best not to ask why.

'Oh, hello Mr Charles.' Alice-Miranda smiled at the old man. 'It's a bit wet to be out in the garden, isn't it?'

'I don't mind working in the rain. At least it's not cold,' he replied cheerfully. Decades of outdoor labour had rewarded him with deep lines on his forehead and around his cornflower-blue eyes that sparkled on this dreary morning. 'Well done for what you did yesterday. I hear you girls saved that family's life.'

'If it wasn't for Alice-Miranda being ridiculously brave and making the rest of us feel as if we could do anything, things mightn't have turned out nearly so well,' Millie said.

Caprice rolled her eyes. 'I don't have time to hear this *again*,' she grumbled and, shoving Millie out of the way, took off towards the back doors of Winchesterfield Manor.

'Excuse you!' Millie shouted after her.

Charlie shook his head. 'Miss Millie, you shouldn't let Caprice push your buttons. It isn't worth it.'

'So I'm told,' the girl replied with a sigh. 'I just can't help myself, but I promise I'll try not to let her get to me.'

Millie and Alice-Miranda said their goodbyes and ran to catch up to Caprice. The three of them sped past the portraits of generations of head-mistresses with their stern expressions and beady eyes, dripping water on the carpet as they went. It was funny to think that Miss Grimm would one day have her picture up there too, but hopefully she wouldn't look anywhere near as terrifying.

'Hello Mrs Derby,' Alice-Miranda said, announcing their arrival.

'Good morning, girls. Please take off your rain-coats and leave your umbrellas in the stand,' the woman said. She glanced up from her notebook and gasped. 'Good heavens. What happened?'

'Ask Caprice,' Millie said, glowering at the girl.

'I think I'd prefer not to.' Louella offered them a packet of wet wipes from the top drawer of her desk, then hurried around and set to work eradicating the mud from Caprice's and Millie's dresses. Alice-Miranda took one and attended to their grubby legs. 'At least you appear somewhat respectable now,' Louella said, stepping back to appraise them. 'Miss Reedy will see you shortly. She's meeting with Miss Grimm at present.'

Although Ophelia Grimm was technically still on maternity leave with baby Aggie, she had recently resumed some of her duties. Truth be told, she was itching to return to work. Ophelia had been biding her time, trying to find the right moment to inform Livinia that her tenure was about to be cut short.

Millie sat beside Alice-Miranda while Caprice took a seat at the opposite end of the room, as far from the other two as she could get.

'I should probably head back – we've got Science first lesson and you know how Mr Pratt doesn't like us to miss out,' Alice-Miranda said.

Millie reached across and grabbed her friend's hand. 'Please don't go,' she implored. 'Miss Reedy will definitely be more reasonable if you're here. You tend to have that effect on people.'

Louella Derby suddenly stood up and, without a word, dashed out of the room. Meanwhile, on the other side of the wall, it sounded as if a fight had broken out.

'Why did you employ her without having me interview her?' Miss Reedy's voice boomed.

She might as well have been standing right beside the girls, such was the tremor.

Alice-Miranda looked at Millie, who glanced over at Caprice, who raised a perfectly arched eyebrow back at her.

'There was simply no time, Livinia,' Miss Grimm replied loudly. 'I didn't want you to have to pick up more classes and Philomena had a heavy load. You couldn't possibly have done all of that on top of running the school. Anyway, you were at the conference. I was doing you a favour.'

Alice-Miranda grimaced. 'That doesn't sound very good,' she whispered, wondering if she and the girls should step out of the room.

'Well, she's not right,' Miss Reedy retorted. 'She's presumptuous and over-confident, and I have a very bad feeling about the whole situation.'

Louella Derby walked back into the room, wiping her mouth with a tissue. She straightened her skirt and sat down at her desk, only to be startled by the angry voices coming from the other side of the wall.

'You've done nothing to convince me that I should terminate the woman's employment, and we are obligated to give her a three-month probationary period. I can't get rid of her simply because you have a bad feeling,' Ophelia protested. 'We'd be sued and rightly so.'

The display case in the hallway, which boasted an array of highly polished trophies and sparkly awards, rattled as if a giant had stamped their foot.

'Well, you wait and see. She's going to be a disaster. I know it,' Livinia retorted, and the rest of the conversation subdued to a dull murmur.

Louella looked at the girls, her pointer finger aloft. 'Not a word to anyone about this. If I hear one whiff of gossip about what went on in there, I'll tell Miss Reedy that you were listening at the door. Do you understand?'

Millie and Alice-Miranda nodded.

'If you want to appear on that television talent quest, Caprice Radford, you'd better answer me,' Louella hissed.

Caprice's head bobbed up and down as the door to the study opened.

Mrs Derby smiled. 'Good. Miss Reedy is ready to see you now.'

✩

An hour or so later, Ophelia Grimm was about to rush out the door for Aggie's paediatrician appointment when she remembered something important. In the heat of her argument with Livinia, she'd forgotten to mention that she'd declined several enquiries from reporters seeking to interview the girls about the fire. She raced back to the office, but Livinia was gone. Louella was nowhere to be found either. Ophelia scribbled a note and placed it in an envelope marked 'Livinia Reedy – URGENT', then wrote Louella a message to make sure it was delivered as soon as possible. Ophelia sped to the flat and, in her haste to get to the car where Aldous and Aggie were ready and waiting, left her phone sitting on the kitchen bench.

With the front office empty, no one saw the figure enter and scoop up the letter for Livinia as well as the note addressed to Louella. Sometimes, one just happened to be in the right place at the right time.

Chapter 9

Alice-Miranda was despatched back to class with little more than a stern look and a flick of Miss Reedy's hand, while Millie and Caprice had been ordered into the study. The tiny girl decided to leave the umbrella for Millie in case the rain started again and, after farewelling Mrs Derby, walked out into the quadrangle, eager to get to her Science lesson. Mr Pratt had promised something fun last week as part of their unit of work on electrostatics and she always looked forward to his experiments. She skipped along the path, hoping she hadn't missed too much, and was pleased to see Miss Wall and Mrs Clinch walking ahead of her. She quickened her pace to say hello to the pair, who appeared to be in the middle of an animated conversation.

'Well, I'm glad that Ophelia has seen sense to make you her deputy,' Caroline Clinch said. 'It's the step up you need. You did a wonderful job with the girls on the leadership camp.'

'Thank you, Caroline, but I'm technically working for Livinia at the moment.' Benitha adjusted her baseball cap and pushed a rogue strand of hair behind her ear. She had recently replaced her rather tired school-issue tracksuits with a range of luxe activewear in Winchesterfield-Downsfordvale colours in a bid to give herself a more professional edge. 'I'm not sure what will happen when Ophelia is back in the hot seat. I imagine I'll be demoted and Livinia will officially become her deputy even though we both know I'd do the best job.'

'Gosh, I hope that's not the case,' Mrs Clinch said. Her nostrils flared as though she'd caught a whiff of an open sewer. 'Honestly, the power has gone straight to Livinia's head, and while Josiah is a sweet man, his teaching standards are nothing short of woeful – especially his practical work. It's patently obvious to all the staff and surely Ophelia sees it too.' The woman shook her head. 'We have to get rid of her. She's been here too long. In fact, I even heard Mr Trout say *he'd* had enough and that man is practically unoffendable.'

'*I* heard she was seriously annoyed about the new English teacher,' Benitha said.

Caroline nodded. 'You should have seen her giving the poor woman the third degree at supper last night. She's obviously jealous of Tabitha's talent and the fact she's newly graduated with a lot of innovative ideas, but that's precisely what we need around here – fresh blood.'

Alice-Miranda wished she'd made herself known before now. Hearing how unhappy Miss Wall and Mrs Clinch were about Miss Reedy and Mr Plumpton made her stomach churn. Staff morale was important in every organisation – she'd learned that from her parents. Miss Reedy had been so off hand towards Miss Crowley this morning too. None of it augured well. Alice-Miranda took a deep breath and said a rather loud hello.

The two women leapt into the air.

'Where did you come from, ghost child?' Benitha demanded.

'I accompanied Millie and Caprice to a meeting with Miss Reedy. I'm just on my way back to Science class,' Alice-Miranda replied. 'Mrs Clarkson gave me permission.'

'Oh okay,' Benitha said, softening. 'Great job yesterday, by the way. What you girls did was very brave.'

'And a touch foolish,' Caroline added. 'But you're all fine, thank goodness for that.'

'Yes, we are,' Alice-Miranda said with a smile. She hurried off to class, feeling rather out of sorts for having overheard the second uncomfortable conversation of the morning. Miss Reedy and Mr Plumpton were part of the heart and soul of Winchesterfield-Downsfordvale – she couldn't bear the thought of losing either of them, but it sounded as though the rest of the faculty had other ideas. Alice-Miranda didn't like feeling that the school was out of balance and at the moment the scales seemed heavily weighted against Miss Reedy, that was for sure.

*

A few minutes after ten o'clock, Millie and Caprice scurried through the lab door, having missed more than half of their lesson.

'What happened?' Alice-Miranda whispered to Millie when the girl hopped up onto the stool beside her. Mr Pratt was busy with the Van de Graaff generator, making Sloane's hair stand on end at the front of the classroom. The rest of the children were laughing and lining up for their turn, although the man assured them there was some serious learning to be done among all the fun.

'Miss Reedy was snappier than a Patagonian toothfish. She's making us do ten hours of school and community service and I'm banned from riding until it's done,' Millie moaned. 'Caprice isn't allowed to do the television show unless she finishes hers too. It's supposed to be on in a couple of weeks, so it's going to eat into her rehearsal times,' the girl added, brightening.

'That seems a bit harsh, especially considering the part you played in saving the Abbouds yester-day,' Alice-Miranda said with a frown.

'Miss Reedy didn't even mention that. She was in a filthy mood,' Millie said. 'Probably because of the fight with Miss Grimm.'

'I can't stand it, Millie. The idea of the teachers falling out with each other is too awful for words.' Alice-Miranda's mind was a whirl. When she'd first arrived at Winchesterfield-Downsfordvale, the staff and students were utterly miserable and she couldn't bear for the school to become unhappy again. While she wasn't planning to tell Millie about what she'd overheard on the way back – because that would be gossiping – something had to be done.

'Girls, would you care to share whatever it is you're discussing with the rest of us?' Mr Pratt asked. His white hair was standing on end and his moustache appeared to be levitating above his top lip. 'Something more important than my class, hmm? For which there will be a quiz at the end of the lesson, to be completed in your *neatest* handwriting.'

Millie bit her lip in an effort to quell the laughter that was bubbling up inside her. The man looked ridiculous. And why a Science teacher was so fussy about their penmanship was beyond her. It had never mattered an iota to Mr Plumpton.

'Sorry, sir,' Alice-Miranda said. 'Millie and I were discussing the importance of loyalty and a happy school environment, but you have our full attention now.'

'You can save your philosophising for when you are doodling in Art class,' the man said. He waved the wand of the generator, creating a giant spark that sent several of the girls ducking for cover.

There was a swift knock at the door before Miss Reedy walked into the classroom. 'This looks interesting,' she said with a furrowed brow.

'It's *always* interesting in my classes as well as highly educational and lots of fun too,' Mr Pratt replied. 'Would you like to join us?'

'Another time perhaps,' Miss Reedy said, clutching her clipboard to her chest. 'I need to speak to the girls who were involved in the fire yesterday.'

Caprice's face fell as a giddy murmur reverberated around the room. 'They're probably going to get a bravery award,' one of the girls whispered, which only caused to further sour Caprice's mood.

Millie followed Alice-Miranda to the door with Chessie and Sloane behind them. Jacinta was in another class and was already waiting for them outside Miss Reedy's office on the ground floor of Caledonia Manor. Livinia held the door open as the girls filed inside. There weren't enough chairs for them, so they stood in a semicircle in front of her desk.

The teacher sat down and clasped her hands. 'Girls,' she fizzed, all traces of her earlier bad mood banished. 'I had a very exciting phone call this morning from none other than Tilde McGilvray. She would like to interview you all for the show.'

'Oh, I love her!' Sloane exclaimed. 'She's so positive and all the segments on her show are good news stories, which makes for a refreshing change from all the bad things that get reported every day. Because, as a young girl, I really don't want to know about currency crashes or car crashes or any other crashes for that matter. I'd much rather hear about the boy who takes his dog to visit the old people's home or the woman who's been providing morning teas for the shopkeepers in her village for fifty years. Those stories restore my faith in humanity and inspire me to be a better person.'

The other girls looked at her curiously.

'Who are you and what have you done with Sloane Sykes?' Jacinta demanded.

'Very funny,' Sloane said, rolling her eyes. 'I just think Tilde McGilvray is an inspiration. I watch her show whenever I can and you might be interested to know that it's the only current-affairs program approved by Mrs Clarkson. What's wrong with that?'

'Nothing at all,' Alice-Miranda said, 'and I agree with you that Ms McGilvray is terrific. She once did a story with Daddy when Kennington's provided groceries to a family whose house had burned down in Highton Mill.' As the words flew out of her mouth, Alice-Miranda realised how remiss she'd been. 'Goodness, Daddy would do the same thing for the Abbouds. That would be a great help to them.'

'Best not to get ahead of yourself, Alice-Miranda, though it is a lovely idea,' Miss Reedy said, peering over the top of her glasses. 'I'm glad that you're all excited about the interview. Now, the crew are due to arrive at five o'clock and will set up in the sitting room of the boarding house. Ms McGilvray wants you girls in your normal habitat. I'm sure she won't ask you any tricky questions, so just be yourselves and answer honestly and plainly – but not too plainly, Sloane and Jacinta. Do you understand?'

The girls looked at each other and then at Miss Reedy and gave a nod.

Livinia smiled. She was quite excited herself, though it was hard to ignore the little voice in her head reminding her that she hadn't yet told Ophelia the plan. It was through no fault of her own. She had tried several times to call the woman but hadn't been able to get through nor leave a message.

'Make sure that you are in full uniform and looking immaculate. I know this is about your brave deed, but you are also representing Winchesterfield-Downsfordvale,' Livinia said. 'Now, off you go to morning tea. I noticed that Mrs Jennings just received a delivery from the junior school kitchen and it smelt to me like freshly baked brownies.'

Millie licked her lips. 'Thank goodness it's not leftover scrambled eggs,' she murmured as the girls filed out. She realised Alice-Miranda wasn't among them and poked her head back inside the doorway. 'Are you coming?'

'I'd like to have a quick word with Miss Reedy. You go ahead,' Alice-Miranda replied, answering Millie's curious look with a smile. She waited until the door was closed before approaching the acting headmistress's desk.

'How can I help you?' Miss Reedy said, offering the girl a seat.

'I'm a bit worried about you and Miss Grimm,' Alice-Miranda replied. Over the years the two women had seemed to go from miserable enemies to, at the very least, respected colleagues – perhaps even friends – but that all seemed in doubt today. 'When I went with Millie and Caprice to the office earlier, we couldn't help overhearing your argument. Mrs Derby told us not to speak a word of it to anyone, but I thought it would be all right to talk to you seeing as you were involved.'

Livinia sat back in her chair and folded her arms. 'I see.'

'Miss Crowley seems awfully nice and I didn't think it was like you to jump to conclusions about people that way,' the child offered.

'Well, I just don't agree with Miss Grimm's decision to appoint the woman without my input. I am acting headmistress, after all,' Livinia replied. 'Miss Crowley will have an opportunity to prove herself, don't you worry about that. I'm not a complete dragon, although you girls might think otherwise. Now, run along, Alice-Miranda. I have some urgent work to attend to.'

Alice-Miranda hesitated. She wanted to say more – Miss Wall and Mrs Clinch's words were playing on her mind too – but repeating them seemed risky in the extreme. Poor Miss Reedy was completely unaware the staff were against her.

The woman had already buried her head in some paperwork. 'Is there anything else?' she asked, without looking up.

'No. Thank you for listening, Miss Reedy,' Alice-Miranda said, and scampered from the room.

Livinia rested her elbows on the desk and massaged her temples. As far as she could tell, she was doing a fine job of running the school, but Ophelia didn't seem to recognise her contribution at all. At least the Tilde McGilvray interview might go partway to smoothing things over, and of course she'd give Tabitha Crowley a fighting chance. Livinia had been a new teacher herself once, full of ideas and brimming with optimism about the children whose lives she would influence. Tabitha just needed to learn that there was a hierarchy, that's all.

Chapter 10

Myrtle Parker hung up the telephone and walked into the sitting room, where her husband was reading a book. 'That was Sue,' she said.

Reg glanced up at his wife, who he thought looked rather lovely today in a sky-blue dress. She'd recently stopped wearing quite so much floral after he'd suggested she shouldn't stand next to the curtains or he wouldn't be able to find her. 'You're going to have to give me more than that, dear. There are at least five Sues in your orbit.'

'Sue Trelawny. She volunteers doing the tea rounds at the hospital in Downsfordvale,' Myrtle explained.

'Skinny Sue,' Reg said with a grin.

'Slim Sue,' Myrtle corrected.

'As opposed to Salty Sue, Silly Sue, Smart Sue or Stout Sue,' Reg said.

Myrtle exhaled. 'Please, Reg, they all have surnames, and if you ever call them any of those monikers, I will promptly divorce you.'

'Yes, dear,' he said, returning to his book, 'but I did learn them from you.'

'They don't have to know that,' the woman said, plonking herself down on the floral settee opposite. 'Well, aren't you interested to hear why she called?'

'Not particularly, but I gather you're going to tell me anyway.' The man put down his book on the small table next to him and looked at his wife expectantly.

'It's about the Abbouds,' Myrtle said, plumping the cushions beside her. 'Sue says that Mehmet is in a very serious condition, and his poor wife and children have been discharged with nowhere to go. *Nowhere* – can you imagine? Apparently, the family isn't fully insured. It's a disaster,' Myrtle clucked, shaking her head. 'We must do something.'

Reg pushed himself up out of his chair and made his way across the room.

'Where are you off to?' Myrtle asked.

'I'm going to Downsfordvale to pick them up,' Reg said, walking into the kitchen to collect the car keys. 'Isn't that what you're saying? We've got two spare bedrooms and we can make up the airbed on the floor for the little ones.'

'Heavens no!' Myrtle blanched and took off after him, her hands flapping by her sides. 'That's a terrible idea. What about my ornaments? The woman has small children – *several* of them.'

Reg walked back into the sitting room and sat down on the lounge with a *whump*. 'Do you have a better idea? It's very uncharitable to leave the family homeless.'

Myrtle let out a long sigh. 'I'm playing bridge with Henny and Hephzibah this morning. I'm sure that something will come to mind while I'm driving.'

'I might go and see Stan then,' Reg said. His brother-in-law lived at Wood End, and while it was quite a walk, he could do with the exercise.

'You most certainly will *not*. I won't have you rambling that far. You're still recovering, Reginald. The doctor said that you must take things *slowly* and understand that you'll never be the man you were before the accident, which is why I no longer give you any jobs – I couldn't stand having that hospital bed back here in the sitting room. You have no appreciation for how hard it was doing the housework around you for all those years.' Myrtle leaned down and kissed her husband's forehead. 'Why don't you come for a drive with me to Caledonia Manor? The ladies would love to see you and we could do with a fourth player for cards.'

'Only if you take me to see Stan tomorrow,' the man said. 'And I really wouldn't mind if you gave me odd jobs to do here and there, Myrtle. It will make me feel useful again. After three years in a coma, I need to get on with things.'

'Well, you do have that other ridiculous project I've been turning a blind eye to,' Myrtle tutted.

Reg grinned. 'The most fun I've had in years.'

'It's unbecoming for a man of your age,' Myrtle sniffed, 'but I won't stop you. I promised myself that, if you ever woke up, I'd agree to anything, just to have you back again. And perhaps there are one or two things you could do to help around the house.' She fetched her handbag from the hallway while Reg collected his jacket.

Myrtle popped a pillbox hat onto her head and opened the front door, giving their beloved gnome, Newton, a smile on the way out.

'My, my, I wonder who that is visiting Ambrosia?' she said, squinting at the shiny Aston Martin sitting in the driveway of Wisteria Cottage.

Reg followed her out the door. 'Whoever it is, I wouldn't mind swapping vehicles.'

'Don't be so silly, Reg,' Myrtle scolded. 'You'd look absurd, like a desperate old man trying to recapture his youth.'

'Nothing wrong with that, dear.' He chuckled, locking the door behind him. 'Nothing at all.'

'Why are you really here, Neville?' Ambrosia Headlington-Bear dumped the giant bouquet of flowers into the kitchen sink and turned to face her ex-husband. They'd been divorced for over a year now and their only communication had been via the lawyers.

'I just wanted to see you and Jacinta,' he said. 'I couldn't wait until the weekend, not after what happened yesterday.'

'How did you find out about that?' She flung a tea towel over her shoulder and filled the kettle.

'That's a new look for you,' he said with a rakish grin.

Ambrosia narrowed her eyes at him. 'I thought you didn't want to have anything to do with either of us.' She was determined not to cry, but this was the first time she'd even laid eyes on Neville since he'd told her that he wanted a divorce. She'd almost fainted when she'd answered the front door. And there he was, looking better than ever. She'd forgotten how much she'd loved those brown eyes that saw right through her. Ambrosia did her best to ignore the fact that her favourite car was parked in the driveway too. It meant nothing to her – not any more. She had made her own life with Jacinta and they didn't need Neville. She turned away and dabbed at her eyes. He didn't deserve her tears.

'Could we see Jacinta after school?' he asked.

'Absolutely not,' Ambrosia said firmly. 'I don't want you upsetting her. What's the real reason you're here? Did your latest girlfriend dump you while you happened to be passing through the neighbourhood?'

He sat down at the kitchen table. 'I've missed you,' he said, looking up at her with his big brown eyes.

Ambrosia felt her heart flutter.

'Haven't you missed me just a little?' he asked.

Ambrosia couldn't take it any more. 'Please leave,' she said, shaking her head. 'You can't be here. You can't do this to us. I won't have it.'

Neville stood up. 'All right, I'll go, but I will come and see Jacinta at the weekend. I promised her.' He kissed Ambrosia softly on the cheek, then walked down the hall and out the door.

Ambrosia locked it behind him, then sank to the floor. 'Why?' she raged as she crumpled into a heap and sobbed her heart out.

Chapter 11

'Good morning, girls.' Tabitha Crowley beamed at the group in front of her. 'I'm so pleased to be here, but first things first, I'd better get to know your names, hadn't I?' She cast her eyes across the room, hoping that her studiousness the previous evening would reap rewards. In her experience, it made the children feel ten feet tall if the teacher knew them almost instantly. It made them far more pliable too.

There were several girls she was certain of – Alice-Miranda being one of them. When she'd picked up the official school photograph of the secondary students, she realised that the girl who had been mentioned several times at supper wasn't a relative of the Fayle sisters but rather the youngest student ever to have started at Winchesterfield-Downsfordvale at the tender age of seven and one quarter. Her academic ability had seen her accelerated to senior school much earlier than expected. Tabitha couldn't help wondering at the wisdom of having a ten-year-old girl in classes with thirteen- and fourteen-year-old peers, but if Miss Grimm had decided it was the right thing to do, then who was she to question it? Interestingly, the senior school classes were vertically integrated anyway, meaning the children were with a mixed range of ages depending on their lessons. For a school that seemed quite traditional in almost every other way, the class groupings were a surprise.

Tabitha smiled as she looked from student to student, rattling off their names with lightning speed and accuracy. She was doing exceptionally well until she wasn't.

'Excuse me, Miss Crowley, my name is Caprice, not Millie,' the willowy girl said, smiling sweetly. 'Can I also take this opportunity to apologise for what you witnessed at breakfast? Millie and I had a small misunderstanding. We usually get on like a house on fire.'

Millie almost choked. 'That's an unfortunate analogy, Caprice, given what happened yesterday, but don't worry, Miss Crowley, mixing us up is an easy mistake. Caprice and I are almost twins,' the girl said to great guffaws from her classmates.

Caprice glowered at Millie then turned back to Miss Crowley, her face a picture of serenity.

Miss Crowley frowned. 'I'm terribly sorry. I know exactly who you both are, but I just had the names muddled in my head. It won't happen again.'

Tabitha was silently berating herself. She hated getting off on the wrong foot with her students and it was doubly silly seeing that she'd witnessed the pair's spat in the dining room this morning. It was obvious there was no love lost between the girls and she would have to work even harder now to win their trust. Tabitha resumed acquainting herself with the students and breathed a sigh of relief when she got to the last child and hadn't made another mistake. 'Now that we've got the introductions out of the way, let's get started, shall we?' Tabitha said, and directed the girls to take out their workbooks.

Millie was still smarting over her punishment from Miss Reedy. She hoped the woman wouldn't object to her helping out at the stables for her school component, and shelving books at the village library as community service. Ten hours was a long time when she could probably only do one hour a day, if that. At least Miss Reedy hadn't disqualified her from the television interview this evening. That was something to look forward to.

'So, tell me about the text you're reading as a class,' Tabitha said. She was eager to hear the girls' opinions. It wasn't a book she would have chosen, but as Miss Reedy pointed out, she couldn't very well go and change things willy-nilly halfway through the term.

'Mrs Reeves only gave it to us last week and it's horrible,' Sloane said. 'I'm never going to finish it.'

'I agree,' Ivory moaned. 'The characters are awful and I don't like the premise at all. Surely the kids could be more civilised and work out who was in charge rather than it becoming a free-for-all.'

Tabitha wasn't a fan of *Lord of the Flies* either but had thought the girls must have been studying it all term. An idea popped into her head. She had written a unit of work a year ago and had been itching to teach it again. Now was her chance. 'Okay, change of plans,' she announced with a clap of her hands. The girls looked at the woman eagerly. 'We're going to examine the way the illustrations enhance the text in a range of picture books, especially in relation to various themes.'

'Do you mean books like *The Giving Tree*?' Alice-Miranda asked. 'There are lots of lessons to be learned there. My granny read it to me when I was very little and we talked about the selfishness of the boy and the way the tree never stopped giving right to the end, when all that was left was a stump.'

Tabitha grinned. Her misgivings that the child might not belong in the secondary school evaporated at once. 'Exactly like that.'

'Awesome!' Sloane clenched her fists. English had never been her favourite subject and the idea of analysing picture books appealed to her a lot more than reading a whole novel.

A ripple of excitement rolled around the classroom.

Millie was telling Alice-Miranda about one of her favourite picture books from childhood when she noticed Miss Reedy standing in the doorway. The woman was watching intently but was yet to alert anyone to her presence.

'Right, Caprice, could you collect all the copies of *Lord of the Flies* and pop them into the store-room?' Miss Crowley scanned the bookshelves behind her desk and began pulling out slender volumes. 'Now, I want to integrate a range of other disciplines into our work as well. You might like to respond to the text by writing a play, poetry or even music. You could create your own illustrated picture book or undertake a science experiment. I'm open to all ideas.'

Jacinta frowned. 'So we're not just going to answer an endless list of comprehension questions and write essays?'

Tabitha shook her head. 'You'll never do that in my class if I have a say in it. And I can't believe in this day and age anyone teaches like that.'

'Miss Reedy does and Mrs Reeves,' Sloane said. 'It's *so* boring.'

Millie stole a peek at Miss Reedy, whose face resembled a thundercloud.

Tabitha turned and startled when she realised the woman was there. 'Hello Miss Reedy, can I help you with anything?'

Livinia pursed her lips. 'I just wanted to see that you had things under control.'

'Oh yes.' Tabitha began to pass out books to the girls. 'Perhaps you'd like to join us?'

'Sadly, I don't have time. I do, however, look forward to seeing a detailed program of this exciting new unit of work – the one with no comprehension questions or essays – on my desk at lunchtime,' Livinia said, then spun on her heel and stalked off.

Tabitha Crowley's stomach flipped. It was plain to see that she was going to have to work twice as hard to win Miss Reedy's approval, but if that's what she had to do, then so be it. She marched back to the whiteboard and smiled at her eager students. 'Shall we get started?'

Alice-Miranda hoped the girls did their best and made the unit a great success for Miss Crowley's sake. The woman was clearly taking a big risk.

Millie looked at Alice-Miranda and grinned. 'I like Miss Crowley a lot, even if she did call me Caprice.'

Chapter 12

Charlie Weatherly climbed down the ladder and stepped back to admire his handiwork. The sign had taken months to arrive, but it looked a treat and the weather had cleared long enough for him to put it up.

'Hello Mr Charles,' Alice-Miranda said with a wave. 'That looks great.'

'Well, it says what it is,' the man replied, rocking on his heels. 'I like that.'

The girls had been wondering whether their senior boarding house was going to be named after a former headmistress or a pupil of renown, but in the end Miss Grimm and the Fayle sisters had decided that Caledonia Stables was best and not too easily mixed up with the newer stables that still housed horses over at the junior campus.

'How are you and the girls feeling after your heroics?' the man asked.

'We're fine, but the Abbouds have been on my mind all day,' the tiny child admitted.

'Yes, it's a worry. Mehmet is one of loveliest fellas I've ever known and the man can cook, that's for sure,' Charlie said. 'Something smells good in there today too.'

'It's spaghetti bolognaise and garlic bread. I can recommend both.' Alice-Miranda was glad to be able to say that honestly. She'd bolted down her lunch and was now on her way up to Caledonia Manor to see Miss Hephzibah and Miss Henrietta, armed with the latest Highton's catalogue that her mother had sent. She wanted to give it to them before afternoon lessons began.

The girl waved goodbye to Charlie and wandered up the driveway and through the main entrance of the manor, down a long hallway and to the door marked 'Private'. She knocked once and waited.

Alice-Miranda felt something tickle her bare leg and looked down to find a black kitten.

'Hello Cleopatra. That naughty Fudge hasn't been chasing you again, has he? I think he's staying with Mrs Howard this week, so you should be safe enough.' She picked up the purring creature as Miss Hephzibah opened the door.

The woman's eyes crinkled like a concertina fan as she embraced the child, cat and all. 'Good afternoon, darling girl.'

'I hope I haven't come at a bad time, but I just got the mail at lunch and Mummy sent this for you.' The child passed Hephzibah the fat brochure. 'She said in her note to let me know if there's anything you and Miss Henrietta would like, and I'll organise to have it sent right away. Mummy would usually do it, but she and Daddy have gone on a big adventure trekking in the Andes for a whole month.'

'Oh, how lovely.' Hephzibah smiled. 'I don't think I'll ever get this old brain around that modern-day online shopping – much better to have a book to look at. Come in and have a piece of cake,' she said, standing aside to let the girl through. 'I baked it this morning.'

Alice-Miranda glanced at her watch. She still had twenty minutes before her PE class and she'd already changed into her uniform. 'Thank you, that would be wonderful,' she said, and followed the old woman into the huge country kitchen, where she was surprised to see Mr and Mrs Parker sitting at the table with Miss Henrietta. There were plates and tea cups and a deck of cards set off to the side.

'Reg, it's just not possible that we have the family stay with us,' Myrtle said with a sniff. 'I've told you that already. Please don't bring it up again – I can only tolerate so much guilt.'

'I still can't believe there's not a spare house in the village,' Henrietta said, twisting her wedding ring. 'The older girls have to go to school. The last thing their mother needs is to be worried about that as well.'

Reg looked over and grinned. 'Hello young lady. Aren't you a sight for sore eyes?'

Alice-Miranda hurried around to give the man a hug. He whispered something to her and she smiled conspiratorially before he drummed his forefingers on the tabletop and pretended to hit a high hat – except that he actually did tap his wife on the head.

'Stop that, Reginald,' the woman admonished, and was swiftly placated by a hug from Alice-Miranda.

The girl gave Henrietta a squeeze too then sat down at the end of the table, in time for Hephzibah to place a wedge of hummingbird cake in front of her.

'Oh, this looks delicious. Thank you,' Alice-Miranda said. She picked up her fork and dug in. 'Have you heard anything more about the Abbouds?' When Myrtle explained what her friend Sue had told her, the girl frowned. 'But that's terrible. We have to do something.' She wondered if she could organise the groceries from Kennington's without her parents' help. 'Maybe there's a house in the village that's vacant or up for rent.'

Myrtle shook her head. 'We rang the estate agents and tried the council too and apparently there's not a one. I still find that very hard to believe, but that's what we were told.'

The group had intended to play bridge that afternoon, but once Myrtle relayed what Sue had told her, they'd decided to brainstorm ways to help the Abboud family instead and had spent quite a deal of time on the telephone making enquiries.

'Believe me, we have tried all avenues.' Myrtle got up and bustled over to the kettle to refill the teapot. 'The Abbouds will likely have to leave Winchesterfield. Even Downsfordvale didn't sound promising, but at least I've managed to secure some donations of baby goods, which are being delivered to the hospital today.'

Alice-Miranda's eyes widened. She swallowed her mouthful and set down her fork with a delicate *tink*. 'We could have a clothing drive at school. If every girl donated one item, that would go a long way to filling the children's wardrobes.'

'A marvellous idea,' Henrietta said, clapping her hands.

'That sounds relatively easy too,' Reg said.

Myrtle nodded. 'And I can spread word in the village to see if we can get some clothes for Ada.'

'It's still not fair that the Abbouds will have to move away,' Alice-Miranda said. She looked at the adults and their serious faces. 'The fire was an accident. They shouldn't be punished for that.'

'Accident or not,' Myrtle said with a sigh, 'I'm afraid life often isn't fair.'

Chapter 13

Alice-Miranda's last lesson of the day was PE and involved a challenging obstacle course and cross-country run devised by Miss Wall. Back in the classroom, Millie thought her brain was going to explode as Mrs Clinch explained quadratic equations for the umpteenth time and she still didn't have the foggiest. She'd have to ask Alice-Miranda to help with her homework again and see if she could make heads or tails of things.

The friends had passed each other on the way to last period and agreed to catch up at the stables after school. When Alice-Miranda had visited the Fayle sisters at lunchtime, Millie had gone in search of Miss Reedy to ask if she could muck out the stalls and feed the ponies as part of her punishment – that way she could see Chops even if she couldn't ride him. Fortunately, the woman's mood had lifted and she agreed, commenting that she was impressed Millie had wanted to make a start on her service work so soon.

Alice-Miranda was going to pay Bony a quick visit and check that the stone bruise on his foot was healing. When she and Millie had been out riding a week ago, the poor boy had managed to get a large pebble lodged in the cleft of his near front hoof. Charlie had offered to phone the vet, but Alice-Miranda opted to make a poultice and keep an eye on him. It wasn't the first time the pony had suffered the injury and she was keen to see if she could deal with it herself. The good news was that Bony had been improving each day.

'Hello!' Alice-Miranda called, her voice echoing through the stone building.

Bonaparte whinnied loudly in reply, then thrust his head over the timber stall door and snorted.

'Well, good afternoon to you too.' Alice-Miranda walked over and gave the pony a rub on his nose. 'I don't suppose you've seen Millie?'

Bonaparte reached around and nibbled the girl's hair.

'Oi, stop that,' she said. There were a few long strands dangling from the beast's lips. She hurried off to the feed bins and lifted several lids before finding a stash of carrots.

Outside, a rhythmic *kerthumping* sound gave away Millie's location. Moments later, she trudged in, pushing a wheelbarrow piled high with fresh straw bales. The new stablehand, a stout young woman named Dervla Nichols, was walking beside the barrow and holding on to the load to make sure it didn't topple over on the uneven cobblestones.

Millie let go of the handles with a grunt, dropping the cargo to the ground. She wiped the back of her sweaty forehead with her hand and sighed. 'Maybe I should have volunteered to tutor one of the junior girls instead.'

'I can help,' Alice-Miranda offered. She held out the carrot to Bony, who hoovered it from her hand in a heartbeat.

Millie fetched a pair of scissors from the store-room to cut the twine on the bales while Dervla began to unload them, one outside each stall. 'Thanks, but if Miss Reedy thought I was getting off lightly, she'd double my sentence,' Millie grumbled. 'Anyway, we can't stay long this afternoon. We need to get back for the interview.'

Alice-Miranda glanced up at the clock on the wall. 'We've got an hour or so. It won't take me long to check Bony's foot and then you can give me something to do.'

Millie grinned. 'There's a big pile of manure that needs to be moved.'

Alice-Miranda giggled. 'Well, Daddy always says that shovelling dung is something everyone should do once in a while.'

'Just maybe not every day.' Dervla rolled her eyes, having spent the afternoon mucking out the stalls herself.

'How are you enjoying the place, apart from the manure?' Alice-Miranda asked.

Dervla had previously worked for Evelyn Pepper for eighteen months and had found it increasingly difficult to juggle her studies with the demands of her position. The property, Chesterfield Downs, was owned by Queen Georgiana and housed her prized racehorses. Alice-Miranda and Millie often rode over there to visit Bony's boyfriend, a retired champion called Rockstar – one of Her Majesty's most successful competitors. The pair adored each other, which was odd, as Bony didn't adore anyone very much.

The young woman stopped to retie her ponytail. 'Actually, it's a doddle here compared to the racing stables. I wish I'd snared this job years ago, when I first started university. There's a lot less poop here than over there, that's for sure.'

Alice-Miranda had been fascinated to learn that Dervla was soon to graduate with a double degree in forensic science and criminology. She'd mentioned that she was keen to work for the intelligence service.

'I heard about what you girls did yesterday in the village. Everyone's talking about it,' Dervla said.

'Anyone would have done the same, given the circumstances,' Alice-Miranda said. She walked into Bony's stall and clipped a lead rope onto his halter, then fastened it to a round hook so she could examine his foot. She ran her hand down the pony's front left leg and he lifted it up for her. Alice-Miranda then took the hoof pick off the ledge inside the stall and gently prodded the soft triangular section of his hoof, called the frog. For the first time since he was injured, Bony didn't flinch. Instead he raised his tail in the air and trumpeted so loudly it sounded as if Charlie had started up the tractor outside.

'You are a disgrace, Bonaparte Napoleon Highton-Smith-Kennington-Jones.' Alice-Miranda fanned her hand in front of her face. 'What a stinker!'

An equally loud noise sounded from the stall next door.

'Was that you, Buttercup?' Alice-Miranda said.

'I don't think so,' Dervla laughed. 'All the other ponies are out in the paddock.'

'Was that *you*, Millie?' Alice-Miranda giggled.

'Maybe . . . Okay, fine, it was me,' Millie confessed. Peals of laughter rang out from Dervla and Alice-Miranda. 'It's because of those awful eggs this morning,' Millie added sheepishly. 'It's been like the roaring forties today. I accidentally let one rip in Maths and Mrs Clinch thought she'd torn her trousers. You should have seen the woman – she was prancing about, trying not to let anyone get a look at the back of her pants until she could find a hand mirror to investigate. It was lucky I didn't wet my pants laughing too, then of course Sloane dobbed me in.'

'Poor Mrs Clinch,' Alice-Miranda chortled. She picked up a brush and gave Bony's neck a rub-down.

Dervla opened the stall door and collected his feed bin. 'Have you heard any news about the Abbouds?'

Alice-Miranda frowned. 'Mr Abboud is still in intensive care. Mrs Abboud and the children have been discharged. Sadly, I've heard on good authority from Mrs Parker that they have nowhere to go. It's the most desperate situation.'

Millie's head popped around the stall door. 'What about the flat here, above the stables?'

It was a good idea, but Dervla had just moved in, and Alice-Miranda doubted that a family of five children and their mother – including two infant babies – would cope very well in the dusty, draughty building, not to mention the smells from downstairs.

'That's ridiculous – there has to be somewhere that poor family to go,' Millie said. 'I mean, how many people live here at school?'

Alice-Miranda's eyebrows jumped up. 'Oh, Millie, you're a genius!' She quickly untied Bony and scampered out of the stall. 'Sorry for bailing on the manure, but I need to see Miss Grimm urgently. I'll be back at the boarding house in time for the interview and I promise I'll help on the weekend.'

'What did I say?' Millie called after her.

'I'll tell you later, if it works out,' Alice-Miranda replied with a hearty wave. She couldn't believe no one had thought of it earlier. It was perfect. Now she just had to convince Miss Grimm, although it crossed her mind that perhaps it was Miss Reedy she should have been asking.

Chapter 14

Alice-Miranda ran around the back of Winchester-field Manor to Miss Grimm and Mr Grump's flat, where she could hear the baby crying inside. She rapped hard on the door and waited. A minute or so later, it swung open and Mr Grump appeared, holding Aggie on one shoulder with a tea towel slung over the other.

'Good afternoon,' he said, breaking into a wide grin. 'You're looking hale and hearty after yesterday's adventure. To what do we owe this pleasure?'

'Hello Mr Grump, hello Aggie.' Alice-Miranda tickled the toddler's chubby bare leg. 'I was hoping to speak with Miss Grimm, if I may. I have an idea and I need to talk to her about it right away.'

A delicious smell of roasting meat filled the air.

'Come in. Ophelia's just ducked through to her office to meet with Miss Wall, but she's due back any time now.' Aldous Grump swung Aggie down onto his hip. The baby took one look at their visitor through her teary blue eyes and her frown instantly dissolved.

'Hello lovely girl.' Alice-Miranda held her finger up and Aggie smiled, reaching out to grip it tightly before attempting to pull it into her mouth. Alice-Miranda laughed. 'I think that might taste like Bonaparte's dusty coat. Are you hungry?'

'She's always hungry, and around dinnertime she's Grump by name and by nature.' Aldous chuckled. Aggie squirmed and wriggled, eager to go to the girl, so Aldous passed her over and quickly set about mashing the potato, pumpkin, peas and carrots in the saucepan on the side of the sink.

Alice-Miranda closed her eyes and opened them with a 'boo' and was rewarded with several bouts of rapid-fire giggles from Aggie. Their game continued until Mr Grump walked over with her dinner. Alice-Miranda wrestled Aggie's kicking legs into the high chair and found a bib.

'Goodness, you're a natural at this,' Aldous said, placing the bowl down and a baby spoon beside it. 'But don't try to feed her or you'll end up wearing it. Little Miss Independent has just discovered that she can do it herself and you won't get that spoon off her for love nor money.'

Aggie picked up the utensil and dug into the bowl, managing to get a substantial lump onto her spoon before she shoved it into her mouth, spilling most of the contents down her front.

'It's very quiet in here,' Ophelia said from the hallway. She walked through into the kitchen and was surprised to see they had a visitor. 'Oh, hello Alice-Miranda.'

'Hello Miss Grimm. I'm sorry to drop in unannounced, but there's something I need to ask you and there's no time to waste,' the child said earnestly.

Aldous Grump greeted his wife with a kiss, then turned his attention to the onion that was peeled and waiting to be chopped on the board near the sink.

'This sounds serious,' the woman said, placing her notebook and pen on the table.

'It is. It's about the Abbouds,' Alice-Miranda said, and launched headlong into her idea, outlining all the reasons why it would work and how the girls could help. By the time she'd finished, Ophelia Grimm was nodding in agreement.

'You're absolutely right – we need to do something immediately,' the woman said. 'I'll call the hospital and speak to the matron. The sooner we can get that family rehoused, the sooner they can start getting their life back on track.'

Aldous turned around with tears streaming down his cheeks. 'Well done, Alice-Miranda.' He wiped his eyes with the tea towel. 'Dratted onions get me every time.'

'It was actually Millie who made me think of it.' At the mention of the girl's name, Alice-Miranda glanced at the kitchen clock. 'Oh dear, I'm going to be late,' she said, jumping to her feet.

Ophelia checked the time and frowned. 'But dinner isn't for another hour.'

'Not for dinner. For the interview with Tilde McGilvray,' Alice-Miranda said.

The woman's eyebrows just about launched off the top of her forehead. 'The *what*?' she demanded.

Aggie took one look at her mother's face and her bottom lip began to quiver. Fat tears pooled in the corners of her eyes. 'I specifically told Livinia I don't want you girls reliving the ordeal and, frankly, journalists are untrustworthy to the core. They're likely to sensationalise the whole thing and we simply can't have that.'

It was hardly a surprise the woman felt that way. When Aldous's daughter died, Ophelia had been ambushed by reporters who wrote awful things. When she'd finally agreed to an interview to try to make things better, the journalist had turned on her and the situation became ten times worse with her and the school being blamed for the child's death. It took years for the enrolments to recover, not to mention the personal toll it had taken on Ophelia.

Alice-Miranda bit her lip. 'But isn't Tilde McGilvray's show all about good news and Miss Reedy *is* the acting headmistress?'

Ophelia stared at the child as if she had just told her she had a ferret sitting on her head. 'I beg your pardon.'

Aldous spun around and waved the knife he was holding in the air. 'Alice-Miranda's right, Ophelia. You put Livinia in charge and, ultimately, she's allowed to make the final decisions. You might not like them, which is why I suggested it would be good for us to go away for a while and leave her to it,' the man said. 'You only have another few months off and you've been doing too much as it is.'

'We're not going anywhere!' Ophelia said sharply. 'Come along, Alice-Miranda. I'll drive you over to Caledonia Stables and I'll speak with Livinia when we get there. This interview is *not* happening and I *will* be back at the helm tomorrow morning.' The woman marched into the hall to collect her blazer and reapply her lipstick.

Alice-Miranda felt a tightness in her stomach. 'Sorry to have caused a problem,' she whispered to Mr Grump.

The man smiled and offered her a wink. 'She'll calm down eventually,' he whispered in reply.

'I heard that, Aldous,' Ophelia said, walking into the room to pick up her handbag and car keys. 'And no I won't. In any case, I need to return to work before I go completely mad and drive you mad with me.' With that, she kissed Aggie on the head and stalked out the door.

Chapter 15

Ophelia Grimm pulled up outside Caledonia Stables, beside a news truck with a satellite dish on its roof in the courtyard. As the woman turned off the engine and dialled the hospital's number, Alice-Miranda scurried out of the car and into the boarding house, hoping she wasn't too late. She was met at the front door by a rather harried Mrs Clarkson.

'Alice-Miranda, where have you been?' the woman asked. 'They're just about to start the interview.'

'With Miss Grimm.' Alice-Miranda's eyes darted around, hoping that Miss Reedy was close by and they could speak in private. 'Is Miss Reedy about?'

'She's in the sitting room with Tilde McGilvray and the rest of the girls,' Mrs Clarkson replied. She was surprised to see Ophelia striding through the front doors.

'Where are they?' the headmistress demanded.

Petunia Clarkson gulped and pointed down the hall. With a brief nod, Miss Grimm charged into the sitting room, where she was confronted with glaring lights, cameras and a crew of four. Alice-Miranda followed her in and caught sight of the girls beckoning to her from the long couch, where they were lined up like a row of babushka dolls. Livinia Reedy was checking their uniforms and making sure that everyone looked their neatest. She turned and spotted Alice-Miranda, concerned by the child's dishevelled appearance.

'Livinia, may I see you outside?' Ophelia barked. *'Now.'*

Sensing that something was amiss, Tilde McGilvray intercepted the woman. 'Miss Grimm, how wonderful to meet you,' she said, oozing charm. She took Ophelia by the arm and gently spun her around, away from the girls. 'Seeing that you're here, would you like to be part of the interview too? The things you've done for this school in the past couple of years – expanding into secondary and working so closely with the boys at Fayle – are exemplary.' Tilde grinned. 'And you know those stories are what I'm all about.'

Ophelia's heart was racing. This wasn't her objective at all, and why was this woman being so nice to her? Weren't all journalists opportunistic twats by their very nature?

'Please, we have room on the couch and I'm sure that our viewers would love to meet the woman who has instilled such selfless values in her students,' Tilde said.

Livinia would have liked the spot on the couch herself, but she was pleased to see Ophelia. She'd left a message with Louella Derby to mention the interview to her as soon as she and Aldous arrived back from Downsfordvale. What Livinia didn't know was that Louella had left early to attend an appointment of her own and the information had never reached their boss. It was no matter, though, as Ophelia had sent her a handwritten message with her thoughts on dealing with the press.

'But . . .' Ophelia rasped. Her mouth was suddenly as dry as a desert. 'But I'd rather the girls *didn't* do the interview.'

Tilde gasped. 'Why ever not? They're heroes and the world needs all the good news stories it can get. Besides, my sources tell me that just a few minutes ago you offered accommodation to the Abboud family. Perhaps, if you're not keen about the children being interviewed, I could have a one-on-one with you instead.'

Miss Grimm was dumbstruck. How Tilde McGilvray knew about her conversation with Mrs Abboud was a complete mystery. The woman was clearly not to be trifled with. 'N-no, that's not what I want,' Ophelia replied.

A pubescent-looking producer held up his hand. 'Tilde, we're going live in thirty seconds.'

'Miss Grimm, I must ask you to take your seat or step out of the frame,' Tilde said, and practically pushed Ophelia down beside Alice-Miranda. She hurried over to perch on a wing-backed armchair. 'Girls, are you ready?' she asked, her eyes blinking wide like a porcelain doll. She stared down the barrel of a camera lens. 'Good evening and welcome to *Tilde's Toast of the Town*, where we celebrate six good news stories of the day. To begin with, we have a tale to warm the cockles of the hardest of hearts. I am here in the senior boarding house at Winchesterfield-Downsfordvale Academy for Proper Young Ladies, where we are joined by the headmistress, Miss Ophelia Grimm, and the five girls who saved the lives of an entire family yesterday from a house fire in the village of Winchesterfield.' Tilde smiled at Ophelia. 'Miss Grimm, you must be very proud of the girls and what they did?'

Ophelia stared at the camera, completely dumbstruck.

'Miss Grimm?' Tilde repeated.

Alice-Miranda gently prodded the woman's leg.

'Um, yes,' Ophelia squeaked, her voice barely audible.

When it was clear that was all she was going to get, Tilde swiftly turned to the girls, who thankfully were much better at speaking on camera. She asked each of them a question and was pleased to see them bouncing off one another, talking about what had happened.

'We're terribly glad the family is okay,' Alice-Miranda added, 'although Mr Abboud is still in a serious condition. We are all sending our very best wishes for his speedy recovery.'

With everyone's attention focused on the interview, no one noticed a figure slip into the room. Caprice's eyes narrowed in envy. It wasn't fair that these girls were being interviewed by Tilde McGilvray – *she* was a good news story too. Except she'd just received some very bad news. The television talent quest she'd been invited to take part in had been postponed indefinitely. She stood in the shadows, making sure that Miss Reedy didn't spot her, and waited for her chance. She had a brilliant idea, as long as Tilde asked the right questions.

'I imagine you girls have been thinking about what else you might do to help the family get back on their feet,' Tilde said.

The friends glanced at one another. Alice-Miranda had already decided she would speak to her father about Kennington's providing groceries for the Abbouds, but as the girls hadn't regrouped since breakfast there had been no discussions about what else they might do. She thought it best not to mention the clothing drive on television as she was certain they could get enough donations from the girls at school and there was a risk of the family being inundated by the general public.

'We could hold a fundraiser,' Sloane said, and the rest of the girls nodded.

'Maybe a cake stall?' Chessie suggested.

Jacinta scoffed. 'That wouldn't raise nearly enough money.'

'It would have to be BIG!' Millie said, sweeping her arms in a wide arc and almost walloping Sloane in the face. 'And fun so that everyone gets involved. I'm sure it costs a lot to rebuild a house and restaurant.'

'Perhaps we should talk about it off camera with Miss Grimm and Miss Reedy first,' Alice-Miranda advised.

'Concert!' one of them yelled. The girls turned to each other, confused about whose idea it was.

'A concert!' Millie repeated, her eyes widening. 'For everyone.'

'But with really good singers and bands – not just kids, but proper stars. They always raise lots of money, don't they?' Jacinta said. 'It could be like a festival.'

'The kids should be in it too – the Winchester-Fayle Singers can make their comeback,' Sloane said excitedly, then grimaced as her stomach cramped. Unfortunately, this morning's scrambled eggs were about to unleash their second wave of spite. Sloane clutched at her tummy as she let one rip.

For a second there was a stunned silence. Ophelia Grimm stared at her shoes in horror. Millie twisted her lips to stop from laughing while Chessie peered down the row, wondering who the culprit was. Sloane thought she might die right there and then on national television.

But Tilde McGilvray, ever the professional, piped up with a giggle. 'Apologies for the noise, viewers. You can't see him, but the school dog – what's his name, girls?' She looked at the children expectantly.

'Fudge!' Alice-Miranda jumped in. 'His name is Fudge.'

Tilde giggled again. Millie did too. 'It seems Fudge is a windy hound. Cheeky boy – go on get out of here,' she said, pretending to shoo him away. Jacinta's mouth opened. She was about to say that she couldn't see Fudge anywhere but Tilde was too quick. 'So, a festival?' the woman said, turning back to the girls. 'What a brilliant idea.'

Standing off-camera near one of the light tripods, Livinia Reedy had been swept up in the girls' enthusiasm and was nodding and smiling. It was only when she noticed the look of horror on the headmistress's face that Livinia made a cutting motion across her neck. She'd have to talk Ophelia around and it was probably best not to do it now.

Caprice smirked to herself. She would be the star of the show – an up-and-coming actress and singer – winner of the junior section of the National Eisteddfod. It was perfect. With her plan in place, she slipped out of the room.

'Well, you heard it here first, ladies and gentlemen,' Tilde said in a sparkly voice. 'Winchesterfield-Downsfordvale will be hosting a concert to raise money for the Abboud family. Is there a date you have in mind?' The woman looked at the headmistress, who seemed to be shrinking in on herself.

'What?' Ophelia blanched.

Tilde chuckled. 'When you decide, just let me know and I will happily spread the word. Perhaps I could emcee for you and telecast it as a special?' She turned to the camera and smiled. 'Viewers, I'm sure you will agree what an impressive group of children and teachers we have here at Winchesterfield-Downsfordvale.'

Back at their flat, Aldous Grump had switched on the television in the sitting room while he and Aggie played a game before bedtime. The baby girl rolled over and sat up, then pointed at the screen. 'Mama!' she said.

Aldous peered at the set, not sure what had surprised him the most – his wife's unscheduled television appearance or the fact their daughter had just uttered her very first word.

Chapter 16

'And we're out,' the executive producer called. The rest of the episode had been pre-recorded and was being controlled by another producer back in the television studio.

Tilde McGilvray stood up and smiled at the girls and Miss Grimm. 'That was fantastic,' she said.

'Really?' Miss Grimm blinked like a deer in the headlights. She stood up, smoothing her skirt. 'We clearly have very different definitions of success. How on earth are we going to organise a concert? It's preposterous. The costs will be exorbitant, let alone the time it would take to pull it all together.' The woman glared at Millie, who hid behind Jacinta. Never mind that she had come across as a complete idiot, sitting there with her mouth opening and closing like a gasping guppy.

'We can do it, Miss Grimm,' Alice-Miranda said. 'I'm sure that Uncle Lawrence will have some contacts, and Miss Crowley was very excited about getting the Winchester-Fayle Singers back in action.'

'That hardly makes a world-class show, does it?' the woman griped. She spotted Livinia lurking among the crew. 'And we haven't consulted the Abbouds about any of this. It could come across as awfully patronising.'

Alice-Miranda bit her lip. In all their excitement, she and the girls hadn't considered that at all.

Ophelia arched an eyebrow at Livinia. 'A word. *Now*.'

As the two women disappeared into the corridor, Alice-Miranda walked over to Tilde McGilvray and held out her hand. 'Thank you very much for the interview, Ms McGilvray.

You ask such insightful questions and I do hope that Miss Grimm will come around to the idea of the festival.'

Tilde smiled, her white teeth gleaming under the stagelights, and took the child's hand in hers, her gold bracelets jingling. 'It was lovely to meet you, Alice-Miranda, and I mean what I said about spreading word about the concert. I'm happy to help,' the woman said, handing the girl her card.

'Did anyone else see Fudge in the room?' Jacinta asked with a frown on her face.

The girls burst out laughing. 'We'll explain later,' Chessie said, as Mrs Clarkson gathered them together. It was almost dinnertime and she had a surprise in store.

After they bade farewell to Ms McGilvray and the crew, the girls walked past Mrs Clarkson's office. The door was ajar and it was clear that Miss Grimm and Miss Reedy were in the middle of a pitched battle. While Mrs Clarkson disappeared into the dining room with Sloane, Chessie and Jacinta, Millie grabbed Alice-Miranda's arm and the pair hung back.

'I thought it would be a good way to acknowledge what the girls have done and get the school some free publicity. We're not full at the moment, and you and I both know that it takes a lot of funds to run this place – especially since the expansion,' Livinia said loudly.

'But I left a note for you,' Ophelia fumed.

'Yes, and I have your note right here. You specifically told me that I should proceed if the opportunity for a suitable interview should arise.' Livinia went to pull the paper from her pocket but couldn't find it. She thrust her hand into her other pocket then opened the notebook she was carrying. She was certain she'd picked it up from her desk in Caledonia Manor.

'So you've resorted to lying to me,' Ophelia snapped. She sighed and shook her head. 'I need an ally who works *with* me, not against me, Livinia. Now the girls will be all het-up about a concert that's not happening.'

'I think it's a wonderful idea,' Livinia retorted.

'Well, I don't,' Miss Grimm countered.

Millie and Alice-Miranda looked at one another. 'Oh, this is worse than I'd managed,' Alice-Miranda said, wringing her hands.

'And what were we thinking, saying we should have a concert and not just a concert – a festival?'

Millie said, berating herself. 'That's something professional event organisers do, not kids.'

The office door swung open and the girls jumped out of sight, behind a tall pot plant. Ophelia Grimm stalked down the hallway and exited the building.

Alice-Miranda wanted to make sure Miss Reedy was all right. 'You go ahead,' she said to Millie. 'I won't be long.'

Millie agreed, but only because whatever Mrs Jennings had cooked smelt absolutely delicious and she was starving.

In actual fact, Mrs Clarkson's surprise was that Mrs Smith had taken charge of dinner for the night and had whipped up her famous lamb roast accompanied by baked potatoes and cauliflower cheese with lashings of gravy. To top it off, there was steamed chocolate pudding and ice-cream for dessert. After this morning's egg-tastrophe, Mrs Jennings had been sent for some more mentoring with Ginny at the junior school.

Alice-Miranda hurried back to find Miss Reedy sitting with her head in her hands at the desk. Her misery seemed amplified against the cheery surrounds of Mrs Clarkson's office, with its bright yellow polka-dotted stationery and the framed poster on the wall with the slogan 'It's a good day to be happy'. 'Excuse me, Miss Reedy,' she said, knocking on the door, 'are you all right?'

Livinia looked up and hastily brushed the tears from her eyes. 'I'm fine, Alice-Miranda,' she said. 'You should be at dinner. Off you go.'

'I'm afraid I might have said something out of turn,' the child said, inching into the room. 'I was the one who mentioned the interview to Miss Grimm, but I had no idea it would cause problems between the two of you.'

Livinia sighed. 'It's not your fault. Miss Grimm and I have a difference of opinion, that's all.' She was racking her brain, trying to remember where she'd left Ophelia's note. As soon as she found it, she intended to show the woman and demand an apology.

'Well, if it means anything, I think the interview went swimmingly and Ms McGilvray asked terrific questions,' Alice-Miranda said.

Livinia stood up and walked to the doorway. 'No, it was a mistake. And so is the fundraiser – it's far too much work and, really, it's not up to the school to rescue the Abbouds.'

'But the whole village wants to help,' Alice-Miranda said. 'I'm sure if it was the school that had a fire, everyone would rally behind us.'

Livinia sighed again. The child was right, of course, but now wasn't the time to further blot her copybook with Ophelia. 'Run along and have your dinner before you miss out,' she said, mustering a half-hearted smile. 'And, please, no more talk about the concert – we don't want the students getting themselves into a lather about something that's not going to happen.'

'Yes, Miss Reedy.' Alice-Miranda nodded, though she was disappointed to hear the woman was giving up so easily. 'Oh, and I'm sorry Miss Grimm's decided to come back early from her maternity leave. I think you've been such an innovative acting headmistress. Our Friday afternoon clubs have been very popular with the girls and we've so enjoyed your assemblies. At least now you'll be able to concentrate on your classes and not be torn in ten different directions.' Alice-Miranda flashed her a smile and darted out into the hall.

A deep frown puckered the woman's brow. Ophelia was coming back early? This was certainly news to her. When was Ophelia planning to tell her that and how on earth did the child know?

Alice-Miranda hurried to the dining room, wondering how Miss Reedy and Miss Grimm could be so confused about the same note. She had a strange feeling that there was something else amiss, but right now there were more pressing matters on her mind.

Chapter 17

Alice-Miranda stared at the blank page in front of her. She'd just read an intriguing picture book about a fox and a bear and their journey together, though it didn't take long for her mind to wander back to the feud between Miss Grimm and Miss Reedy and the part she'd played in fuelling it. She tapped her pen rhythmically on the pad of paper, puzzling over how she could fix things between the two women.

Millie nudged her friend and pointed out the window. 'There's some good news.'

Alice-Miranda pushed back her chair and scurried over to take a closer look. Jacinta and Chessie followed. Sloane, meanwhile, was busy chatting to Miss Crowley about creating a collage using mixed media to represent the various themes of the story she'd chosen. Alice-Miranda stood on her tiptoes and peered out the window to see Mrs Abboud hop out of a minivan with Mrs Parker. There was another lady in a sedan behind them. Minutes later, with a mountain of baby equipment unpacked, the ladies took the twins and little Hatice out of their car seats. There was no sign of the older Abboud girls, but perhaps they were at school.

'That is a relief. I'm so pleased Mrs Abboud took up Miss Grimm's offer,' Alice-Miranda said, turning to her friends.

'It's fine for now, but they won't be able to stay in that flat upstairs forever,' Jacinta said. 'I don't imagine it would be terribly big and they are a large family.'

Tabitha returned to the front of the room and asked the girls to take their seats. 'I just wanted to congratulate you on how hard you've all worked today,' she said, fiddling with her bracelet. 'I can see that many of you are making great headway on the unit already.'

Alice-Miranda felt a twinge of guilt. She'd barely achieved a thing, which wasn't like her at all.

'And I'd also ask you to spread the word that the first rehearsal for the Winchester-Fayle Singers will take place this Friday after school, here in the music room down the hall,' the woman said.

'Will everyone be involved?' Jacinta asked innocently.

Caprice sniggered. 'What Jacinta really wants to know is whether her boyfriend from Fayle will be coming over.'

'Oh yes, the boys will be joining us,' Tabitha said with a grin.

'Is the concert still going to happen?' a small girl called Lettie asked from the front row. Even though the other students hadn't watched the television show last night, news of the festival had spread like wildfire.

'I think it should. I'm sure that it would raise lots of money,' Miss Crowley said. 'Well done, Millie, for thinking of it.'

Caprice rolled her eyes.

'I'm afraid that Miss Grimm and Miss Reedy aren't very keen,' Alice-Miranda said. 'Maybe if we formed a committee and organised everything ourselves, they might change their minds.'

Tabitha chewed on the end of her pencil. She didn't want to overstep the mark, being new and all, but if she could help the girls pull off something amazing then hopefully the school would keep her. 'Girls, I think we should do it,' she said finally. 'We have to at least try.'

A ripple of excitement ran through the room.

'Yes!' Millie hissed, clenching her fists.

'You'd better get in touch with your uncle, Alice-Miranda, and see if he has any contacts for singers or bands,' Sloane said. 'I'm voting for Pretty in Pink and The Stingrays – they're both awesome.'

Tabitha looked at the child curiously. Those were two of the most popular groups in the world at the moment. Sloane was likely aiming a little too high. 'Might I ask who your uncle is, Alice-Miranda?'

'Lawrence Ridley,' Millie answered for her. 'And his son, Lucas, is Jacinta's boyfriend.'

Tabitha gasped. 'He's gor . . . very talented and I'm sure he's well connected too.'

'You were going to say gorgeous, weren't you?' Millie grinned with all her teeth. 'And he totally is. My mum says she'd leave Dad in a heartbeat for Lawrence if he ever divorced Charlotte.'

Miss Crowley's face turned the colour of an overripe tomato. 'I'm sure your mother's joking.'

'I wouldn't count on it,' Millie said with a glint in her eye.

Jacinta raised her hand. 'Miss Crowley, the lesson's over.'

'Oh, so it is,' the woman said, grateful for a change of subject. 'Now, girls, I'm going to make an announcement about singing practice at dinner tonight. Alice-Miranda, would you like to see who wants to be involved in the committee?'

'I'll get on it,' the girl promised with a nod. There was still a niggle in the back of her mind about Miss Grimm and Miss Reedy, but hopefully she could talk them around. If the girls organised everything, there was no reason for them to say no. A family's wellbeing depended on it. If Mr Abboud woke up to find that his home and restaurant were being rebuilt, that would go a long way to making him feel better. Granny Valentina always said that it was important for people to have something to look forward to.

Chapter 18

Alice-Miranda had a spring in her step as she set off back to school from the village. Her lesson this afternoon had gone especially well, and she was leaping and skipping in time to the beat in her head. She couldn't remember loving anything as much – except for riding, but she'd been doing that since she was a toddler. This was new and a bit tricky and probably the most challenging thing she'd tried her hand at in a very long time, although organising the concert was going to take every ounce of skill she and the other girls had too.

It felt fun to have a secret. Well, there were three people who knew – actually now four as she'd recently spilled the beans to Neville Nordstrom. They'd been writing to each other since the leadership camp in Scotland, and Alice-Miranda was hoping that her parents would allow her to have a few friends over to stay during the next term break. Neville was one of the kindest boys she'd ever met, and he was sweet and funny too.

Alice-Miranda had almost reached the end of Rosebud Lane when she spotted a girl with long dark hair scamper from around the back of a pretty stone cottage, the front of which was partly covered by a trellis of pink roses. Alice-Miranda recognised the house as belonging to Mrs Goodman. Mr Parker had told her some fascinating stories about the woman but, strangely, she was yet to meet her. The dark-haired girl dragged a schoolbag out from under a hydrangea bush, then ran swiftly down the road, turning left into the high street.

It took a moment for Alice-Miranda to realise that it was Zahra Abboud. She ran after her, thinking they could walk to Caledonia Manor together, given the Abboud family had moved into Mrs Reeves's old flat that morning.

'Zahra!' Alice-Miranda called, but the girl didn't stop. If anything, she increased her pace and was heading in the opposite direction to school.

Alice-Miranda dashed past the Munzes' general store and the Abbouds' burnt-out home and restaurant across the road. The place was cordoned off with police tape as it was still deemed a crime scene until the authorities finalised their investigations. Zahra turned another corner and ran into the front courtyard of the village primary school, where she dumped her bag on the ground and sat on a bench under a tree. There were several children in the playground and a young supervisor kicking a ball on the grassy area.

Alice-Miranda hesitated at the gate. 'Zahra,' she called again, waving her arm in the air.

The girl looked up. There was something in her eyes – terror, Alice-Miranda would have said, which was strange because she wasn't there to do her any harm.

Alice-Miranda hurried over and sat down beside the girl. 'I thought it was you. How are you feeling?'

'Fine,' Zahra said quietly, staring into the street.

'I saw you just now, coming out of that cottage at the end of Rosebud Lane,' Alice-Miranda said.

Zahra shook her head. 'No, you didn't.'

Alice-Miranda thought it highly peculiar for the girl to deny the plain truth, but before she had time to ask anything more, Zahra hastily gathered her things and ran to a silver minivan that had rounded the corner. The girl jumped into the front passenger seat and pulled her seatbelt over her shoulder.

'How was your Maths tutoring?' the woman asked. 'Does your teacher want to talk to me?'

'It was fine,' Zahra replied, crossing her fingers. 'And no, he doesn't.'

'Where are the other students from the group?' Mrs Abboud asked, scanning the playground.

'Over there somewhere,' Zahra said, gesturing to the children running on the grass.

'Isn't that Alice-Miranda, from the boarding school?' The woman squinted out the window at the tiny girl, who gave a full-bodied wave.

Zahra shrugged.

'My goodness, Zahra, have you forgotten your manners? If it wasn't for that girl and her friends, we would all be dead. Except for you because you were not home when the fire started and still you do not tell me where you were.' Ada hopped out of the car and walked around to the footpath. 'Alice-Miranda!' she yelled, waving.

The girl skipped to the car, her chocolate curls bouncing. 'Hello Mrs Abboud. It's wonderful to see you,' the child said. 'How is the rest of the family?'

'We are all healthy and now we have a roof over our heads too, thanks to you,' Ada said. 'Mr Abboud is still sleeping, but they tell me it is for the best until he has recovered some more. I have not been able to thank you for what you and your friends did for us.' There was an overwhelming sadness in her dark eyes.

'It was Jacinta who spotted the smoke first – we're just glad that she did. And it's silly for the flat to be empty. At least now Zahra and Esma can still go to school and you'll be close enough to be able to supervise the rebuilding,' the child said.

Mrs Abboud swallowed hard. 'I am afraid we cannot afford to – there is too little insurance and our savings will not cover the costs.'

Alice-Miranda glanced at the car, where Zahra was avoiding looking at the pair of them. 'Don't worry, we have a plan to get the money you need,' she said.

Mrs Abboud shook her head. 'You have done more than enough already. We cannot accept it. Mehmet would be angry with me for taking advantage.'

'But it's not just me and the girls, Mrs Abboud. We're going to involve the whole community and I know that if the shoe was on the other foot and someone else was in need, you and Mr Abboud would be the first to step up. You held that fundraiser to help repair the village hall after the floods, and you send left-over food from the restaurant to the homeless shelter in Downsfordvale each week,' Alice-Miranda said. 'Please let us help you this time. Besides,' she added with a grin, 'the plan is for something that will be lots of fun, so it's a win-win for everyone.'

Ada frowned. 'Only if you promise it will not be too much work for you. I can help – and the girls too. You must let me know what we can do, then perhaps I will not tell Mehmet straight away. He will need time to come to terms with the news and then I know he will be so happy that we can reopen the restaurant. It is his life.'

Alice-Miranda held out her tiny hand. 'Promise,' she said with a smile.

Ada enveloped the child in a warm embrace. 'Thank you, for everything,' she whispered, and stepped back. 'Would you like a lift to school? I can drop you on the way. We are going to the hospital.'

Alice-Miranda declined the offer, opting to walk to clear her head. 'If you need any baby-sitters, I'm sure there are lots of girls who would be only too happy to help.'

Mrs Abboud nodded then hopped into the minivan. Alice-Miranda waved as the Abboud family puttered off down the road. Zahra didn't look up once. Alice-Miranda wished she'd had longer to speak to the girl. She resolved to find her later and talk to her alone. It seemed they both had a secret, and she could only hope that Zahra's wasn't going to land her in any trouble.

Chapter 19

Alice-Miranda arrived back at school an hour before dinner and went straight to Miss Reedy's office in Caledonia Manor. She was anxious to talk about the concert. If Mrs Abboud was happy for the girls to hold a fundraiser, then with any luck the teachers wouldn't stand in the way. Given that Miss Crowley had offered to help them organise it all, they wouldn't be adding to everyone's workload. Just as she reached up to knock, the door opened and Miss Wall walked out, almost barrelling into the child.

'Oh, sorry, I didn't expect anyone to be standing there,' the teacher said. It seemed she had traded her school-issue PE kit for three-quarter navy leggings and a loose white singlet over the top of a collarless royal-blue T-shirt. Alice-Miranda noticed the woman's face was shiny and red, and surmised that she must have just come from the sports field to see Miss Reedy.

'Hello Miss Wall, you're looking lovely today,' Alice-Miranda replied. She thought the effort the woman had put into improving her attire since becoming deputy headmistress was admirable. The tiny child peered around the woman's imposing form. 'I wanted to talk to Miss Reedy about the concert for the Abbouds. Actually, while I have you, what are your thoughts?' It occurred to the girl that, if she could get some of the staff onside, then perhaps it would be easier to convince Miss Reedy and Miss Grimm that it was a good idea.

'Hmm, I'd rather not say until I know how the headmistress feels about it,' Benitha replied with pursed lips.

'That's unfortunate because she's not keen at all,' Alice-Miranda said. In truth, she was surprised Miss Wall would take such a diplomatic stance since the woman had always been one to speak her mind, whether her view was popular or not. 'She thinks it's too much work and too big a distraction, but I believe it would be great for our leadership skills,' Alice-Miranda said. 'And you of all teachers would know how important that is after the Future Leaders Opportunity Program in Scotland.'

'I'll think about it, but I wouldn't get your hopes up if I was you,' the teacher said, and hurried away.

Alice-Miranda stood in the hallway, gazing at Miss Reedy's door. She reached up to knock again but was distracted by footsteps on the timber floor. It was Mr Plumpton, waving his hand as he hurried towards her.

'Livinia's raced off to an appointment in Downsfordvale,' the man puffed. 'Why don't you leave her a message?'

Alice-Miranda wondered why Miss Wall had been in the woman's office and hadn't mentioned anything about Miss Reedy not being there.

'Is everything all right?' Mr Plumpton asked.

The child nodded, then noticed a splodge of green goop on the teacher's forehead. 'Thank you, Mr Plumpton, that's a great idea. Um, you might want to take a look in the mirror,' the child added, pointing at his brow.

She fished out a clean handkerchief from her pocket and offered it to him.

Josiah touched his forehead, then examined the tip of his finger. 'Dear me. Slime mishap in the lab last period. Thanks for telling me. I wouldn't want to go to dinner looking like an alien,' the man said with a chuckle. He dabbed at the spot and promised to return the girl's handkerchief the next morning. 'Oh, and between you and me, I think the concert is a wonderful idea,' he said. 'Livinia does too, but she's had a difficult time of things lately and has been a bit out of sorts. I know she's doing her best to convince Miss Grimm.' Josiah had been concerned to overhear Miss Wall and Miss Tweedle whispering about his wife earlier in the day. When he'd confronted the pair, they denied everything, but he could have sworn he'd heard Livinia's name.

Alice-Miranda smiled. 'Don't worry, Mr Plumpton, I wasn't planning to give up. Quite the contrary.'

'I'm glad to hear it,' the man replied with a wink.

Further along the corridor, hidden behind a potted palm, a figure dashed away and out of sight, a great big grin plastered across their face.

Inside the office, Alice-Miranda quickly located a pen and notepad. She scribbled a message and was about to leave when she saw something she shouldn't have. It couldn't be helped, though, as it was sitting right there on top of everything. It was a note from Miss Grimm clearly telling Miss Reedy that the girls weren't to do any press and it was dated yesterday.

Alice-Miranda bit her lip. Why would Miss Reedy go against Miss Grimm's instructions and claim that her note had said otherwise? The girl folded her own message and wrote Miss Reedy's name on the back, then left it on the desk. She exited the office, almost bumping headlong into Miss Crowley. The corridor was busier than the high street this afternoon.

The woman smiled cheerfully. 'Hello Alice-Miranda. I was wanting to have a word with Miss Reedy. Is she free?'

Tabitha Crowley looked lovely today with her hair pulled up in a high bun, encircled by a length of pink velvet ribbon. She wore a stylish suit in the same shade that saw cigar pants and a cropped jacket paired with a lime-coloured silk blouse and matching heels.

'She's not in at the moment,' the child replied. 'But she's certainly in hot demand. Mr Plumpton said that I should leave her a note. I'm very glad to have run into you. I saw Mrs Abboud in the village and she's given us her blessing for the fundraiser. Mr Plumpton said he thought it was a good idea too, so all we have to do is bring Miss Grimm around.'

'That's fantastic news!' the woman said, her hazel eyes sparkling.

'We could gather the girls who want to help with the organising and have a meeting now if you're free,' Alice-Miranda said.

Tabitha had been thinking exactly the same thing. She'd already finished her marking for the day and lessons were set for the next week. All she had left to prepare was some music for the singing group, but that could wait until tomorrow.

'If you don't mind walking down to Caledonia Stables, we could make a start before dinner,' the girl suggested.

Tabitha grinned. It felt good to be part of something again. At her last school, perhaps because she'd only been on a contract and knew it wasn't likely to last forever, she'd always been a bit of a square peg, but here the girls and staff were so welcoming. Well, almost all of them. Miss Reedy wasn't her closest ally, but her husband was kindly, and Tabitha was sure that, if she won him over, his wife would follow suit. Tabitha was thrilled that she was able to teach the way she wanted to, and now there was an exciting project that she could sink her teeth into – two, if she included taking over the Winchester-Fayle Singers.

'You know, Miss Crowley, you remind me of someone,' Alice-Miranda said, tilting her head to one side, 'but I can't put my finger on who it is. I'm sure it will come to me soon.'

'They say all of us have a twin somewhere out there in the world,' the woman replied.

'A doppelganger.' Alice-Miranda nodded. 'I have one and I owe her a letter. Her name's Britt Fox and we were at a leadership camp together in Scotland for the Queen's Colours Program a little while ago. She lives in Norway. From the time we met, everyone said that not only did we look alike, our mannerisms were similar too. But Britt's a much more adventurous dresser than I am. She's helping me expand my fashion choices and take greater risks.'

'I'd love to meet her one day. She sounds fabulous,' Tabitha said, smiling at the delightful thought of two Alice-Mirandas. 'Now, let's make a start on this concert, shall we? I've got a few ideas, but I imagine you girls will have loads more.'

The pair walked out of Caledonia Manor and wandered down the drive. As they passed a guard of stone lions, Tabitha spotted Caprice Radford ahead of them and shuddered. Two of that child, on the other hand, was definitely two too many.

Chapter 20

'So, what's this all about?' Millie rushed into the sitting room, drying her hair with a towel. She'd just returned from a vigorous hour and a half of tennis training and, having caught a whiff of her armpits, decided she needed a shower before dinner or no one would want to sit with her.

Alice-Miranda explained to the room of twenty girls that Mrs Abboud was open to the idea of a fundraiser, but only if she could help. 'I think we should form a committee,' she proposed, 'or else there'll be too many cooks and everyone will be getting in the way of each other and then nothing will happen at all.'

'The first thing we need is a date,' Chessie said, turning to a fresh page in her open notebook. 'So we know how long we have to get things organised.'

The rest of the girls agreed.

Miss Crowley took out her term calendar and quickly scanned the weekends until the break. 'As far as I can see, Sunday the thirteenth looks like the best option,' she said. 'There's nothing else scheduled.'

'Fine, pencil it in,' Sloane said, reclipping one of the barrettes she'd recently taken to wearing in her hair.

Alice-Miranda bit down on the end of her pen. 'What roles do we need for the committee?' she wondered aloud. She'd seen her mother and father head up enough of them to know that specific responsibilities were important and supporting one another was paramount to the success of any activity.

'We need a chairperson,' Millie said. 'Which, for the first time in village history, won't be Myrtle Parker!'

The girls laughed.

'I don't know how she'll cope with not being the boss,' Ivory commented as she retied the cerise-pink ribbon around her ponytail. 'Wait until she hears that the concert is being run by children. She'll be aghast!' The girl pressed the back of her hand to her forehead and pretended to faint.

'There has to be a treasurer to look after the money side of things,' Sloane suggested, only to be greeted by a room full of wary faces. 'I don't want to do it,' she said, throwing her hands up. 'It's far too much responsibility than I'd care to take on, and I know you're all thinking it was my mother who tried to get Fayle closed down so she could sell the land and make a fortune. She might be my mother, but I can assure you that I don't have the same greedy genes.'

'It's fine, Sloane,' Alice-Miranda said gently. 'No one was thinking that at all.'

Caprice snorted. 'Speak for yourself.'

Sloane turned to fix the girl with a steely glare. 'Considering you weren't even here when that happened, I'd keep my mouth shut if I was you.'

Caprice folded her arms. 'It's going to be so much fun telling all these school stories to

Gloss and Goss when I'm the most famous singer and actress in the world.'

Sloane's jaw dropped.

'Don't worry, no one reads that rubbish,' Millie whispered to her. 'At least no one with any sense. Come on, let's get back to business.'

Alice-Miranda gave Millie a wink, thankful that another potential explosion had been averted.

'We need a secretary to take all the notes from the meetings,' Millie said, and glanced over at Chessie, who was furiously scribbling down everything the girls were saying onto her notepad. The others followed Millie's gaze.

Chessie looked up, wondering why the room had fallen silent, then grinned. 'I'd be happy to do it.'

The newly founded committee got to work. Their discussions ricocheted from advertising and media to signage and risk assessment, which everyone agreed was a total bore. Fortunately, Miss Crowley offered to do the paperwork for that. Before long, Chessie had compiled quite a list.

In the end they voted Alice-Miranda to be the chairperson, Chessie as secretary, Millie was the treasurer, Sloane was in charge of promotions,

Ivory and Susannah put their hands up for venue management, Danika was in charge of technology and Shelby was to look after the car park. Caprice appointed herself as the head of talent as she was the one with the most contacts in the business. When Millie pointed out that it was Alice-Miranda who probably had the best connections, Caprice promptly reminded everyone that her mother was the famous television chef, Venetia Baldini, which solved the catering issue right away. The children brokered a deal that, if Caprice could get her mother to organise the food, she could program the show – on the proviso that the entire committee would have input on the acts. The girl agreed, though only because she had already decided on at least a dozen songs she was planning to perform. Everyone else came under a team leader, so there were plenty of girls ready to do the legwork.

'What are you putting your hand up for, Jacinta?' Millie asked.

The girl startled from where she'd been giving the carpet her full attention. 'Sorry, what did you say?'

'Your job?' Millie said with a frown.

'Oh.' Jacinta shrugged. 'I don't mind. You choose.' Since Mrs Parker's revelation about Lucas the other night, she'd barely been able to think of anything else. It hadn't helped that her father had telephoned again this afternoon and asked if there was any chance he could pick her up after school tomorrow and take her for a milkshake. Jacinta hadn't known what to say. He interpreted her silence as a yes and said that he would arrange it with the school. Jacinta wanted to tell her mother, but was worried she'd be upset. Part of her badly wanted her father to be the man she'd always hoped he would be yet there was every chance he could disappoint her again. Why did grown-ups have to be so ridiculously complicated?

'How about you organise other activities?' Millie said. 'If it's going to be a proper festival, we'll need a whole bunch of stalls with things like face painting and craft. What about a kissing booth? I know a few girls who'd pay good money to peck Lucas on the cheek.'

The girls giggled and some guffawed. 'Jacinta would, that's for sure,' Sloane teased.

'I don't have to pay for mine,' Jacinta retorted and was met with raised eyebrows and catcalls.

She blushed a deep shade of red and shook her head. 'The stalls are a great idea. I'll work on that, but there won't be any kissing at this festival.'

'We need a name,' Chessie said. 'Who knows, if it goes well, it could become an annual event and we could choose a different cause to support every year.'

'That's a brilliant idea,' Alice-Miranda said, rubbing her hands with excitement. 'Once we've done it this time, it will be so much easier with the next one as we'll know what we're doing. Okay, does anyone have a thought about the name?'

'What about Kids for Kids?' Danica said.

'Boring!' Caprice bleated. 'And we're not just doing things for kids, we're doing them for a whole family.'

'I wonder if we could play on the school name,' Alice-Miranda said. 'Winchesterfield . . .?'

Jacinta's eyes brightened. 'The Fields Festival, or Fields of Fun?'

'I love those!' Alice-Miranda gasped. 'Chessie, can you note both of those ideas down so we can all think about it and revisit them in a couple of days?' She looked around the group. 'We should probably assign each person a task to achieve before our next meeting too. It's Tuesday today, so how about we reconvene on Thursday after dinner to check in and see how far we've got? In the meantime, I'll speak to Miss Grimm and Miss Reedy about the date and assure them that they don't have to lift a finger – this is all on us,' she said, and turned to the teacher. 'Miss Crowley, could you ask Mr Plumpton and some of the faculty members if they're keen to lend a hand? I know dear Mr Charles will support us, as will Mrs Smith and Mrs Jennings.'

'So long as she's on ticket sales or something and not cooking,' Caprice crowed.

Tabitha smiled and gave a decisive nod. 'And if you'd like me to come with you to speak to Miss Grimm and Miss Reedy, I'm happy to.'

The dinner bell rang, breaking up the party.

'Something smells delicious,' Sloane said with a note of surprise.

'I saw Mrs Smith arrive just after lunch,' Chessie whispered conspiratorially. 'She said she was doing her famous Keralan fish curry.'

'Brilliant.' Millie licked her lips. 'I hope she's made naan bread as well and the pappadums with mint raita – they're my favourite.'

'Perhaps I'll have dinner with you girls tonight,' Miss Crowley said as the group stood up to leave. 'It'll beat tinned spaghetti on toast in my flat.'

Alice-Miranda grinned. 'That would be lovely and, don't worry, you won't be the only staff member there.'

Brimming with ideas and exciting plans, the newly formed committee walked down the hallway to the dining room and, sure enough, found a table full of teachers already inside.

Livinia pushed her glasses up the bridge of her nose, her mind a whirl of confusion. She'd searched high and low for the dratted note after her run-in with Ophelia and couldn't believe it had been sitting in the middle of her desk the whole time. Trouble was, it didn't read the same way she remembered. Her eyes took in Ophelia's distinctive handwriting and personalised letterhead. Yes, she had been in a hurry when she received it, but this note expressly told her not to accept any interviews. How had she got it so wrong? Livinia let out a deep breath and wrung her hands together. She would go and apologise to Ophelia at once. It was the least she could do.

Chapter 21

Jacinta swizzled the straw around in her strawberry milkshake, staring blankly at the bubbles.

'Don't you like it?' her father asked. 'We can get something else.'

The girl shook her head. 'It's fine.'

'How's school?' he said, hoping his daughter would give more than a one-word reply.

They were sitting at a booth at the far end of the Cupcake Cafe, which was busy with parents and children getting snacks after school. A small boy, no more than four years old, began to wail. Jacinta watched him, wondering if he was about to launch into full tantrum mode, but his mother shoved an ice-cream into his hand and he stopped the performance.

'Earth to Jacinta,' her father said, waving a hand in front of her face.

'School's fine,' she replied, returning her attention to the frothy pink drink in front of her.

Neville racked his brain, trying to remember something that his daughter was interested in. 'How's your dancing going?'

'It's gymnastics and acrobatics, not dancing,' Jacinta said without looking up. 'I was the Junior National Champion, not that you would know seeing as though you didn't even bother to watch me compete. You know, I was the only child without any family members there to support me. Thank goodness for Mrs Howard and Miss Wall.'

Neville swept his hand through his hair. 'Of course I remember, sweetheart. We sent you a huge bouquet of flowers afterwards. Your mother and I were so proud.'

Jacinta shook her head. 'Wrong again. You and Mummy were at Cannes Film Festival. Your assistant, Bridget, sent me the flowers.'

Neville groaned inwardly. 'Look, Jacinta, I acknowledge I've been a less-than-ideal father and I apologise for that, but I want to make it up to you,' he said, reaching across the table and taking her hands in his. 'I want things to be different between us going forward. Better.'

'Why now?' The girl sat back and folded her arms across her chest. 'You've never been interested in me. What's changed?'

Neville rested his elbows on the table and cradled his chin in his hands. 'I suppose you get older and people you love aren't around any more and it makes you think about what's important . . . I miss you and your mother. I want us to be a family again.'

'We've never been a family,' Jacinta said, her brow furrowing. 'You and Mummy dumped me in boarding school as soon as I was old enough and hardly ever came to get me for the holidays. When I did go home, I was left with the nanny or your PA. Although there was that one time that the PA thought I was with the nanny and vice versa and I ended up staying home on my own for three days before Great-Aunt Minnie called in and realised that no one was looking after me. How is she, by the way?'

Neville coughed and covered his mouth. 'She's fine. Sends her regards,' he mumbled, taking a sip of his espresso.

'She must be ancient by now,' Jacinta said. 'I remember she smelt funny – like pine trees.'

'You know I never meant to hurt you and I was always thinking of you, sweetheart,' the man said. 'You've got to let it go. Holding on to past resentments isn't good for you.'

Jacinta sighed. 'I have every right to be angry. You've been an awful father.'

Neville could feel a trickle of perspiration running down the back of his neck. He clenched his teeth. 'You're right. I was a terrible father.'

'And husband,' Jacinta added.

'I thought Ambrosia deserved better,' the man said.

Jacinta rolled her eyes. 'No, you didn't. You dumped Mummy on your anniversary and then you stopped paying for me as soon as she got a job,' she said, and took a sip of her milkshake.

'Okay, so my timing was off, but I was in a bad place,' Neville pleaded. 'I'd just done the biggest deal of my life and I didn't know what was next. I felt lost and your mother was so obsessed with being at all the premiere parties and events . . .

I was tired and I just wanted a break from it all,' the man said with a sigh. 'It was impossible to keep up with her.'

It sounded like one excuse after the other and, frankly, Jacinta had heard enough. 'Could you take me back to school, please?' she asked.

Neville looked crestfallen. 'Oh, I thought we could go to Claude's over in Downsfordvale for dinner, seeing that the Middle Eastern place in Winchesterfield burned down. I have permission from Mrs Clark.'

Jacinta finished her milkshake with a loud slurp and stood up. 'It's Mrs *Clarkson*, and the fire is the reason I have to get back. We're organising a fundraiser for the Abbouds to help rebuild their house and business.'

Neville's brow furrowed. 'Why? I don't pay school fees for you to spend your time working on charity events.'

'You don't pay my school fees, full stop,' the girl retorted. 'Mummy does and she thinks it's a wonderful idea. I can't believe you haven't even asked about the fire.'

'What about it?' Neville said, then slapped his forehead. 'You were there, weren't you?

Sorry, I've just got a lot of things on my mind at the moment.'

'Yes, I was there,' Jacinta said, standing up. 'We're organising a concert, but it's sort of more like a festival with lots of activities. I'm in charge of the face painting and I thought we might have a balloon artist and a couple of craft tents to keep the little kids entertained. And I need to talk to Lucas and see if his father has any contacts with some of the performers on our wish list.'

Neville was incredulous. 'You're going to do all that? At least get my PA, Trista, to help you.'

Jacinta wondered what fate had befallen Bridget, her father's previous assistant, who had babysat her more times than she'd seen her own father. The pair hopped into Neville's shiny Aston Martin that was parked outside the cafe.

'I know you're angry with me, sweetheart, but you have to believe me when I say I'm a changed man,' Neville said as he fired up the engine. 'Your mother and I are going out for dinner tomorrow night and I'll be back again on the weekend to take you to sport or out for lunch – you can just let me know what you'd like. And I meant it about Trista helping with your fundraiser.'

Jacinta looked over at him and remembered what Alice-Miranda had said. You can only take people as you find them. 'Thanks, Dad,' she said quietly.

'My pleasure.' Neville smiled across at his daughter. 'I promise you, Jacinta, we're going to be a family again. You just wait and see.'

Chapter 22

By Friday morning, everything was beginning to fall neatly into place. The committee had settled on a name for the festival, the scope of duties and had allocated a task to each of the girls to complete. They were yet to lock in a major act, despite Alice-Miranda putting in a call to her Aunt Charlotte. Uncle Lawrence was in Siberia, filming a romantic comedy set in a fish factory, and it was going to be a couple of days before she could speak to him. Meanwhile, Miss Crowley had managed to recruit Mr Pratt and Mrs Clinch, who were eager to be of service. She neglected to mention that both of them had already lodged several complaints about the noise coming from Mrs Reeves's old flat, where the Abboud family was staying.

In better news, there had been no official word that Miss Grimm had taken back the reins from Miss Reedy, so Alice-Miranda was hoping the headmistress might have reconsidered her decision. Miss Reedy had done a wonderful job as far as she could tell and it didn't seem fair to short-change the woman on what she had thought would be a full year's tenure, particularly over a decision that she was well within her rights to make as acting headmistress. In fact, Miss Grimm seemed to have vanished into thin air and Miss Reedy along with her. Alice-Miranda wondered if Miss Grimm had followed her husband's advice and taken a break away with the family. Whatever the case, Alice-Miranda decided to track down Miss Reedy to secure the seal of approval for the festival.

'We have to get her to say yes soon or else there's no point continuing with the plans,' Millie said as the pair bounded along the path to the junior school. 'Especially now that we've settled on the name.'

'The Fields Festival really is perfect, isn't it?' Alice-Miranda sighed. 'I'd hate to dash everyone's hopes.'

The girls scampered through the back entrance of Winchesterfield House and were surprised to see the hallway and office teeming with people. There were mothers and fathers and lots of girls. Some of the children were dressed in casual clothes while others were in uniforms from various schools. Mrs Derby was attending to a mother and child who were filling in some forms at her desk. Alice-Miranda and Millie waited until they'd taken their seats before stepping up to speak to her.

'Hello Mrs Derby, sorry to disturb you, but we wanted to catch Miss Reedy or Miss Grimm,' Alice-Miranda said.

The woman shook her head. 'I'm afraid there's no chance of seeing Miss Grimm today or tomorrow or . . .' She glanced at the calendar on her computer screen and winced. 'Or until the end of next week.'

'What's going on?' Millie asked, gesturing to the room of people.

Louella leaned across the desk. 'Your television appearance has sparked an avalanche of enrolment enquiries and Miss Grimm is positively overwhelmed with interviews,' she whispered. 'Frankly, I don't know how she's managing with everything and the baby – thank goodness Mr Grump is on hand. Honestly, working mothers are incredible. It's terrifying.'

Alice-Miranda couldn't help noticing the dark rings beneath Mrs Derby's eyes and the worry lines etched on her brow. 'Where's Miss Reedy?' she asked. 'Shouldn't she be conducting the interviews?'

'She's out there somewhere running the school as far as I know,' Mrs Derby said, waving a hand. She took up an envelope on the side of her desk and handed it to the girl. It was addressed to Miss Reedy in Miss Grimm's handwriting. 'Would you mind giving this to Miss Reedy when you next see her? I can't possibly leave this madhouse.'

'Are you feeling all right, Mrs Derby? You look a bit off-colour,' Alice-Miranda said. She'd seen the woman nibbling on a dry biscuit and spotted a glass of something resembling ginger ale on her desk too.

'I'm fine,' Louella replied with a pinched smile.

The room seemed to be growing more and more restless by the second.

'Excuse me,' a woman said haughtily, elbowing Alice-Miranda out of the way. 'How much longer will the headmistress be?'

'Excuse you,' Millie muttered. She had half a mind to elbow the woman back.

Louella ran her finger down the list in front of her. She'd allowed half an hour for each interview, but Miss Grimm had been averaging around forty-five minutes and was now two hours behind schedule. The interviews would likely run until after six, which was a terrible thought, especially given the way Louella was feeling. 'I'm afraid there are still several families in front of you at this stage.'

Alice-Miranda had an idea, but there was no time to discuss it. She stood on a chair and clapped her hands. 'Hello everyone, my name is Alice-Miranda and this is Millie and we're going to take you all on a tour of the junior school.'

'We are?' Millie asked.

Alice-Miranda gave a quick nod. 'Everyone except the family with the next appointment,' she said, looking to Mrs Derby for their names.

'Mr and Mrs Davies and Annabelle,' Louella said.

'Oh, aren't you the girls who saved that family in the fire?' a man with an impressive handlebar moustache piped up.

Millie nodded, and there was a ripple of excitement around the room.

'You were so brave,' a small girl with long dark braids gasped.

'You and your friends are the reason we're here,' a woman with a severe black bob added.

'Well, let's get moving, shall we?' Alice-Miranda hopped down off the chair as Millie ran to fetch one of the school umbrellas from the stand by the door. She figured they'd need something for the group to follow given she and Alice-Miranda were still somewhat vertically challenged.

'Just keep an eye on this,' Millie said, and thrust the object skywards.

'Don't open that in here, young lady,' said the man with the moustache. 'It's bad luck.'

Millie grinned. 'I wasn't planning to.' She did, however, fleetingly wonder whether she had opened an umbrella inside or walked in front of a black cat right before Caprice had arrived at the school.

Louella Derby stood up and looked over the heads of the crowd to catch Alice-Miranda's eye. 'Thank you,' the woman mouthed before dashing off in the direction of the staff bathroom.

Chapter 23

The two friends quickly conferred and settled on taking the group through the library, which had lost its Goldsworthy prefix after Alethea left the school and her father was sent to prison. They were greeted in the foyer by Mr Gordy Winslade, the recently appointed librarian. For a while there, Miss Reedy had looked after the collection on top of her English classes. However, it had all got a bit too much. The woman was a whiz, not a magician, so before embarking on maternity leave, Miss Grimm decided that a specialist staff member would be a valuable addition to the school.

'Good afternoon,' the man said warily, tugging on his silver beard. 'What's all this?'

Alice-Miranda quickly explained. She and Mr Winslade were old friends. Prior to coming to work at the school, he had been in charge of the Highton Mill Public Library in the village adjacent to her family home, Highton Hall. It was Alice-Miranda's mother who had alerted the old man to the opportunity, and they'd all been thrilled when he got the job.

'Oh, splendid,' the man enthused. 'I'd love to talk about the library – you know it's my favourite place in the world. Well, not just this library, although it is special in its own way. I love *all* libraries. Wherever there are books, there is knowledge and information, emotions, imagination, characters and pagination.' His voice was getting higher and higher.

As it sounded as if the man was about to break into song, Alice-Miranda tugged on his sleeve. 'I'm sorry, Mr Winslade,' she whispered, 'but we don't have long as Millie and I will need to get to assembly and we still have lots to see.'

Mr Winslade blushed. 'Forgive me, child. It's just that once you get me started, it's hard to get me to stop, and I can't wait to be able to help all of you find stories that you love or information you need.'

'He's an odd little man,' the haughty woman said, loud enough for all to hear. This time she earned herself arched eyebrows from every parent in the room. 'Don't look at me like that. He *is*,' she protested.

'He's also one of the kindest people you'd ever meet,' Millie said. 'We're big on that at Winchesterfield-Downsfordvale.'

As the group exited the building and crossed the flagstone courtyard towards the classrooms, Miss Reedy came striding up to them. 'What's all this?' she asked over the top of her glasses.

Millie explained what they were doing, which saw Miss Reedy's eyebrows jump up in surprise. She'd offered to take tours for Ophelia, but the woman had turned her down, saying that Livinia had enough on her plate. She thought they were getting back on an even keel after she'd apologised for the mix-up with the note – despite the fact it was Ophelia who should have been eating humble pie when all the enrolment enquiries began rolling in.

Alice-Miranda turned to the assembled crowd. 'Please allow me to introduce Miss Reedy, our acting headmistress while Miss Grimm is on maternity leave. Miss Reedy is the most marvellous English teacher.'

'Why aren't you in there conducting the interviews if you're the headmistress?' one of the fathers chuckled. 'Are you only pretending?'

Livinia smiled tightly. 'I think you'll find that it's much better to have your interview with the real McCoy. I'll just get on with running the school while you're keeping her busy.'

The group of parents and children stood in a huddle, some pointing out parts of the campus, others blank-faced.

'Miss Reedy, we actually came over to talk to you before assembly if we could,' Alice-Miranda said.

'It's about the festival,' Millie added, taking advantage of the fact that Miss Reedy might think twice about saying no in front of all the prospective students and their parents.

'We discussed that on Monday evening, girls, and now is not the time to raise it again. You know

Miss Grimm's feelings on the matter,' Livinia said with a pointed look.

There was a general rumbling of discontent through the group.

'That's a pity,' a man in a pinstriped suit said loudly. 'We saw the girls talking about it on the telly and were so impressed. That's one of the reasons Barbara and I decided to enrol our little Tuesday here.' He glanced at the girl beside him, who was in possession of two long plaits that reached almost to her knees.

Livinia swallowed hard. Her husband had been rabbiting on at home about the event, saying that all of the staff thought it was a wonderful idea, but she'd also told him in no uncertain terms that it wasn't going to happen.

'But we've organised everything,' Millie said in a wobbly voice. The festival meant so much to her – to all of them – that she hated the thought that it might not go ahead. 'We have a commit-tee and Alice-Miranda is the chairperson and I'm the treasurer and everyone has jobs and we even have the most fantastic name – The Fields Festival. It's a play on Winchesterfield. And we're going to have it in the field in the front of the school. Miss Crowley's been helping us.'

Livinia frowned. 'Has she now?' As a new member of staff, surely the woman had enough to do already – and she was yet to have her first rehearsal with the Winchester-Fayle Singers.

'We've got The Stingrays,' Millie blurted.

Alice-Miranda's eyes were the size of dinner plates while several of the girls and mothers behind her squealed loudly. Or perhaps they had come from the two fathers at the back, who were clenching their fists like excited schoolgirls. 'Really?' she mouthed to Millie, wondering if her friend had somehow received an update.

Millie shrugged while the gaggle of parents began talking over the top of one another and saying how they were going to get their tickets right away. It was bedlam. Livinia Reedy couldn't believe her ears. The idea that they would have The Stingrays at the school was thrilling. They were the biggest band in the world at the moment, and while she was no aficionado of pop music, she had been known to sing along to them on the radio and they always made her smile.

'Who else have you secured?' she asked.

Alice-Miranda jumped in quickly with the list she had so far, which mostly included locals and, of course, Caprice.

'And we're hoping to get Nick Waterford,' Millie added. 'He's a good friend of Alice-Miranda's parents.'

'Millie,' Alice-Miranda whispered sharply, 'we don't know for sure yet.'

'It doesn't matter,' Millie whispered back. 'I think Miss Reedy's going to say yes anyway – just look at her.'

'Oh my word.' Livinia suddenly felt faint. He was more her style. She'd loved Nick Waterford since she was a young girl. She'd been to several of his concerts and thought he was incredible. He was getting on a bit now, but the idea of having him at the school was almost too much. Her spine tingled at the prospect.

'I almost forgot,' Alice-Miranda said, pulling the envelope from her pocket. 'Mrs Derby asked me to give you this.'

Seeing Ophelia's handwriting, Livinia opened the letter and read it very carefully. She wasn't about to be caught out a second time, though she was surprised by the contents. 'Well, girls, it sounds as if you have everything in hand,' Livinia said, finally allowing herself to smile.

'You mean we can go ahead?' Millie asked, glancing at Alice-Miranda.

Miss Reedy nodded and held up the letter. 'I have Miss Grimm's blessing right here. She says she's reconsidered, so you can make your announcement in assembly.' It was going to be a very happy assembly indeed, as she'd also planned to acknowledge the girls for their bravery too. The announcement of the festival would be the icing on the cake.

'Yes!' Millie fizzed, high-fiving Alice-Miranda.

'And I'll be taking over liaising with your committee,' Miss Reedy added. 'Miss Crowley has enough to do settling in.'

Millie and Alice-Miranda looked at one another.

'This is excellent news,' said the man in the suit, and his sentiments were echoed around the group.

Livinia Reedy bid them farewell and dashed away. Perhaps Mr Grump had managed to change his wife's mind about the event, but whatever the reason, she was glad the woman had. The school would be full in no time flat and she was certain Ophelia would recognise how much the television interview and festival had to do with that. There was no way Benitha Wall would be continuing as deputy. The position would be Livinia's – of that she had no doubt.

Chapter 24

Tabitha Crowley hobbled up the path, cursing her choice of shoes. She'd have to remember to wear sensible ones given the walk between the two campuses. She was about to duck upstairs to change into some flats when Hephzibah Fayle appeared in the hallway.

'Excuse me, dear,' the old woman called, bustling over to her. 'This came for you and had to be signed for.' She held out a large brown envelope. 'I hope you don't mind, but I thought it was easier than sending the poor man away only to have to return tomorrow, especially as it looks as if it might be important.'

Tabitha caught sight of the logo in the top-left corner and drew in a sharp breath. She wasn't fond of official documentation. In her experience, it never brought good news. 'Thank you,' she said, taking the envelope.

'Please join us for supper on Sunday, dear,' Hephzibah said, her blue eyes shining. 'I'm going to do a pork roast with crackling and baked vegetables. It's Mr Pratt's favourite.'

Tabitha nodded absently, her mind elsewhere. She thanked the woman again, then powered up the stairs to her flat, opening the envelope before she had unlocked the door. The letter was from the solicitor's firm Brown, Brown and White. Tabitha scanned to the bottom of the page, barely believing her eyes. She read it again, slowly this time. According to Mr Brown, they hadn't been able to locate her for the reading of the will, which made sense as it took place while she was moving to Winchesterfield.

Tabitha stared at the number, counting the zeros over and over. It hardly seemed real, having scrimped and saved every cent she could since her parents' accident. It had happened during her last year at school and it always surprised her that she'd not only completed her final exams, but had excelled in them. Her mother and father had endured an up-and-down life, financially speaking. Her father, Anthony, was a wheeler and dealer and had invested heavily in the property market right before the biggest crash since the Great Depression. Her parents had lost everything and it was only because her mother, Tripp, had paid her school fees years in advance that she was able to keep her position after they died. But Tabitha was a pragmatic soul and not prone to melodrama. Besides, her parents had left her in boarding school from the age of nine while they pursued the next deal and the next after that. She'd learned to be self-sufficient. They loved her – that was never in doubt. She just didn't suit their schedule or lifestyle.

So, while Tabitha missed them, life had gone on. She'd been far more upset when her great-aunt had passed away recently. It was Aunty Verve who had made sure that she always had somewhere to go for the holidays, who she spent Christmases with and from whom spectacular gifts would arrive on her birthday.

But this was completely unexpected and more than she would ever need. A single tear spilled onto her cheek. She could finally put down roots. She could enjoy her work and concentrate solely on her career – perhaps even do some travel. Tabitha clutched the letter to her chest and looked skyward. 'Oh, Aunty Verve, thank you. Thank you so, so much.'

'Well, that was a waste of time,' Jacinta sighed as the group left the meeting room in Caledonia Manor, where Miss Reedy had just spent the last hour going over everything they'd already organised with Miss Crowley.

'Miss Crowley should have been there,' Sloane said. 'She knows all that stuff. And what was Miss Reedy talking about us having The Stingrays and Nick Waterford on the bill?'

Millie grimaced. 'I may have said something when Alice-Miranda and I were trying to persuade her that the concert should go ahead.'

'And no, they're not booked,' Alice-Miranda said, 'but there's still time.'

'Good one, Millie.' Sloane groaned, then turned to Alice-Miranda. 'I hope your uncle is up for some smooth-talking because I don't fancy our chances of getting The Stingrays – they're the most famous band in the world, and isn't Nick Waterford about a hundred?'

'He's not *that* old,' Millie said, rolling her eyes. 'My parents like him and we need parents to bring kids, so there has to be something in it for them.'

'Except that we *don't* have him,' Sloane countered.

'I'll speak to Aunt Charlotte tonight to find out whether Uncle Lawrence has had any luck,' Alice-Miranda said.

The girls were due to meet the rest of the Winchester-Fayle Singers in the music room at five o'clock. They raced upstairs and along the corridor, where they could hear the piano, and were surprised to discover Miss Crowley sitting behind the keyboard instead of Mr Trout. The woman stopped when she spotted the girls.

'Come in, everyone,' she said, beckoning them over. 'I hope you had a productive meeting. I'm sorry I wasn't able to join you.'

'We were too,' Sloane said as the girls sat down.

Jacinta made a beeline for Lucas, who was sitting beside Sep in the front row. 'Hi,' she said, tapping him on the shoulder. He grinned at her but there was something in his eyes that caused Jacinta's stomach to tighten. 'Is everything okay?'

Lucas nodded. 'Better now that you're here,' he whispered.

Jacinta bit her lip then smiled as he jumped up to get her a chair.

'How's things with your dad?' he said quietly as Miss Crowley directed Millie to pass out the sheet music.

'He's taking me to acrobatics tomorrow,' she said. 'You know it's the first time ever.'

'Wow, that's amazing,' Lucas replied. 'Would you believe that my mum's going to be here tomorrow too?'

Jacinta was taken aback. 'I thought she was in New York.'

'She was, but Aunt Lily's been in hospital and Uncle Heinrich needs some help with my cousins,' Lucas explained. 'She's bringing Jasper and Poppy over with her as well as her new fiancé, which is exciting and kind of terrifying.'

'But you've talked to him before?' Jacinta said.

'Only on the phone and that's different to meeting someone in person. What if I don't like him or he doesn't like me?' Lucas said uneasily.

'He's not going to like you Lucas,' Jacinta replied, causing the boy to frown. 'He's going to *love* you, just like everyone else – me especially,' the girl said, her cheeks flushing. 'Maybe I can come and see you tomorrow, meet your mum's fiancé and make sure that he's good enough for her. It would be great to catch up with Jasper and Poppy as well.'

Alice-Miranda was perched behind the pair and couldn't help catching the end of their conversation. 'Jasper and Poppy?' she said, leaning forward. Lucas and Jacinta quickly relayed what was going on but left out the mushy bits.

Lucas's aunt and uncle and their children lived on the farm at Highton Hall, the Highton-Smith-Kennington-Joneses' estate. Alice-Miranda had known them all her life and they were like family to her too. She'd only met Lucas a few years ago, and at the time he was a very angry young man. He'd never known his father, who they later found out was the famous movie star Lawrence Ridley. For quite a while Lucas was upset with his mother for keeping the truth from him, but in the end it all worked out and Lawrence married Alice-Miranda's Aunt Charlotte. Father and son had become very close and now Lucas and Alice-Miranda were cousins by marriage.

'Is Lily all right?' Alice-Miranda asked. 'I'm surprised Mrs Oliver didn't mention it, but perhaps she's had a lot on her plate since Mummy and Daddy have gone away.'

Lucas nodded. 'It was a slightly complicated appendicitis, and as Heinrich's been harvesting, Mum's offered to help out.'

'When's your mother getting married?' Jacinta asked, praying it wasn't too soon.

'Next school holidays,' Lucas said. 'I'll be going to New York for the wedding. Then I'm off to stay with Dad and Charlotte and the twins for the rest of the break.'

Jacinta felt her stomach knot again. His whole family was going to be in America now.

Alice-Miranda couldn't help noticing the worry seeping into Jacinta's features, and she had a feeling it had everything to do with what Mrs Parker had said last weekend. She hoped it wasn't true for both Lucas and Jacinta's sakes.

Lucas's dad had gone to Fayle, so she couldn't imagine there was any reason for him to leave. It was family tradition and he was a star student.

Once Millie had finished passing out the sheet music, Miss Crowley stood at the front of the room with a broad smile on her face. 'Listen up, everyone,' she said with a clap of her hands. 'I'd like us to learn some new songs for the concert. We need to rehearse at least twice if not three times a week, and I'll do my best to find times when there's nothing else on.'

Lucas reached across and squeezed Jacinta's hand. 'Finally, we'll get some time together,' the boy whispered in Jacinta's ear. She could feel her cheeks blaze, but he was right – it was the best news she'd had in ages.

'Okay, is everyone familiar with this song?' Tabitha said, playing a few bars on the grand piano.

'This is my mum's favourite,' Sloane said. 'If it's on the radio, she turns it up super loud, which is a blessing because her voice is a cross between a strangled cat and a dying elephant seal.'

'Don't be ridiculous,' Sep said, turning to shoot his sister a glare. 'It's much worse than that.'

The rest of the class burst out laughing.

George Figworth raised his hand. 'I don't think I can sing this, miss,' he said, his lip trembling.

'Why on earth not?' Millie asked, wrinkling her nose.

Figgy sniffed. 'Because it's about a cat and mine died.'

'Oh, George, I'm so sorry to hear that,' Miss Crowley said. She racked her brain to think of another song that might be suitable. The poor lad looked as if he was about to cry. Rufus Pemberley began to giggle. 'And what's so funny, young man?' Tabitha challenged. 'Losing a beloved pet is no laughing matter.'

Rufus nudged Figgy on the leg and this time the pair of them burst out laughing.

'I see.' Tabitha breathed deeply. 'Very funny, boys.'

'How juvenile,' Caprice said with a flick of her copper tresses. 'Just throw them out, Miss Crowley. We don't need them.'

Figgy and Rufus pulled faces at the girl and mimicked flicking their hair in big, flouncy flourishes.

'Right, we should make a start.' Tabitha walked back to the piano and stood in front of the keys.

She was still floating after her news and nothing was going to put a dampener on her day.

The woman's happiness was apparently contagious. Figgy proved to have the kind of voice one considered a gift, and when combined with Caprice and the rest of the group, she had tingles several times.

Jacinta looked at Miss Crowley and for the first time that day noticed the teacher's gold necklace. It had a crest and a bar hanging from it and closely resembled the one her Great-Aunt Minnie wore. She remembered the woman saying it was one of a kind, but people often claimed such things. As Lucas leaned in to whisper in her ear, his arm touched hers and Jacinta forgot all about the necklace. She could have sworn she felt a spark, but that might have just been the fireworks that were going off inside her chest.

Towards the end of the session, Tabitha was positively beaming. The kids were good – there was no denying it. And there had been no more shenanigans from the lads. She always found that, if you made your expectations clear from the outset, it was better for everyone. This was going to be fun.

Chapter 25

On Saturday morning it seemed like everyone had somewhere to be. Millie was off to compete in a tennis tournament in Upping Brougham, Sloane and Chessie were playing soccer against the girls from Sainsbury Palace, Caprice had demanded an extra singing lesson with Mr Trout and, to everyone's surprise, Jacinta's father had stuck to his word and driven her to Downsfordvale for her acrobatics lesson. The boarding house was all but deserted except for Alice-Miranda. Not one to hang about at a loose end, the tiny girl changed into her jodhpurs and boots and made her way to the stables. She could hear someone singing along to the radio and realised that Dervla was in the tack room.

'Hello,' the child said, poking her head around the corner. The woman was surrounded by a mountain of mess.

Dervla spun around. 'Hello there,' she said, turning down the volume on the radio. 'I'm in the middle of a major clean-out – not that it was my idea.'

'Would you like some help?' Alice-Miranda asked.

'Thank you, but I can manage.' Dervla flashed a smile as she wiped her sleeve across her brow. 'Miss Reedy seems to have a bee in her bonnet the past few days. She sent me the longest list of chores. I gather she's planning to bring by some parents of prospective students, but I'm putting my foot down at sanding and staining the stable timber-work. That's definitely outside my job description and I have to study for my final exams.'

'How peculiar,' Alice-Miranda said, her fore-head puckering, 'especially as Mr Charles did all that last year.'

'I almost choked when I read her note ordering me to cover prep time for the junior girls for no extra pay. I can tell you right now that is *not* happening,' Dervla said, her mouth set in a grim line.

'Mmm.' Alice-Miranda frowned. She had a strange feeling that something wasn't quite right about the situation. It was odd that, while Miss Reedy's temperament had improved over the past few days, her demands of the staff had reached extraordinary heights. Alice-Miranda had overheard Miss Tweedle complain to Mr Pratt about having to wash the girls' smocks, while he bemoaned a directive to catalogue the entire contents of the Science storeroom. Perhaps the stress of running the school was beginning to get to the woman.

'But don't concern yourself with my worries,' Dervla said, mustering a smile. 'What are you doing here?'

'I was planning to take Bony out as long as his foot is better,' Alice-Miranda said.

'I can guarantee he's back to his usual self,' Dervla said with a roll of the eyes.

Alice-Miranda looked up from where she was sorting the pile of bridles that was sitting on the floor. 'Oh no, what has that naughty boy done now?'

'Let's just say I have a lovely bite mark on my bottom and he's not getting any treats today.' Dervla picked up a saddle and lifted it onto a peg.

'Bonaparte!' Alice-Miranda chided. She took a step towards the tack-room door. The sleepy beast opened one eye but quickly closed it again when he realised he was in trouble. 'I'm so sorry. I hope he didn't draw blood. The little monster's been known to.'

Dervla hefted another saddle onto a higher peg. 'It's a bit sore and I think I'll end up with a spectacular bruise, but no one is going to see it. Where are you off to on your ride?'

Alice-Miranda untangled a bit from the leather headpiece and placed it on a hook. 'I was considering a visit to Mr Frost over at Wood End. Do you think Bony will be okay going that far?'

'He's fine,' Dervla said. 'I had to get the vet out to Buttercup this morning. She cut her leg on some wire in the paddock and it needed stitching. While he was here, I had him take a look at the ratbag's foot. He wanted me to congratulate you on your treatment regime and said that he couldn't have done it any better himself. Then he grumbled something about ten-year-olds putting vets out of business.'

Alice-Miranda grinned and took up Bony's bridle. 'That's not happening any time soon, but I do like the idea of being a vet. Millie's mum's one and she's fantastic with all animals. I'm glad to hear that Bony's okay, but that's not good about poor Buttercup. Will she be all right?'

Dervla nodded. 'She's in the stall at the end getting lots of treats, which has put Bony's nose right out of joint.'

'Honestly, that beast of mine has no manners and it doesn't seem to matter what I do, he never improves.' Alice-Miranda cast Bonaparte a reproachful look, but he ignored her again. 'How have your classes been this week?'

Dervla placed the last saddle onto its peg and began untangling a pile of lead ropes. 'We've been studying handwriting. It's fascinating stuff. There are some people whose copying skills are incredible, but there's usually something that will give them away,' the young woman said, her eyes glinting. 'It can be the subtlest loop or dot. I never thought

I'd love such intricate work, but it's something I could see myself specialising in.'

Alice-Miranda nodded. 'I'll keep that in mind next time I try to forge my parents' signatures.'

'You? I don't believe it for a second. I, on the other hand . . .' Dervla shrugged and a mischievous smile played on her lips. 'Mildred Jelly had no idea how many times I got out of swimming in that arctic pool over at Sainsbury Palace – until she realised there was no way my mother was able to get the notes written and sent to school in time for the morning of my PE lessons. She threatened to expel me, but my parents talked her around. Dad reasoned that getting one over on the headmistress was a sign of intelligence. I ran into Mrs Jelly a year ago, and she wasn't the least bit surprised to hear what I was studying. She said I was criminal in the making during my time at school, which I took as a compliment.'

'I'd argue that half the battle in becoming an excellent criminologist would be the ability to put yourself in the wrongdoer's shoes,' Alice-Miranda said. She thought of all the crimes and mysteries she and her friends had solved over the years and wondered if a life in criminology might suit her too – so long as she could be a vet on the side who dabbled in acting and competed in the odd Olympic event for horseriding.

The girl took Bony's bridle and saddle and stepped into his stall. At the sight of his mistress and her riding gear, the naughty pony perked up and didn't even try to bite her when she fastened the girth strap. She led him into the centre of the stables, where Dervla gave her a leg-up and tucked a couple of carrots into the saddle bag for later.

'He doesn't deserve them, but he might be easier to manage with some enticements.' Dervla patted the pony's side. 'Take care, and don't let this monster get up to any mischief.'

'Thanks. I'll be back before two,' Alice-Miranda said. She was keen to pop over to Fayle with Jacinta and Millie later in the afternoon. The girl clicked her tongue and Bony walked out into the morning sunshine.

It was another Goldilocks day with crisp air and warm rays. The pair jogged along the trail towards Gertrude's Grove. Bony snorted and stopped to paw at the ground a few times, then he tugged hard on the reins.

'I suppose you'd like to go faster,' Alice-Miranda said, and was met with a loud whinny. 'Suit yourself but remember not to overdo it.'

She urged the pony into a canter across the Grove. He ducked and wove through the forest before they came to the river. The bridge had been rebuilt since the flood, when Mrs Parker and Ambrosia had been stranded in Myrtle's hatchback high in a tree downstream. Bony clip-clopped across the new timbers. Alice-Miranda smiled at the long line of willows swaying gently in the breeze like hula dancers and remembered her shock the first time she and Millie had visited Wood End and met Stan Frost, only to find that Reg Parker had woken from his years-long coma and was out here with him. Bonaparte whinnied as the house and garden hove into view.

'What are you carrying on about?' she asked, reaching forward to give him a pat. Her eyes scanned the front paddock and the driveway down to the house. 'Oh my goodness, how on earth did you two get up there?'

Mr Frost's goats, Cherry and Pickles, were renowned for their ability to infiltrate the oddest places – counting the shed, car roofs and the highest branches among their accomplishments – and today they were standing on the ridge capping at the very top of the house. The pair of them could balance better than the most daring tightrope walker.

Alice-Miranda pressed Bony into a slow canter, giggling as she wondered how the little rogues were going to get down this time. She tugged on the reins and Bony pulled up near the back door. As she jumped down from the saddle, Mr Frost's cocker spaniels, Maudie and Itch, burst through the screen door, barking and wagging their stumpy tails at top speed. They wound in and out of Bony's legs while the pony nipped at their curly coats.

Stan Frost emerged from the house, wearing overalls and a red checked shirt. His grey hair was parted at the side and combed neatly into place and his blue eyes twinkled with delight. 'This is a lovely surprise.'

'Hello Mr Frost,' Alice-Miranda said, hitching the reins up onto the bridle. 'Shall I put Bony out with Cynthia?' The grey donkey was in the closest paddock, making the most awful racket.

'We'll never be able to hear ourselves think if you don't.' Stan gave Bony a pat on the neck and earned himself a quivering lip and a glare for his trouble. 'The old girl has quite the soft spot for your Bonaparte and look at her – I don't know how a handsome fella like him can resist that old bag of bones.'

'I think Cynthia's charming,' the child replied, 'even if she is a bit of a nag.'

Alice-Miranda led the pony to the gate, which Stan unlatched and pushed open for them. She let Bony go, but instead of charging away to eat the lush pasture, he hovered close, keeping one eye on his mistress and the other on Cynthia, who was still hee-hawing and snorting on the far side of the paddock.

'Off you go, Bony.' Alice-Miranda patted his rump, but he refused to move. As soon as Alice-Miranda and Stan closed the gate behind them, the donkey charged towards Bony, chasing him around and around, all the while sounding like an old set of bellows. Alice-Miranda and Stan turned to watch, laughing at Cynthia's antics. Eventually, after half a dozen circuits, Bony gave up and stood under the oak tree in the middle of the field, where Cynthia caught up to him. The donkey rubbed her head all over his neck and nibbled on his mane. He let out a giant sigh but took it nonetheless.

'Can I interest you in a cold drink or a cup of tea?' Stan asked.

'A cup of tea would be just the thing,' the girl said, dusting her hands. 'I want to hear all about Ursula and how her study is going. I hope she comes to work at Winchesterfield-Downsfordvale again soon but as a teacher this time.'

The man's once estranged daughter was currently undertaking her teaching degree and had enjoyed a short stint doing some relief work in the boarding house when Mrs Howard had been away. She was very popular with the girls, who would all love it if she got a permanent teaching position at the school once she was qualified.

'And I want to know about what happened last weekend,' Stan said, bending to pick up a watering can he'd left in the garden bed. 'Reg called to tell me the news. That was a very brave thing you girls did.'

Stan set the watering can down on the back porch, then pushed open the door into the cosy kitchen with Maudie and Itch dancing at his feet. The dining table was loaded at one end with boxes and scattered the length of it were photo albums and sheaves of printed pictures.

'Don't mind the mess,' he said, putting the kettle on. 'I'll clear us a spot. It's amazing how many photographs you end up with over the course of a lifetime. Well, you did in the old days before everything went digital. I must say it's been a trip down memory lane. Trouble is, there's so much and Ursula won't want it all.'

'What about the village historical society or the Queen's Preservation Trust for anything about Wood End, seeing that you've gifted them the property in the long term?' the girl suggested.

'Now, why didn't I think of that?' Stan said with a smile. 'I do have quite a few pictures of the village over the years too.'

'I'm sure Mrs Parker would be thrilled to add it to the collection,' Alice-Miranda said.

Stan shook his head. 'How did I not know that my sister-in-law would be in charge of that? She might want some of the pictures for herself, especially the ones of her and Beryl in happier times.'

'That's a lovely idea. I think the family photos are the trickiest, really – holidays and the like.

Perhaps, after you've given Ursula and Myrtle a look, you might get the rest scanned and then they won't take up so much space,' Alice-Miranda said. 'We have an archive at Highton Hall and a clever lady called Mrs Pennington comes twice a year to catalogue everything. But I suppose our house isn't exactly ordinary and then there are the archives for Kennington's and Highton's as well, which Mrs Pennington takes care of too, but that's her proper job.'

'Most people don't come from important families like yours,' Stan said with a grin. He cut two slices of cake and poured the boiling water into the teapot.

'Do you really think that?' Alice-Miranda frowned. '"Important" is such a funny word. It makes us sound as if we think we're better than everyone else and that's not true at all. Our ancestors just happen to have done some interesting things, which have given several generations of our family considerable creature comforts, but Mummy and Daddy have always told me that with privilege comes responsibility. They're now the custodians for the generations to come. I will be too one day, and it will be up to me to keep the businesses running so that all of the people who rely on Highton's and Kennington's are looked after,' the girl prattled. 'Highton Hall is a beautiful place that should be preserved forever – and perhaps the day will come that I don't live there, but we can gift it to the people so everyone can enjoy it.'

Stan gazed at the child in wonder. 'Are you certain you're not really an eighty-year-old woman masquerading in the body of a small child?'

Alice-Miranda chuckled. 'I'm going to be eleven next birthday. I can hardly believe I'm as old as that!'

The man began shifting a couple of piles when something caught the girl's eye. It was a black-and-white photograph of a band. She picked it up and peered at it closely. There was a newspaper article featuring the same photograph underneath. Alice-Miranda read the caption and gasped. She gasped a second time when she spotted a photograph of a young woman dressed in flared jeans and a cheese-cloth top with a flower crown on her head. She turned to Stan with wide eyes. 'Is that . . .?'

'Oh, you don't want to look at that rubbish,' Stan said, taking the photo and tucking it into the pile at the opposite end of the table. 'Young people never think anyone over the age of twenty have done anything interesting. Besides, if I told you, you wouldn't believe me.'

'Please, I'd love to know,' Alice-Miranda said, carrying the plates of cake and tea cups and saucers to the table. 'I'll swap you a story. You might find it quite fun, I think.'

Stan set the teapot and milk jug on a placemat. Alice-Miranda shuffled onto the seat at the end and Stan sat down adjacent. 'All right, I'll tell you, but only if you promise to keep a secret,' the man said.

Alice-Miranda grinned as he poured the tea. 'It's a deal.'

Chapter 26

Jacinta stared at the plate of spinach-and-ricotta ravioli in front of her. If she spun it around slightly, and leaned her head on an angle, she could just make out a face. Except that when she looked closely, she realised it reminded her of Myrtle Parker. The girl blanched and quickly swished the pasta pillows around. No one needed that woman staring up at them during dinner.

'Darling, are you going to eat your meal or play with it?' Ambrosia asked.

Jacinta glanced at her mother's cannelloni, which had hardly been touched. 'I could ask you the same thing, Mummy.'

Neville wiped his mouth with the white cloth napkin, leaving a smear of Napoletana sauce. 'I don't understand what's wrong with you two. This food's fantastic and completely unexpected in a tin-pot village like this.'

Ambrosia smiled. 'I told you this place had a well-deserved reputation for excellence.'

He reached across and patted her hand, though Ambrosia was quick to withdraw hers. The awkward silence that ensued was interrupted by the shrill ringing of Neville's phone. He hastily pulled it from his jacket pocket and rejected the call. 'Sorry,' he said with an apologetic smile. 'Work never stops.' When his phone rang again, Neville rolled his eyes and switched it to silent mode.

'I don't think your *phone* ever stops,' Jacinta said. 'You must have had twenty calls from Jamie when we were going to and from acrobatics. I couldn't help noticing his name kept popping up on the screen.'

Neville nodded. 'He's looking after a deal we're on the verge of securing. I just wish he'd learn to think for himself and leave me in peace, but it should all be done and dusted soon.'

'Don't let us stop you,' Ambrosia said, taking a sip of her sparkling mineral water. 'It might be something important.'

'Jamie can wait. We're having a special evening – no work allowed.' Neville grinned and Ambrosia felt her breath catch in her throat. When his phone continued to vibrate persistently, Neville turned it off. He'd pay for that later, but he didn't want to ruin their dinner.

With her stomach churning like a water wheel, Jacinta had barely eaten all day. Her father had picked her up from school that morning and they'd driven to Downsfordvale, where he watched her entire acrobatics lesson, beaming like the proud parent she'd always wanted him to be. On the drive home, he'd waxed lyrical about her extraordinary talent to the point where Jacinta demanded that he stop speaking – it was too much. How could this man, who hadn't shown the slightest bit of interest in her since the day she was born, suddenly start behaving like the father of the year?

He'd taken her back to the village, where she'd met Alice-Miranda and Millie, and the three of them had gone to Fayle to see Lucas, Poppy and Jasper. Except that Lucas had spent most of the time with his mother and stepfather-to-be, Blair, who seemed like a really great guy. He and Lucas looked to be getting on extremely well, which only served to make Jacinta more nervous that Lucas might go and live with them in New York. Still, she couldn't bring herself to say anything. She was afraid that, if she uttered the words aloud, it was far more likely to come true. She couldn't bear to lose Lucas, especially not now, yet she couldn't tell him the things she really wanted to either. It was all so awfully confusing.

While Alice-Miranda and Millie had walked back to school, Jacinta had decided to stay the night at her mother's for a change of scene but was surprised to find her father on the doorstep with two enormous bouquets of flowers – pink peonies for Ambrosia and brightly coloured gerberas for her. Then he'd whisked them off to Enzo's Trattoria, an Italian restaurant in Willow Dale, a gorgeous little village half an hour away. Now here they all were, together, and Jacinta had no idea what any of it meant.

The girl stabbed a piece of ravioli with her fork, then set it down on the side of her plate. 'Daddy, why are you here?' she asked, finally mustering the courage.

'Sweetheart, your father didn't take us to dinner for you to give him the third degree,' Ambrosia remonstrated gently.

Jacinta shot her mother a glare that would have stopped a rabid rottweiler in its tracks. Her lips tightened and she swirled her food around again. This time she chose not to search for faces.

Neville cleared his throat. 'How's your work going?' he asked, his gaze lingering on Ambrosia long enough that her cheeks caught fire.

'Oh, um, fine,' she faltered.

Jacinta looked up sharply, cross that her mother was being so coy. 'It's better than fine. Mummy has been shortlisted for a big award in fashion journalism and I think she's got a very good chance of winning. She's terribly clever and everyone loves her articles. She's excellent at getting to the heart of matters and her interview with Christian Fontaine was nothing short of amazing. She got him to talk about things that no one else could. It's a pity she hadn't realised years ago how talented she is because she's much happier now she has a fulfilling job and purpose in life,' Jacinta said. 'And she's a far better human being too.'

'Darling, please,' Ambrosia protested. 'Was I really so terrible before?'

Jacinta could feel the heat creeping up her neck and blinked back tears. 'You were both horrible. I used to lie awake in bed at night, wondering why you ever had me.'

'Do you remember all those months she had colic as a baby?' Neville said, gazing into Ambrosia's eyes. 'Believe me, Jacinta, there were plenty of times your mother and I wondered the same thing, didn't we, Amby?'

Jacinta's jaw dropped and she looked at her parents in disbelief. 'Gee, thanks!' The girl stood up so abruptly her chair fell behind her.

'Jacinta, sweetheart, where are you off to?' Neville said. 'I have something for you and for your mother.' He reached inside his jacket and pulled out two small jewellery boxes, setting them down on the table. 'I was only kidding, Cinta. Mummy and I loved you even when you kept us awake all night,' he said, pouting. 'Don't you want to see what I got you?'

Jacinta burst into tears and ran to the bathroom. Ambrosia folded her napkin and stood up.

'Now where are you going?' Neville said in bewilderment.

'She's upset,' Ambrosia hissed. 'Neville, for goodness sake, why did you have to say that?'

'Oh, come on, you know I didn't mean it,' he said, rolling his eyes.

'Do I?' She looked at him and shook her head. 'Jacinta is right to ask what you're doing here. *I* don't understand, Neville. You told me I was no longer welcome in our marriage and you kicked me out. Thank heavens I had the cottage, or I would have been on the street. You haven't even sent your own daughter as much as a birthday or Christmas card since we split up and now you're here, acting as if the past few years didn't happen. We're divorced, Neville – don't you remember you had the lawyers deliver the papers *tout de suite*?'

'I told you. I miss you and Jacinta,' the man pleaded. 'I know I can't undo all of the hurt, but people can change, Amby. You have, and Jacinta isn't nearly as painful as she used to be.'

The woman took a deep breath. 'My name is Ambrosia, and when you talk about Jacinta like that I have a hard time believing you're remotely interested in her. If you want our old life back, then I have to tell you it's never going to happen. I'm not that woman any more, Neville. I was a terrible mother and a dreadful person – Jacinta's absolutely right about that – and the one good thing that came out of what you did was that I began to realise what I'd become and who I wanted to be and they weren't the same person. If you want to be part of Jacinta's life, you're going to have to behave like a proper father.' With that, Ambrosia stalked off to find Jacinta, who was in the ladies' room, tearing tiny pieces of toilet paper and throwing them bit by bit into the bowl while reciting 'he loves us, he loves us not' under her breath.

A waiter approached Neville at the table and offered him the dessert menus.

'Not now,' he snapped, then sighed. 'Sorry, please just leave them here. My wife and daughter will be back soon.' He took out his phone and stared at the thirty missed calls and messages. This was going to be much harder than he'd imagined.

Chapter 27

On Saturday evening, Alice-Miranda sent a message around the boarding houses that there would be a committee meeting on Sunday after breakfast. Now that the festival was proceeding full steam ahead, they didn't have long to put all their plans in place. Following on from their discussions with Miss Reedy on Friday afternoon, she and Millie had made an executive decision that their next gathering would be girls only – with the exception of Miss Crowley. She'd also spoken to her aunt and wanted to share the good and bad news.

Alice-Miranda had left a note for Miss Crowley in the teachers' communication box, which was located in the foyer at Caledonia Manor. The girls weren't allowed up to the staff accommodation floor, but there was a letterbox they could use if they needed to speak to a staff member.

At ten o'clock, with everyone assembled in the sitting room of Caledonia Stables, Alice-Miranda called the meeting to order.

'Do you think we should wait for Miss Crowley?' Chessie asked, her eyes on the door, hoping the woman would be there soon.

'Another minute or so,' Alice-Miranda replied. 'We have a lot to get through and I didn't hear back about whether she was intending to come. She was going to finish up the risk assessment so we could submit it to Miss Reedy and Miss Grimm.'

'Oh, come on,' Caprice whined, folding her arms. 'I haven't got all day. I have a singing lesson at eleven-thirty.'

Chessie listed the attendees and passed around agendas that Alice-Miranda had prepared, outlining what they needed to get through.

Alice-Miranda glanced up at the clock on the wall. 'All right, let's make a start. We can bring Miss Crowley up to speed if and when she joins us. Item one, how are we progressing with facilities?'

Ivory stood up and distributed copies of a schedule she and Susannah had been working on. 'Charlie thinks we'll need twenty portaloos in addition to the toilets in the sports hall and the block down on the oval, so we've approached two companies in Downsfordvale. With everyone's approval, we'll get them organised tomorrow. Also, when we told them why we were having the festival, both companies offered to bring the loos for free. They're quite fancy, actually, with mirrors and hand basins and super smell eradicators and they would have cost a fortune if we had to pay.'

Alice-Miranda scanned the notes. 'This is fantastic. Well done and that's terribly kind of those companies.'

There were lots of other logistical issues to consider, such as dealing with the rubbish and which areas the public would be able to access, but it seemed that Susannah and Ivory had anticipated everything. And better still, there was already considerable buzz about the festival thanks to Tilde McGilvray spruiking it on her show. She'd also confirmed her availability to emcee the event. Almost everyone they'd approached had offered their services for free, all in the name of helping the Abboud family.

Technology and car parking were equally well thought through. Shelby had talked to Mr Munz about enlisting some villagers to assist as traffic marshals, and the man had leapt at the chance to help. He volunteered his son, Otto, too and had assembled a long list of ladies and gentlemen from the Bridge Club who were eager to help on the day.

Chessie had worked with their Art teacher, Miss Tweedle, to develop a logo for the festival flyers and other promotional material, but they couldn't finish the details until the talent was confirmed. That was problematic because they needed to advertise as soon as possible. They also had to set their ticket prices, which was under Millie's purview. The girl had already met with Mrs Clinch to go over the numbers, wanting to ensure the festival was affordable and accessible to all while maximising the potential funds to be raised for the Abboud family. There was so much to think about.

Caprice frowned. 'I thought we had that crusty, old Nick Waterford and The Stingrays?'

'Well, the good news is that we have Nick Waterford,' Alice-Miranda began, and a cheer went up around the room.

'And the bad news?' Sloane asked.

'You didn't get The Stingrays, did you?' Caprice looked at Millie and laughed. 'I knew you wouldn't.'

'No, but I have another idea,' Alice-Miranda said.

Caprice exhaled loudly. 'I suppose I could headline alongside Geriatric Nick because I –'

'Won Junior Champion at the National Eisteddfod,' Sloane said, rolling her eyes. 'Seriously, you don't have to keep reminding us, Caprice. It's not as if anyone has forgotten and they're not likely to with you harping on about it. The thing is, people outside of the eisteddfod circuit won't have heard of you, so we need another act that people *will* know. A household name.'

'Please don't argue,' Alice-Miranda said. 'There's still lots to get through. We've already lined up a talent quest, the Winchester-Fayle Singers, the Downsfordvale Concert Band and, trust me, I have something else in mind.'

'Who's going to pay good money for that?' Caprice griped. 'I thought the whole idea of this concert –'

'Festival,' Millie corrected.

Caprice glowered from beneath her copper fringe. '– *festival*, was to have proper acts and make it exciting. At the moment it sounds like a boring country fair.'

Alice-Miranda bit her lip. 'We have to keep in mind the *reason* we're having the festival is to raise money for the Abbouds. People will come because they want to help them get back on their feet.' She turned to Jacinta, who was picking at the quick around her nails and staring out the window. 'What other activities have you managed to line up, Jacinta?'

The girl blanched. She hadn't organised a thing. She'd been so mixed up about her father and Lucas that she hadn't given the festival a thought. 'Um, Daddy said that his personal assistant would help me with everything, so I'll call her this afternoon.'

'But it's Sunday,' Millie said.

Jacinta shrugged. 'If she's my father's personal assistant, I can guarantee she'll be available.'

'What about some stilt walkers?' Millie suggested. 'I've seen them at fairs and kids love them.'

Jacinta's face immediately brightened. 'I could do that. We have stilts at my acrobatics class.'

'Face painting is always a hit,' Sloane said.

There was a murmur of approval all around.

'Miss Tweedle is incredible. Remember when she painted faces at the dog show? Figgy looked like a Dalmatian who'd just emerged from a bar brawl and Rufus had that pink-eyed bulldog effect. They were hilarious, but she made all the little kids look cute,' Millie said.

Alice-Miranda's eyes lit up. 'And cuddles for Fudge or, even better, a petting zoo. We could get some lambs and chickens and other adorable, furry things.'

'What about craft or cooking tents, where you can learn something new like decoupage or bead-making?' Ivory said. 'There's a fantastic shop in Downsfordvale. I wonder if the lady who owns it would be interested in having a stand.'

The ideas kept coming and before long it was clear Jacinta wouldn't need her father's PA at all. Last on the agenda was food. Caprice's mother had organised ten different street vendors, offering a wide selection of culinary treats from stone-fired pizzas to nachos, burgers and fries, donuts, as well as vegan and gluten-free options. Venetia also offered to host a *Sweet Things* tent, which, given the popularity of her television show, should be a hit with the festival-goers.

'Fantastic work, everyone,' Alice-Miranda said, and tapped her pen against the clipboard in her lap. 'We should meet again tomorrow afternoon to keep up the momentum.'

Chessie closed her notebook and grinned. 'It's pretty amazing what we're doing. We're going to make a difference for the Abbouds while also creating an event for people in the village and further afield. It all feels so grown up and makes me wonder what we'll be able to achieve when we're adults.'

'We're very fortunate to be given so many opportunities at school,' Alice-Miranda agreed with a smile.

Miss Reedy strode into the room, her lips pursed. 'What's the meaning of this?'

'Hello Miss Reedy,' Alice-Miranda said brightly. 'We thought you and Mr Plumpton had gone away for a weekend sojourn.'

'We cut it short,' the woman replied. 'I couldn't relax with everything that's happening.'

She left out the part about having seen a note from Miss Grimm to Miss Wall, asking if they could meet in private on Sunday for lunch. Livinia had checked the staff communication box just before she and Josiah left on Friday afternoon and it was right there, open for anyone to see. It had gnawed at her the whole time and, despite her husband's protestations that it was probably nothing, the thought that Ophelia was making plans with Benitha behind her back was too much to bear. The strangest thing was that, when they'd returned to campus and she asked the PE teacher what she was up to today, Benitha said she was off to watch the rugby tournament in Downsfordvale. There was no mention of a luncheon with the headmistress. Livinia had called over to Ophelia's flat, ostensibly to let the woman know she was on-site in case there was anything she needed her to do, but Ophelia said that she, Aldous and Aggie were having a quiet day at home with no plans.

Miss Crowley rushed in through the double doors. 'Sorry I'm late,' she puffed. 'I popped over to Downsfordvale to buy some groceries and only just got your message, Alice-Miranda.' She stopped in her tracks when she realised Miss Reedy was also in the room.

Livinia smiled. 'Hello Miss Crowley.'

'Good morning, Miss Reedy,' the woman replied, bracing herself to be given her marching orders.

'Miss Crowley has been instrumental in helping us with all of the official documentation, such as risk assessments and the like, for the school to organise insurance,' Alice-Miranda explained.

Livinia hadn't thought of all that. Filling in screeds of paperwork that did nothing to actually make an event one bit safer was a pet hate of hers. If Tabitha was willing to take that on, she wouldn't say no. 'Wonderful,' she said.

'We've just about finished our meeting,' Alice-Miranda said, hopping up. 'But perhaps the other girls could go, and Millie and Chessie and I can bring you up to speed.'

Caprice was out the door like a shot. She had ten minutes to get to her singing lesson. The rest of the students gathered their paperwork and were off too.

'Well, let's hear what you've achieved then,' Miss Reedy said, taking a seat.

Tabitha perched on a chair opposite and Alice-Miranda started from the beginning.

Chapter 28

Zahra Abboud placed the last piece of the puzzle into the jigsaw she'd been helping her three-year-old sister to complete.

'Again,' Hatice declared, promptly tipping the pieces back onto the grass.

Zahra looked at her watch. 'No more. You and Esma need to go upstairs to Mama.'

Hatice's bottom lip began to quiver and fat tears pooled in the corners of her eyes. 'I want to do it again. Please, Zah Zah,' the girl begged.

Zahra sighed. 'Okay, one more time and then we're going inside.'

In the back garden of Caledonia Manor, while Zahra and Hatice solved the jigsaw puzzle on the lawn, six-year-old Esma had found a black kitten to play with. She was waving a dandelion to and fro while the feline chased after it. Little puffs of white floated on the breeze as the kitten caught the head in its claws, dismantling it more and more with each pass.

After their meeting with Miss Crowley had finished, Alice-Miranda decided to visit the Fayle sisters to see if they'd selected anything from the Highton's catalogue. All her friends were busy, and while she'd offered to help Millie with her chores, the girl had insisted on doing them herself. She'd already completed five hours and was keen to get the rest out of the way before the festival. Chessie had teed up a meeting with Miss Tweedle about her painting for the village art fair, while Sloane and Jacinta were working on their picture-book projects.

Alice-Miranda knocked on the door marked 'Private' inside the manor. When there was no answer, she decided to try the rear garden. It was a beautiful day, so there was every chance Miss Hephzibah and Miss Henrietta were outside tending the roses or weeding the beds. As she rounded the corner, Alice-Miranda could hear someone singing. It was beautiful – pure and clear with a timbre like nothing she'd ever heard before. At first, she thought it might be Caprice, but there was something about this voice that was even more beguiling. And then it stopped.

'Oh hello.' Alice-Miranda spotted Esma, who was giggling at the kitten pouncing after the bald stalk dangling from her hand. She knelt down and reached out to the fluffball. 'Are you being a good girl, Cleopatra?'

Esma looked up at Alice-Miranda with big brown eyes. 'Is that her name?'

Alice-Miranda nodded. 'I think it suits her, don't you? She's got long claws, though, so watch out.'

'I know,' Esma said. She licked her finger and wiped at the little scratches on her forearm. 'But I love her.' She considered Alice-Miranda for a moment. 'Mama said you saved us, and that if you hadn't come, we would all be in hospital like Papa.'

Alice-Miranda smiled. 'It was just lucky we were there and could help.'

Esma's shiny black hair was tied in a braid that fell almost to her bottom and she was wearing a pretty yellow dress with silver sparkles. She noticed Alice-Miranda looking at it. 'Do you like my dress? Mama says the girls at school gave us new clothes because ours were burned in the fire, along with my books and toys. I love the sparkles,' the little girl said, touching the silver sequins.

'It's gorgeous on you,' Alice-Miranda said. That dress had been one of her own favourites when she was little. Mrs Shillingsworth had sent it from home to include in the donations. Alice-Miranda snapped off another dandelion and passed it to the girl. 'Was that you singing?'

Esma shook her head. 'Zahra. She *always* sings. Mama tells her to stop and do her study, but Papa likes it. He says it reminds him of his mama, who died in the war before I was born.'

Alice-Miranda smiled. 'I'm sure Cleopatra would love to play another game with the dandelion. I'm just going to say hello to your sisters.'

Esma's eyes twinkled as she waved the stalk higher in the air, watching the kitten jump and tumble in a bid to reach it. Zahra and Hatice were sitting on the lawn near the edge of the stone wall that divided the garden from the field below. Hatice was twisting a jigsaw piece, trying to find the right spot for it.

'Hello,' Alice-Miranda said with a friendly wave.

Zahra looked up and squinted as the sun beat down on Alice-Miranda's back. 'Hi,' she said quietly.

'How are you settling in?' Alice-Miranda asked.

Zahra shrugged. 'Fine. It's a bit crowded but better than the hospital room – at least we all get a bed now.'

'We never got to finish talking the other day,' Alice-Miranda said, settling beside her on the grass. 'What were you doing in Rosebud Lane?'

'Nothing,' the girl snapped, causing Hatice to glance up in surprise.

'I promise I'm not being a busybody,' Alice-Miranda assured her. 'I just don't want you to be in any trouble, that's all.'

'I'm not,' Zahra said, her brow furrowing. 'It's nothing like that.'

'I can keep a secret,' Alice-Miranda said gently. 'I have one myself and it's quite delicious, really, and sort of funny and perhaps a little embarrassing, especially as I'm not very good, but I think with time and practice I might actually be okay. Sorry, I'm waffling, aren't I?' Alice-Miranda giggled. 'It's just that I'd love to know more about Mrs Goodman. She lives in that cottage I saw you coming out of, doesn't she? Mr Parker told me she used to be a famous singer when she was young, but I am yet to have the pleasure of meeting her. Is she giving you lessons? I heard you before and your voice is beautiful.'

Zahra had been staring intently at the ground, pulling blade by blade of grass. She paused and looked at Alice-Miranda with pleading eyes. 'You can't tell my mother. She will be so angry. She wants me to become a doctor or a teacher, but not a singer – she says there is no future in it.'

'But that's what you want more than anything?' Alice-Miranda asked.

'Singing is everything to me,' Zahra confessed with a heavy sigh. As those words left her lips, it felt as though a weight had been lifted off her shoulders. 'I was at Mrs Goodman's when the fire broke out. We heard the sirens, but she had just begun to teach me a new song and I was so in love with it that I wanted to learn the whole thing.' Zahra shook her head. 'My family could have died because of my selfishness yet I don't want to stop – I *can't* stop singing.'

'And you shouldn't,' Alice-Miranda said. 'You have a gift, Zahra – one the whole world should hear.' She tilted her head to one side. 'How did you meet Mrs Goodman in the first place?'

Zahra smiled at the memory. 'I was singing upstairs in my room with the window open and she heard me from the street. When Mrs Goodman next came to the restaurant, she asked if the voice she'd heard belonged to me. At first I denied it, but then she said that, if I wanted, she could help me. I had no idea about her past when curiosity got the better of me and I went to her house and, Alice-Miranda, it's amazing.' Zahra leaned closer, her eyes glittering. 'Her walls are covered in framed posters of all the shows and concerts she's performed. She played recordings on a strange machine that I think must be almost as old as she is. And when she sang it was as if the world had stopped turning. I couldn't breathe. When we sing together, it's the best feeling.'

Alice-Miranda sighed happily. 'It sounds wonderful.'

'Papa used to cover for me, but now . . .' Tears spilled onto Zahra's cheeks. She brushed them away with the back of her sleeve. 'I can't get to my lessons as easily. Mama suspects I'm hiding something – she thinks it's a boy. Yuck.' The girl grimaced. 'I can't tell her because she'll make me stop.'

Alice-Miranda reached out and took Zahra's hands in hers. 'You mustn't stop singing. I can keep an eye on Esma and Hatice for an hour. Could you tell your mother that we're going for a walk to see the rest of the school? It's not a lie if I take the girls to visit the stables to meet my naughty pony.'

Zahra looked at her in astonishment. 'You'd do that . . . for me?'

'Talent like yours should be nurtured, Zahra. Plus, I have an idea,' Alice-Miranda said with a grin. 'Perhaps your mother just needs an opportunity to see how much singing means to you and how good you are. We're having a music festival to raise money to rebuild your house and the restaurant and there's going to be a talent quest.'

Zahra's stomach came alive with butterflies. 'Mama would be so upset.'

'Leave that for me to worry about,' Alice-Miranda said. She leapt to her feet and brushed her hands. 'For now, you need to get to your lessons. Why don't you go and tell your mother we're going for a walk and you can make a beeline to Mrs Goodman's?'

Zahra didn't need to think twice. She was off like a shot and returned a few minutes later. 'Thank you, Alice-Miranda. I owe you one,' she shouted, then disappeared around the side of the building and out of sight.

Chapter 29

Lucas Nixon sat at his desk, trying to concentrate on the essay he was writing about infamous traitors of the twentieth century. It was a timely topic, as he discovered after going for a walk to the village yesterday afternoon.

While he had never met Neville Headlington-Bear, Lucas had seen the man's picture splashed across magazines and newsstands enough times to recognise his face. And then there he was, standing beside a silver Aston Martin, looking as if he'd stepped from the pages of a Highton's catalogue. Lucas had tried not to stare. Instead, his first impulse had been to flee. He'd darted into the Munzes' store to pick up some treats for him and Sep. He bought an ice-cream on the way out and sat on the bench in front of the shop to eat it, which also happened to be directly in front of Mr Headlington-Bear's fancy car. It didn't take long for the boy to realise that Neville was now sitting inside the Aston Martin with the windows down.

'She'll come home. Seriously, there's nothing to keep her in *this* place,' the man had said into his phone. 'As soon as she does, I expect that money to be in my account. I just hope I won't have to keep up the charade for too long.'

Lucas should have got up and walked away at that point, but he wasn't averse to the odd bit of eavesdropping, especially when it concerned his girlfriend's estranged father. Why would Neville receive money if he and Ambrosia reconciled? Lucas wondered. It didn't make any sense. He leaned back to hear more.

'She's quite the talented acrobat,' Neville continued. 'Gosh, no. There's no way I'm putting up with her whining at home – she can stay at school. Anyway, it's just a means to an end.'

It had taken all of Lucas's willpower to refrain from turning around and telling the man exactly what *he* thought right then and there. Jacinta wasn't whiny; she was brave and funny and had more talent in her left pinky than her father would ever have. Not trusting himself to keep quiet, Lucas had thrown the rest of his ice-cream in the bin and stormed off. He'd tried to call Jacinta, only to be told that she'd joined her parents for dinner. So, he'd spent a sleepless night worrying about what to do. Now it was Sunday afternoon and his stomach was tossing and turning like a washing machine on rinse cycle.

Lucas put down his pen and hurried to the phone box at the end of the hall. There was only one person who would know what to do, and he needed to speak to her right away.

Lucas telephoned Caledonia Stables and spoke to Mrs Clarkson, who said that Alice-Miranda had taken the Abboud girls for a walk to see the horses. But he didn't want to wait until later to speak to her. Jacinta had said she was going to call on Sunday night and he needed to know before that if he should warn her or not. He quickly signed himself out and sped through the school grounds into the village, towards Winchesterfield-Downsfordvale. He was surprised to see Zahra Abboud, wearing headphones and humming to herself, with a spring in her step. Wasn't she meant to be with Alice-Miranda?

He ran past her, then veered left through the school gates, where the playing fields, sports hall and Winchesterfield Manor went by in a blur. He charged on, not even stopping to say hello to Mrs Howard, who was tending the roses at the front of Grimthorpe House. She yelled out to him, but he just gave a wave. As the stables hove into view, he hoped his cousin was inside. Lucas ran into the building and stopped. He bent forwards, holding his sides and gasping for breath. All he could hear was his heart beating in his ears. 'Hello?' he called feebly.

Millie's head popped up over the stall door at the end of the row. 'Oh, hi Lucas. What are you doing here?'

'I need to talk to Alice-Miranda,' he puffed.

'She was here a little while ago with Esma and Hatice, but they've gone back to Caledonia Manor,' she said, throwing a forkful of straw into the air.

Lucas groaned. 'Thanks,' he said with a sigh, and turned to leave.

'You know, Jacinta thinks you're going to live in New York with your mother,' Millie said. She opened the stall door and emerged with a wheelbarrow full of soiled bedding.

Lucas spun around, aghast. 'What?'

'Mrs Parker was blathering about it the other day. She said you're going to live with your mum in America once she's married.' Millie fixed him with a no-nonsense stare. 'Is that true?'

'No . . .' Lucas said weakly. 'Maybe?'

Millie put her hands on her hips and arched an eyebrow. 'Well, which is it?'

Lucas sighed. 'Mum asked me to think about going on exchange for a year so I can spend some time with her and Blair. Fayle has a brother school, you see, called Passmore. But I haven't said yes yet.' He hadn't even mentioned any of this to Sep, so how Myrtle Parker knew was anyone's guess.

Then again, she didn't have the nickname Nosey for nothing.

'Lucas, Jacinta's going to be devastated even if it's only for a year.' Millie took up the handles and pushed the barrow towards the entrance.

The boy walked along beside her. 'She's going to be more upset when she finds out what her father's up to,' Lucas said, then realised he hadn't planned to tell anyone but Alice-Miranda.

Millie's face darkened. 'Why? What do you know?'

'Forget I said anything,' Lucas mumbled, taking a step backwards, 'and don't breathe a word of this to Jacinta.'

'Hey, you can't tell me half a story,' Millie protested, but the lad was out of the building like a shot. He ran and ran through the school until he reached Caledonia Stables and was heading for the mansion. Or he was, before Jacinta's voice pulled him up short.

'Lucas!' she called, waving her arms as she hurried up the driveway towards him. 'What are you doing here?'

He stopped and turned around. 'Oh . . . hi.'

Jacinta took in his red face and his grey T-shirt that was now a patchwork of sweat stains.

He looked down and noticed what she'd noticed. 'I was just out jogging and, um, I thought I'd take a new route,' he said, cringing inside.

'You, running?' Jacinta laughed. 'You're beginning to sound like my father and all the tall tales he tells.'

Lucas gulped. 'So, you're on to him then?'

Jacinta frowned. 'How do you mean? We went out for dinner last night and, well, it was a bit tense for a while. I don't think he has the greatest sense of humour but then he apologised and gave me this.' She reached up and touched a gold star covered in diamonds hanging around her neck. 'It's real, you know.'

'So everything's okay between the two of you?' Lucas asked.

'I wouldn't say *everything*, but it's better than I can ever remember.' Jacinta shrugged. 'He gave Mummy a beautiful emerald ring and she was so touched she started crying. He said he wanted us to be a family again and that this time, if Mummy took him back, he'd come and live in the village and see me all the time.'

Lucas bit his lip. That's not what he'd heard.

'What is it?' Jacinta said.

'I just don't want you to get hurt again,' he began.

Jacinta nodded. 'He promised that he's a different person, and Alice-Miranda always says you can only take people the way you find them. I don't want to be mad at him forever.'

Lucas could only agree. He'd spent ages being upset with his mother for not telling him the truth about his dad, but then he'd realised that it was a huge waste of energy. Everyone had their faults, and there was nothing to gain from telling Jacinta what he'd heard – only heartache. Perhaps he'd misunderstood. The fact he hadn't told her what he was thinking of doing was also eating away at him. It was all such a mess.

'Do you want a drink? We can get some water,' Jacinta offered. 'Mrs Clarkson is in the sitting room. She won't mind if you come in.'

Lucas shook his head. 'I'd better be getting back. I've got an essay to finish for first period tomorrow.'

Jacinta's face fell. 'Is everything okay? You seem ... I don't know ... weird,' she said, searching his eyes. 'Was there something you wanted to tell me?'

'No . . . nope, nothing at all,' he said, dying inside. His life had been reduced to a bad teen movie, where his brain and body were completely disconnected and the girl of his dreams was about to dump him for being a total imbecile. 'I'd better go.'

Lucas turned and sprinted down the driveway while Jacinta stood there, watching him shrink into a dot on the horizon. It was pretty obvious to her that Lucas was hiding something, and she suspected she knew exactly what it was.

Chapter 30

Alice-Miranda held on to Esma and Hatice's hands as they skipped around into the back garden at Caledonia Manor. She was expecting Zahra to meet her there at three. But what Alice-Miranda didn't expect to see was Ada Abboud and the twins. The babies were lying on a blanket on their tummies, kicking their legs and gurgling in the middle of the lawn with their new double pram parked nearby.

'Mama!' Hatice pulled away and ran towards her mother.

'Hello girls,' Ada called, getting to her feet. She enveloped Hatice and gave her a kiss on the head. 'It was such a beautiful day I couldn't resist the sunshine and this garden is quite something.'

Esma dragged Alice-Miranda towards her mother. 'We met Bony,' the girl said. 'He's Alice-Miranda's pony and he's very naughty.'

'He showed us his teeth like this.' Hatice bared hers and made a whinnying sound.

Ada laughed. 'Did you give him a treat?'

Hatice shook her head. 'Alice-Miranda did, but he tried to chomp her finger. He has very bad manners.'

'And stinky poos.' Esma fanned her hand in front of her face. 'Like the twins.'

'I don't think you can talk.' Ada grinned. 'Where is Zahra?' she asked, looking behind them.

'She ducked off to the bathroom,' Alice-Miranda said, wishing the girl would appear. She hated telling tales, even when they were for a good reason. Fortunately, Esma and Hatice had spotted Cleopatra at the far end of the garden and ran off to play with her. 'How's Mr Abboud?' Alice-Miranda asked. She sat on the blanket and reached out for Hamza's tiny hand.

'The doctors are happy with his progress. They may even bring him out of the coma later in the week,' Ada said. She picked up Miray and cuddled the snuffly infant to her chest.

'That's good news. The festival plans are coming along well too,' Alice-Miranda said.

'You must let me know how we can help,' Ada said. 'Perhaps I can cook if we can find some babysitters.'

Alice-Miranda nodded. She launched into a detailed description of everything the committee had planned but made the mistake of glancing at her watch.

Ada's eyes narrowed. 'Where is Zahra, really?' she asked.

Right at that moment, Zahra sped around the corner. Seeing her mother, she quickly tore off her headphones and dumped them and her backpack among the dahlias. 'Sorry, I had to get a drink,' she puffed.

Ada raised an eyebrow. 'And go to the toilet?'

'Yes, I was busting,' the girl replied, flashing her mother a smile.

Alice-Miranda sighed with relief. 'I was just telling your mother about the festival.'

Zahra hoped she hadn't said anything about the talent quest.

'Your mother thought she might help with the food,' Alice-Miranda said, her brown eyes wide.

Ada stood up and placed Miray into the double pram that had been part of Mrs Parker's procurement. She then lifted Hamza in beside her. 'Come along, Esma, Hatice,' Ada called. 'I need to make a start on supper.'

The pair lingered, not wanting to leave their new friend.

'Thank you for looking after the girls,' Ada said, smiling at Alice-Miranda. 'You are our guardian angel.'

'Mrs Abboud. Would it be all right for Zahra to come and have dinner with us in the boarding house tonight?' the girl asked.

'Oh, I am afraid I need her to help me with the children,' Ada replied. Spotting the disappointment on her oldest daughter's face, she added, 'But perhaps another time. I know it is hard for Zahra to always be minding the little ones.'

'Thank you, Mama,' Zahra said, brightening.

Ada walked ahead, pushing the twins while Esma and Hatice danced along beside her.

'How was it?' Alice-Miranda whispered.

'Wonderful,' Zahra said, beaming. 'I have a new song and it's exquisite.'

'You know, Esma and Hatice might still spill the beans,' Alice-Miranda said. 'In any case, you should tell your mother about your lessons.'

Zahra nodded. 'I will, but not just yet. It would be far better that she sees me perform on the day and then afterwards I will tell her everything and deal with the consequences. I promise.'

Percy Pratt leaned his elbows on the desk and rubbed his throbbing temples. He'd been marking all afternoon and had already downed two paracetamol to deal with the pain, but there was one more thing he had to finish before he could rest. He picked up his pen and began to write. It was all going well until the phone rang, causing him to smear the page.

'Drat it!' Percy cursed. He pushed back his chair and hurried over to answer the call. 'Hello Mother,' he sighed. 'Of course I was going to ring you. It's . . .' He pulled the phone away from his ear as the elderly woman berated him for his tardiness, which was not fair at all. Percy's life was as neat and tidy as the bottles lined up by order of height on the shelves in the Science storeroom. His living quarters were immaculate too. The single bed was made with perfect hospital corners and topped with a hand-made crocheted rug his mother had insisted he bring with him. There wasn't a speck of dust despite his penchant for collecting all manner of scientific curiosities, which adorned the coffee table and bookshelves. He had mazes and several versions of Newton's cradle with the silver balls he liked to set off all at the same time. There were balancing men and spinners and magnets suspended in liquid, some of which he had made himself.

His eyes fell upon the framed poster he'd purchased at the Science fair a few weeks back. It was hanging proudly on the wall with a host of others, proclaiming that *If you're not part of the solution, you're part of the precipitate*. When he'd shown it to Josiah on their way home, the man had stared at him blankly. He'd had to explain what it meant and was greeted with hearty guffaws. Honestly, the fellow was a disgrace to the profession.

'Mother, I have something I need to finish. I'll call you back later,' Percy said, and hung up the phone.

He considered the ruined page, then bunched it into a little ball and tossed it away. It rolled and skipped to the edge of the desk, where it teetered for a few moments before falling through the open window and into the garden below. Percy was so busy redoing his work that he didn't notice it disappear.

Chapter 31

Alice-Miranda glanced at her watch. If she hurried, she still had time to visit the Parkers. She dropped by the boarding house to let Mrs Clarkson know where she was going and bumped into Jacinta, who was standing in the doorway of her room with a peculiar look on her face.

'Is everything okay?' Alice-Miranda asked.

'I don't know,' Jacinta replied in a wobbly voice. 'Lucas was just here and he was acting like a complete weirdo, as if he had something to tell me but couldn't. He's going to live with his mother in America, I'm sure of it.'

Alice-Miranda didn't really have time to talk, but she hated leaving her friend alone in her time of need. 'I was just on my way to visit the Parkers and I'd love some company. Would you like to join me?'

'I'm not *that* desperate.' Jacinta sniffed and mustered a smile. 'But I'll come with you and go and see Mummy. I left a book at her place, which I need to pick up.'

Alice-Miranda grinned and the pair of them set off towards the village. 'How was your dinner last night?' she asked.

'I was sceptical at first,' Jacinta admitted, 'but I think Daddy's really going to try this time. He's even helping me to organise some of the entertainers for the festival – and he's doing it himself, not palming it off on his PA, which never would have happened before. You told me that you can only take people as you find them, so that's what I'm doing. Maybe he's not such a bad person after all and, well, who hasn't been guilty of poor choices? I know I have.'

Alice-Miranda chuckled and gave her friend a squeeze. 'I'm so pleased you're giving him a second chance. Everyone deserves that.'

The girls reached the middle of Rosebud Lane and were surprised to see Miss Crowley in the garden of the cottage next door to the Parkers. It was a quaint stone house with a red front door in the centre, framed by a triangular porch. Symmetrical double-hung windows sat on either side with two identical ones above. Bookended by chimneys, a pretty Virginia creeper had cast its veil over the left side of the building which had been for sale for a little while now, after old Mr Tucker had moved to an aged-care home in Downsfordvale. Miss Crowley was standing beside a tall man in a navy suit and tie.

'Hello girls,' Tabitha said with a smile. 'Lovely afternoon for a walk.'

'Are you buying the house?' Jacinta asked.

'I just came to have a look,' Tabitha said, then led them down the drive and out of earshot of the estate agent. 'Actually, I think I probably will,' she whispered, 'but I want to see if I can do a deal. I'm sure Mr Coburn up there is counting on me being a silly young woman who doesn't know how to negotiate, and I'd like to prove him wrong.'

'Good plan.' Jacinta nodded. 'Who doesn't love a bargain?'

It was right then that Alice-Miranda finally realised exactly who Miss Crowley reminded her of. 'It's Jacinta,' she gasped.

Jacinta looked at her friend. 'Yes, that's my name, don't wear it out.'

'No, I've been thinking ever since Miss Crowley started at school that she reminds me of someone and now I know exactly who it is – it's you,' Alice-Miranda explained.

'Really?' Tabitha said.

'Stand next to each other,' Alice-Miranda instructed.

Mr Coburn walked down the driveway towards the group. 'Is this your sister, Miss Crowley?' he asked.

'See?' Alice-Miranda said triumphantly. 'I'm not the only one who thinks there's a resemblance.'

Jacinta and Tabitha grinned at each other. 'We'll have to do some research,' the woman said. 'It would be lovely to find a long-lost relative or any relative for that matter.'

Mr Coburn handed the woman his card and promised to call tomorrow to see if she had any more thoughts on the house, then he hopped into his shiny red BMW and drove away.

'You know, if you buy this house, you'll be living across the road from my mother,' Jacinta said. 'And next door to Myrtle Parker, which is something to consider carefully, although she's not nearly as bad as she used to be.'

A mop of curly hair popped up over the hedge like a startled meerkat. 'I heard that, Jacinta Headlington-Bear,' Myrtle chided.

Jacinta's eyes widened. 'Oops,' she said, giggling behind her hand.

How long Mrs Parker had been listening was anyone's guess, but Alice-Miranda suspected it was probably from the moment the estate agent's car had arrived outside the house. 'Doing a spot of weeding, were you, Mrs Parker?' the tiny girl asked.

Myrtle drew back her shoulders and brushed a leaf from her hair. 'Yes, absolutely,' she said. 'We have standards to maintain in Rosebud Lane. We're contenders for best kept street in the village this year.'

'How delightful,' Tabitha said, and introduced herself to the woman.

'Well, I just hope someone buys this place soon and brings it up to scratch.' Myrtle tsked.

'It would be a crying shame to have one house letting us down.'

Alice-Miranda smiled to herself. Considering that Mrs Parker's garden had resembled a weedy jungle up until Ambrosia set to work on it – and Mr Parker diligently maintained it – she could hardly comment on the cottage next door, which, apart from the odd stalk of onion grass, was as neat as a pin and almost as pretty as Wisteria Cottage.

'We should be letting you go, Miss Crowley,' Alice-Miranda said. She was eager to find Mr Parker too. As the group was about to part, Neville's Aston Martin swerved into the road before pulling to a stop in Ambrosia's driveway.

'Daddy!' Jacinta shouted. She raced across the road as her parents hopped out of the car. Much to Neville's surprise, she launched herself at his middle and gave him a hug.

'Goodbye, Alice-Miranda. It was lovely to meet you, Mrs Parker. Perhaps I will see you again,' Tabitha said with a smile. She gave Jacinta a wave and began to walk down the lane towards the main road.

'Who was that, darling?' Ambrosia asked, peering across the street.

'Miss Crowley. She's the new English teacher at school. Alice-Miranda thinks she and I could be sisters,' Jacinta said.

'Crowley,' Ambrosia repeated. There was something about the name that rang a bell.

Neville forced a grin to his lips. 'This is a surprise, darling. I thought you had things to do at school.'

'I did, but Alice-Miranda wanted to visit the Parkers, so I decided to see Mummy and pick up a book I left here,' the girl said. 'I'm so thirsty. I hope there's still some of that date-and-walnut loaf left.' She ran down the side of the house and around to the kitchen door.

'Are you coming, Neville?' Ambrosia detected a hint of disappointment in the man's face, but it was of no consequence to her. A couple of dinners and a drive in the countryside did not a new man make. There was a long way to go yet before she'd entertain any thoughts of a reconciliation. 'You'd better get on to that fire twirler you promised Jacinta – you don't want to disappoint her.'

Alice-Miranda was walking up the Parkers' driveway when another car pulled up out the front.

'Stanley Frost, what are you doing here?' Myrtle called out to her brother-in-law. 'If you're expecting a meal, I'm afraid you're barking up the wrong tree.'

'Always a pleasure, Myrtle,' the man called back. He opened the boot and took out a large box. 'I brought you some photographs for the historical society and some I thought you might like for yourself.'

Alice-Miranda giggled. The man's timing couldn't have been better. She had an idea and now she just had to convince Mr Parker and Mr Frost that it was a good one.

Chapter 32

Alice-Miranda slid onto the bench beside Millie, eager to tuck into her roast dinner. The usual dining-room chatter was rather muted this evening, replaced by the sound of chinking cutlery instead.

'Mmm, this smells good,' Alice-Miranda said as she reached for the salt and pepper shakers in the middle of the table. The potatoes were especially crispy and the meat was cooked to perfection. Only the gravy seemed to have a few extra lumps, so Mrs Jennings was definitely improving. Alice-Miranda glanced over at Millie's plate that was already half empty.

'Sorry, I couldn't wait any longer,' Millie said with her mouth full. 'My stomach was grumbling so loudly that Sloane thought there was a thunderstorm coming, but at least I got the rest of my community service out of the way. Honestly, you won't recognise the stables. Dervla had already made a start on the tack room, and this afternoon we cleaned the place from top to bottom and oiled all the woodwork. It looks like new, though it smells foul.'

'Well done, Millie,' Alice-Miranda said. 'Dervla mentioned Miss Reedy had set her a long list of jobs, so she'd have been glad of the help. How are you going with your activities, Caprice?'

'Fine and dandy,' the girl replied curtly. 'I'm almost done.'

But that wasn't true at all. So far, she'd managed thirty minutes of weeding with Charlie and that was it. With all the extra rehearsal time for the festival, she wasn't going to waste a minute on pointless chores. Miss Reedy was so busy at the moment Caprice was hoping she'd forget about the whole boorish business altogether.

As meals were finished, the noise levels rose again with girls chatting about their day. There was much excitement about the festival too. Jacinta waxed lyrical about her father, who had sourced a fire twirler and had promised to hire the country's most renowned balloon artist for her too. 'Daddy said he's going to take Mummy and me skiing later in the year,' Jacinta added giddily. 'They never used to take me when they were married, but he has it all planned.'

Alice-Miranda beamed at the girl. 'It sounds like he's a different person.'

Jacinta nodded, unable to wipe the smile off her face. 'He really is. I just know it.' She stabbed a potato with such force that all four girls looked up from their plates. 'At least that's one part of my life that's on the up and up.'

'Do we have another headline act yet?' Chessie asked Alice-Miranda. They had to get the publicity materials out tomorrow and Tilde McGilvray was going to start promotions on her show this week too.

The tiny girl waggled her eyebrows. 'I do.'

Caprice rolled her eyes. 'Well, who is it?'

'I can't say yet,' Alice-Miranda replied. 'You'll have to trust me on this one. How about we put everything we have on the flyer and just add "plus special surprise guests"? People will be intrigued.'

'Or not,' Caprice snarked.

Once everyone had returned to their meals, Millie nudged Alice-Miranda's leg. 'So, who is it?' she whispered.

'I'll explain all before bed,' Alice-Miranda said with a glint in her eye.

Chessie glanced at Sloane from across the table. The girl had been uncharacteristically quiet during dinner. 'Are you all right?' she asked.

Sloane shook her head. 'No, not really. I went for a walk this afternoon to see Mrs Howard because she's helping me with a sewing project and, when I got to Grimthorpe House, she was having afternoon tea with Mr Trout and Mr Winslade and they were talking about Miss Reedy and it wasn't very nice,' the girl explained. 'They said Miss Reedy had been bossier than ever and had made some very unreasonable demands. Mr Winslade said she'd written him a letter telling him he had to work back every night until seven and keep the library open on weekends too and that there was no room for discussion if he wanted to continue his position as librarian.' Sloane looked at them helplessly. 'That doesn't seem fair at all.'

Alice-Miranda bit her lip. She had a strange feeling there was more to the story than any of them could possibly know.

'And Mr Trout said that he'd received a letter telling him that, if he continued with his choice of extravagant assembly music, he had better start searching for another job,' Sloane added. 'The even weirder thing is that the teachers didn't seem to care that I was there. Mrs Howard was grumpy with Miss Reedy too. She'd punished two of the youngest girls with hours of extra homework and threatened that, if they complained to their parents, they'd be expelled. Again, there was no discussion to be entered into.'

'That is bizarre,' Millie agreed.

'No, it isn't,' Caprice scoffed. 'Reedy has been pretty cranky lately. Look at what she did to us.'

Alice-Miranda shook her head. 'I don't think it's like her at all. Miss Reedy has been so supportive of the festival and I know she's had a lot to do, but that sounds very strange. You said that the teachers received their messages in note form?'

Sloane nodded. 'Mrs Howard said Miss Reedy sent out a message to all staff saying she was so flat out running the school, and Miss Grimm would be busy interviewing new students for the next couple of weeks at least, that she had no time for face-to-face meetings and that all communication would be via handwritten letters until further notice.'

'Wouldn't that take more time than just picking up the telephone or chatting to someone in person?' Jacinta said, scrunching her nose. 'I know it would for me.'

Alice-Miranda could only agree. It was very odd indeed. Something wasn't right and she was determined to find out exactly what was going on.

Chapter 33

Ophelia Grimm stood up and offered her hand to the slender girl in front of her and then to her parents. 'It's been lovely to meet you, Araminta. I look forward to hearing lots of stories about your Cosmo when you start with us next year. The girls adore Fudge, although he has been known to eat more than his fair share of sports shoes.'

'Cosmo's a champion chewer as well,' the girl's father quipped.

Araminta grinned. 'Thank you, Miss Grimm. I'm really excited to be attending Winchesterfield-Downsfordvale and a little bit scared too, if I'm honest.'

'That's absolutely normal,' Ophelia said with a reassuring smile. 'Remember, everyone who's starting new is in the same boat, but our girls are very welcoming. In fact, one of our students – Alice-Miranda Highton-Smith-Kennington-Jones – used to go to Ellery Prep. She came quite early, though, and has been a breath of fresh air.'

The girl's eyes brightened. 'I know of her and I saw her on the television the other night. She's very brave.'

Ophelia nodded. 'She most certainly is.'

The headmistress bid farewell to the family at the study door. She was thrilled to have the daughter of a renowned documentary filmmaker and former prima ballerina starting in the new year. It was by far one her most interesting inter-views yet, and thank heavens for that, as she'd had a few that had almost sent her to sleep. Ophelia poked her head out the door and was pleasantly surprised to see that, for the first time in days, there was no one waiting.

'Mrs Derby, could you come in here once you've finished Araminta Hobbs's paperwork?' Ophelia walked back into her office and sat down heavily at her desk, before sneezing violently six times. 'Oh dear, where did that come from?' She grabbed a handful of tissues from the box beside her. Almost immediately, her head began to spin and it felt as if her brain had been enveloped by a thick fog. Ophelia closed her eyes and had almost dozed off when Mrs Derby entered the room, balancing a cup of tea and a plate of biscuits. There was a notepad tucked under her arm and a pen behind her ear. She placed the refreshments in front of the headmistress and wished she could tell her to go and lie down on the couch for an hour. Unfortunately, that was not about to happen. Ophelia rubbed her neck, which was feeling stiffer by the second. Her throat was sore too and her temples had started throbbing. 'What's next?' she asked.

Louella consulted her notes. 'Your eleven-o'clock appointment is running late. Poor family had a flat tyre, but they should be here within twenty minutes. Then you have back-to-back interviews until six, I'm afraid. Tomorrow and

Friday are no better, but at least you haven't got anything in your diary for the weekend.'

'We can't complain about being popular,' Ophelia said, rolling her shoulders. 'I imagine Livinia has everything else under control.'

Louella chewed the end of her pen. 'Um, well, about that . . .'

'For goodness sake, woman, out with it,' Ophelia snapped. She was dying to drink her tea and eat her biscuits in peace and perhaps snatch five minutes to duck in to say hello to Aldous and Aggie, as she'd hardly seen them all week. It was one thing telling her husband she was planning to return to work, it was another to suddenly start working around the clock.

'There have been a rather large number of requests for meetings with you from the staff,' Louella said. She'd been thinking about whether or not to mention it given how busy Miss Grimm currently was, but several teachers had dropped by more than once to threaten that, if they didn't get an appointment soon, they would burst into one of the woman's interviews and didn't care about the consequences.

'Livinia can deal with them,' Ophelia said, holding up her hand. 'She's technically in charge at the moment, especially as I imagine their issues are about day-to-day affairs.'

Louella picked at the skin around the quick of her thumbnail. 'That *is* the problem,' she said hesitantly. 'They want to talk to you *about* Livinia.'

Ophelia sneezed again and reached for a tissue. 'Well, if that's the case, have them meet with Benitha and I'll make a time to chat to her tonight.' She wondered what Livinia could possibly have done now. Fair enough the two of them hadn't exactly been seeing eye to eye, but that had been sorted out. Livinia had apologised for her error with the note and, although Ophelia wasn't about to admit it to her, doing the television show had been good for the school. With a full complement of students, it would make expanding programs so much easier.

Louella nodded and was about to leave when she remembered something else. She pulled the flyer from the middle of her notebook. 'This is terrific, by the way,' she said, handing it over with a smile. 'Everyone's so looking forward to it.'

Ophelia had just taken a sip of her tea and promptly spat it all over the desk. 'What on earth?

I told Livinia that this was *not* happening. How dare she!'

Louella swallowed hard. 'But ... she said you'd changed your mind.'

'I most certainly did *not*,' Ophelia said, beginning to shake. 'I can't believe she'd try to pull that trick a second time.'

'Hellooo, is there anyone there?' a woman's voice rang out from the room next door. 'Sorry we're late.'

Louella reached across to take the flyer, but Ophelia snatched it away and stuffed it into the top drawer. 'Get a message to Livinia that I need to see her this evening, but I will speak to Benitha first. This has got to stop.'

'But the Fields Festival is all organised,' Louella protested. 'It's on next Sunday and they have some wonderful acts on the bill. I don't think it would do the school's reputation any good to cancel now, especially as it's a fundraiser for the Abbouds and Tilde McGilvray's been talking about it on her show. The tickets are selling like hotcakes.'

Ophelia cradled her head in her hands. 'Fine,' she seethed. 'I just don't understand why Livinia would go against my wishes.' It finally made sense why several of the parents she'd interviewed had been rabbiting on about some silly old singer with a name she didn't recognise. The event must have been arranged a week ago yet no one had thought to mention it to her. Louella was right – there was nothing to be done. However, Livinia had to understand this was Ophelia's school and, while she might be enjoying her time in charge, it would be over very soon. 'Is it hot in here?' Ophelia asked, tugging at her collar.

Louella took a cautious step back. 'I would have said it was a little on the cool side.'

Ophelia was now shaking uncontrollably while beads of perspiration trickled down her temples.

'Miss Grimm, you don't look at all well,' Louella said, taking another backwards step towards the door. The last thing she needed was to catch the flu – that would bring her completely unstuck and she was only just coping as it was. 'You're as pale a sheet.'

Ophelia stood up. 'I need some water, that's all,' she said, before fainting to the floor in a crumpled heap.

Chapter 34

Alice-Miranda felt as if she'd blinked and it was already the weekend. Between lessons, meetings and rehearsals, she'd barely drawn a breath. She'd tried to catch up with Zahra, but the girl was either at school or visiting her father in hospital. Alice-Miranda wondered if she'd managed to get to her singing lessons at all.

She'd tried to see Miss Reedy too, but the woman had taken over Miss Grimm's interviews as well as the running of the school. According to Mrs Clarkson, Miss Grimm had been struck down suddenly with the flu on Wednesday. She was in isolation until she recovered, not wanting to pass the bug to her husband or daughter, who had decamped to the seaside until she was better. Mrs Smith had recently recovered from the same illness herself and decided she was best placed to take care of the woman. Her assistant, Ginny, could hold the fort in the meantime.

On Saturday afternoon, the girls had just finished their committee meeting when Sloane piped up. 'Did you ever speak with Miss Reedy about her letter-writing spree to the teachers, Alice-Miranda?' she asked, reaching for the last scone on the tray. Mrs Jennings had brought them round knowing that the girls would likely miss afternoon tea. 'Because they're still all getting about, looking as if they were the ones who'd lost everything in the fire. Mr Trout almost bit my head off yesterday when I was delivering him a cupcake.'

'No, she's been too busy,' Alice-Miranda replied, closing her folder. 'But I was rather hoping things had settled down.'

'Not from what I've heard,' Ivory said in hushed tones. 'Reedy's reign of terror continues. Miss Wall and Mrs Clinch were talking about it yesterday, saying that if they have to do one more weekend duty they're going to resign.'

'Is that true, Miss Crowley?' Alice-Miranda asked.

The woman looked up from where she was sitting in one of the armchairs. 'Well, I don't want to speak out of turn, but I would have to agree that some of Miss Reedy's instructions do seem a little –' Tabitha paused to choose her words carefully – 'unusual.' She clasped her hands and smiled. 'But we're going to forge on and have a fabulous festival and I'm certain that, when Miss Grimm is back at the helm, things will even out.'

'Or there'll be a revolution,' Millie said. 'That could be fun to watch. Imagine Miss Reedy in a Miss Wall headlock – the woman wouldn't stand a chance!' She launched herself at Jacinta and the two girls began to mock wrestle on the ground, to the amusement of the others.

'I'm sure it's not as bad as all that,' Alice-Miranda said as the group began to drift from the room.

'I'll meet you back here in ten,' Millie said, jumping to her feet and rushing out the door.

Jacinta executed the most graceful of backwards walkovers and headed off to her room while Sloane ferried the empty scone tray to the kitchen. Chessie followed after her, carrying the dirty cups and glasses. Alice-Miranda found herself alone with Miss Crowley for the first time all week. The woman was skimming her notes and writing a list of jobs she needed to do as soon as possible.

'Have you thought more about the cottage?' the child asked.

Miss Crowley nodded bashfully. 'I snuck off after school on Thursday to have another look and put in an offer.'

'That's splendid news,' the child enthused. 'It will be lovely to have a proper space of your own.'

'Actually, I quite like living on campus with lots of people around, but I feel as if I should do something to give myself a bit of security for the future,' the woman explained. 'It's not been a big feature of my life to date.'

Alice-Miranda looked at her quizzically. 'How so?'

'Well, my parents died when I was in my last year of school and I was an only child. My father's latest crazy business venture had just gone bust when the accident happened, so my inheritance was little more than a few pots and pans and my mother's wedding and engagement rings,' Tabitha said. She couldn't understand why she was telling all of this to a ten-year-old, but there was something about Alice-Miranda.

'Oh, Miss Crowley, I'm so sorry. I can't begin to imagine how horrible that must have been for you.' Alice-Miranda perched on the arm of Tabitha's chair and hugged the woman. The thought was not lost on her that she too was an only child, although she'd never felt like one. She had the most wonderful friends and considered everyone who lived on the estate at Highton Hall to be her family. She also had her cousins, Lucas, Marcus and Imogen, and Millie was as close as a sister.

'It was pretty hard, I admit,' Tabitha said, fighting back tears, 'but I had this spectacular great-aunt who I used to spend the holidays with. She was terribly eccentric and smelt like pine cones, which I later discovered was due to her fondness for gin. I called her Aunty Verve, but her real name was Minerva. She lived in a huge Victorian house filled with all manner of antiquities, including a brown bear named Frank who she'd rescued from a zoo in Albania. He'd lived with her as a pet until his death at the age of forty, which was considered a good innings for his kind, and then she'd had him stuffed and put in the sitting room. I know we would never do such a thing these days, but I suppose taxidermy was considered chic back then.

'Anyway, she talked to him all the time as if he was a person. He just scared the socks off me. I think, underneath all the fun and bravado, Aunty Verve was lonely and I was too, so we were a good match.' Tabitha sighed and shrugged her shoulders. 'Aunty Verve didn't have any children of her own, so when she passed away recently, I was stunned to learn that she'd named me in her will. So that's one reason I'm buying the cottage – to make sure I do the responsible thing and don't fritter away my good fortune. I want to look after her legacy.'

'That's a very sensible idea and your Aunty Verve sounds like she was a marvellous lady,' Alice-Miranda said with a firm nod. 'What about Frank? Did you inherit him as well?'

Tabitha chuckled. 'No, I happily did not. I have a cousin who was mentioned in the will too, but I've never met him. He's Aunty Verve's brother's child, but he's a bit of a mystery and considerably older than me. I asked her about him once and she said he was an unusual character and that he'd changed his name and she didn't think it would do me an ounce of good to meet him. She didn't think much of him, though he had a daughter she was fond of.'

'Do you know his name?' Alice-Miranda's eyes widened at the prospect of a long-lost relative. 'Perhaps you could find him. I mean, he is still family, even if your aunt didn't fully approve of him.'

'I suppose I could,' Tabitha said. 'His name is Gilbert Crowley, but I'm not sure what he goes by these days. There was something strange in the will. It stipulated that, if at the time of Minerva's death he was no longer married, his share of the inheritance would pass straight to his daughter. There was a long definition of what constituted a marriage too, which included things like living together as a family, him being a provider and so on. It was quite odd, but then again so was Aunty Verve. I'd have expected something just as batty for me – perhaps that I *wasn't* to be married or

I should have three cats, fourteen chickens and a motor scooter. Thankfully, she didn't impose any conditions on my inheritance.'

Alice-Miranda grinned. 'I think eccentricity is a trait to be valued. Life would be dreadfully dull if we were all the same.'

'I tend to agree, though I'm quite the conform-ist. Everything in its place, "i"s dotted and "t"s crossed. I suppose it's my way of trying to control things. It's silly, really, because if there's one thing I've learned, it's that life is mostly beyond our control,' Tabitha said.

Alice-Miranda nodded. 'I think the most important thing is how we choose to react to whatever comes our way. I'm sure your Aunty Verve would be very proud of what you're doing.'

'Thank you, Alice-Miranda, that means a lot,' the woman said, smiling. She pushed herself up out of the chair, having realised the time. 'I must get going. I've got to meet the estate agent at the house again. He's bringing a local builder to give me some quotes on a few renovations I might have done before I move in.'

Jacinta poked her head around the doorway. 'Good, you're still here,' she said. She'd just changed out of her gym clothes and was now wearing jeans with a pretty white blouse and ballet flats. 'I'm going to Fayle to see Lucas and wondered if you might come with me. It would be great to have some back-up.'

'I'll leave you girls to it,' Tabitha said. 'Oh, that's a gorgeous necklace, Jacinta. Is it an antique?'

'My father gave it to me,' Jacinta said proudly.

Tabitha thought for a moment. 'You know, that looks just like one my great-aunt used to wear. Her name was Verve. That doesn't ring any bells, does it? Seeing that Alice-Miranda thinks we could be related.'

Jacinta shook her head. 'No, but I'll ask Daddy where he got it from.'

The woman said goodbye, leaving Alice-Miranda and Jacinta alone in the sitting room.

'I'd love to come except that Millie and I are going to see the Parkers and we're supposed to be there in ten minutes,' Alice-Miranda said.

'Fine,' Jacinta replied, wrinkling her nose. She'd already tried Sloane and Chessie, but they were busy too. 'I guess I'll go on my own then.'

'Sorry, but this is important,' Alice-Miranda said.

'Whatever.' Jacinta shrugged and charged out the door.

'Jacinta, please don't be upset,' Alice-Miranda called after her, but the girl was already gone.

'Don't worry, she'll be fine,' Millie said, when she arrived a minute later. 'Although maybe she won't.'

Alice-Miranda frowned at her friend as they signed themselves out and walked to the front door. 'What do you mean?'

Millie explained on the way to the village about Lucas's visit to the school last weekend, his bizarre behaviour and how he'd mentioned Neville Headlington-Bear was up to something but had left it at that. The girls both agreed they'd just have to wait and see what happened. Hopefully Lucas was wrong about Neville, and perhaps, if Lucas did spend a year on exchange, Jacinta could go to Mrs Kimmel's at the same time. The girls rounded the corner into Rosebud Lane and almost ran straight into Zahra Abboud. She was wearing a pale blue sundress with a butterfly print and a smart pair of silver sandals. Her long, dark hair was tied in a braid over her shoulder.

'Hello,' Alice-Miranda said with a knowing smile.

'My mother has taken the rest of the children to the hospital to visit my father. She thinks I'm with you, Alice-Miranda. I'm sorry, I should have checked to make sure it was okay to use you as my cover again,' Zahra said, biting her lip.

Millie frowned. 'What are you covering for?'

Alice-Miranda looked at Zahra. 'Millie's my best friend in the world. I promise she can keep a secret.' Zahra nodded her consent and Alice-Miranda told the whole story.

'Zahra should come with us,' Millie said.

Alice-Miranda grinned. 'I don't suppose it would do any harm. You're meant to be with me anyway.'

Zahra was intrigued. Alice-Miranda grabbed her hand and they ran along the lane to the Parkers', where they sped up the front steps and rang the bell. Minutes later, they were greeted by Mrs Parker. She had her sleeves rolled up and was wearing an apron over the top of her lemon-coloured dress. There was a smudge of flour on the woman's forehead and the scent of fresh baking wafted out from behind her.

'Hello girls,' she said, eyeing the trio. 'This is a surprise. Zahra, does your mother know you're here?'

The girl cast her eyes to the ground. 'She knows that I'm with Alice-Miranda.'

'Well, they're in the garage,' Myrtle said, standing aside.

'Thanks, Mrs P,' Millie called as the three girls scampered past the woman, down the hall and out through the kitchen doors.

'My name is Mrs Parker, Millicent,' the woman called. 'And don't you forget it, young lady.'

Millie knocked on the side door of the garage and Mr Parker poked his head around.

'Ready?' he asked.

'As we'll ever be,' Millie fizzed.

Chapter 35

'What's the matter?' Jacinta demanded in the middle of the velvet green lawn. 'A week ago, you were holding my hand and telling me how glad you were that we'd be able to spend time together at rehearsals and this week you haven't come to any of them. If I didn't know better, I'd say you were doing your best to avoid me, Lucas. Miss Crowley probably won't even let you sing with us at the festival, you know.'

'Oooh,' George Figworth teased from above. 'Trouble in paradise.'

Jacinta and Lucas gazed up to find they'd attracted quite the audience, with several boys lining the upstairs windows of the Fayle boarding house.

'Put a sock in it, Figgy!' Jacinta scowled and threw the lad a rude gesture.

'Jacinta,' Lucas chided. 'You'll get thrown off campus if anyone sees you doing that.' Then he looked up at the window and shouted, 'Get lost, Figgy, and take your mates with you!'

Jacinta shook her head, her eyes filling with tears. 'I don't care if someone throws me out. I want to know why you're acting like this.'

'I'm just trying to protect you, that's all,' Lucas said quietly.

'I knew it! You're leaving and going to live in New York, aren't you?' she said, folding her arms tightly.

The boy sighed. 'No, I'm not. Well, not now, anyway. I might when I'm a bit older, but I'd talk to you before I made a decision. I've been thinking that we should do an exchange at the same time, but it would be better if we were in our second-last year, when we'll have loads more freedom.'

Jacinta felt her muscles begin to relax and the blood start flowing again. 'That would be . . .

amazing,' she said, a smile tugging at the corners of her mouth. She dabbed at her eyes with a tissue. 'Well, if it's not that, then what?'

'Come with me.' Lucas took her by the hand and guided her to a garden seat around the side of the building. At least it afforded them some privacy, out of sight of the boys' prying eyes. Jacinta sat on the bench and rubbed her palms on the tops of her thighs. The two of them faced out towards the garden. 'I saw your father last weekend in the village.'

'So?' she said, touching her delicate gold necklace.

Lucas turned to her and took her hands in his. 'Jacinta, I think he wants to get back together with your mum and I'm not sure his motives are entirely pure.'

Jacinta raised an eyebrow and laughed. 'You sound like some knight from the Middle Ages, Lucas. Please, just say what you mean.'

'Your father needs to get back with your mother because of some business deal. He's planning on them moving to the city and then, when the deal is done, he's going to dump her again,' Lucas said.

Jacinta snatched her hands away, her forehead puckering. 'No, he's not. You're just saying that because your mother's getting married and you don't like the guy.'

'But I do,' Lucas said. 'Jacinta, I wasn't sure whether to tell you this or not because I didn't want to upset you, but I promise I heard your father talking on the phone and I'm not making it up. Why would I?'

Jacinta stood up. 'It's not true, Lucas,' she insisted. 'Why would you say such a horrible thing?'

She turned and ran, her feet pounding grass and pavement all the way to Rosebud Lane. She sped past her father's car parked in the driveway and around the back of the house but stopped short when she saw her parents through the glass doors. They were standing in the kitchen, looking at each other. Her father stepped towards her mother and touched her cheek, then he kissed her – and it wasn't a peck either. This was a proper kiss, like in romantic comedies when the two people realise they truly love each other. Jacinta knew that Lucas was wrong. He had to be, or else her father was nothing short of a monster.

Chapter 36

Alice-Miranda, Millie and Zahra were floating on air as they walked back to school.

'That was amazing,' Zahra gushed.

'*You* were amazing,' Millie said. 'You'll definitely win the talent quest and I can't wait to see Caprice's face when you do. She's going to hate you, by the way, but don't worry, she'll still hate me more.'

The girls charged up the driveway, past Caledonia Stables and towards the Manor. As they neared the mansion, they could hear the sound of children's voices, like bell chimes and giggles all mixed into one.

'Oh no, Mama must be back,' Zahra said. Her stomach clenched and she felt as if she had a fever.

'But you're with us, just like you said you were,' Alice-Miranda said, giving the girl a reassuring squeeze.

The trio rounded the corner to find Ada Abboud rocking the twins in their pram while Hatice and Esma chased Cleopatra across the lawn.

'Mama, hello,' Zahra called out. 'How is Papa?'

Ada smiled, her eyes crinkling in the corners. 'Your father is awake and asking after you. He is doing much better,' Ada said. 'I told him that you would come with me tomorrow and then perhaps we will tell him about the festival.'

'How much longer will Mr Abboud have to stay in hospital?' Alice-Miranda asked.

'There is a chance he will be able to come home in another week or two,' Ada said. 'Girls, would you like to join us for dinner tonight? I have made moussaka and I am sure Zahra would enjoy the company, as would I.'

Zahra nodded eagerly. 'Please say yes.'

'That would be lovely, Mrs Abboud. We just need to tell Mrs Clarkson where we are,' Alice-Miranda replied.

'We're technically not allowed on the teachers' floor of Caledonia Manor,' Millie whispered out of the side of her mouth.

Alice-Miranda frowned. Millie was right, but perhaps Mrs Clarkson would make an exception in this case. After all, a couple of weeks ago no one would have imagined a family of six living up there either.

Hatice ran to Alice-Miranda, holding a bright pink dahlia in her tiny hand. 'I picked this for you,' she said. 'From over there.' She pointed at the garden, then tugged on Alice-Miranda's arm, bringing her down to the same level where she whispered in the girl's ear.

'Of course we can,' Alice-Miranda replied. She helped the girl choose another stem, which Hatice gave to Millie. As she did, something caught Alice-Miranda's eye. She peered into the foliage and pulled out a scrunched-up piece of paper, which she opened and pressed flat.

It was a note bearing Miss Reedy's personal letterhead. It looked like she must have made a mistake partway through, but how on earth it had come to be in the garden was anyone's guess. Alice-Miranda looked up to the windows. Then she scanned the page. It seemed a particularly sensitive message to have disregarded so carelessly. Hopefully Miss Reedy had changed her mind about its contents and that was the reason it was tossed away. Alice-Miranda folded the note and popped it into her pocket. But what she'd do about it was another matter altogether.

Percy Pratt walked out of the Science storeroom and down the hall, carrying a box with the chemicals he required for his lessons on Monday morning. He'd decided to get the preparation done this afternoon then tomorrow he was off to the city for a lecture at the Science Museum.

'Oh, hello Mr Pratt,' Josiah Plumpton called out, startling the man and causing him to stumble.

The bottle of sulphuric acid teetered, but Percy managed to regain his balance. He spun around. 'Yes, what do you want?'

'I was wondering if you might like some

company tomorrow,' Josiah said. 'I hear Professor Padbury is a very impressive speaker.'

Percy's eyes narrowed. 'How did you know I was going?'

'Livinia told me. She was the one who suggested I join you – actually, she sent me a note.' The man pulled it from his trouser pocket. 'I saw her for a moment just now and mentioned that I was going to speak to you and she thought it was a splendid idea. Poor love is swamped – I don't know how she's getting everything done with all the interviews on top of running the school. I've barely seen her all week and she can't seem to remember things from one day to the next.'

'Your wife has had a lot of interesting ideas lately, so in that case, I don't suppose I can say no.' Percy rolled his eyes and began walking towards the lab.

Josiah chuckled and hurried to open the door for him. 'Wonderful. What time shall we leave?'

The thought of spending an entire day with Josiah Plumpton was almost too much for Percy to bear, but he had no one to blame but himself. 'Meet me at my car at half past seven,' he said.

Josiah beamed. 'Very well. I'm so looking forward to it.'

Chapter 37

If Alice-Miranda thought last week was busy, the days leading up to the festival were nothing short of a blur. Thankfully, Mr Charles had mobilised a force of volunteers from the village to help get the grounds ready. Everyone was keen to pitch in and Myrtle Parker had insisted on supervising the delivery and placement of the portaloos and marquees, making sure they were installed according to the children's masterplan. Alice-Miranda couldn't have been more grateful, considering the infrastructure was delivered and set up on Friday during lessons.

Jacinta, meanwhile, had spent the week ignoring Lucas. She refused to take his calls and, when it came time for choir rehearsals, made sure to sit as far away from him as humanly possible. Sep had implored her to speak to the lad, but she was still upset with Lucas no matter how much she missed him. He had to understand that you shouldn't go around spreading gossip that wasn't true.

Saturday was chaotic, but the girls couldn't make a proper start on things until after sport. Alice-Miranda had decreed that all committee members would meet on the oval at two o'clock, when they would get to work putting up signs, bunting and decorations, and sound-check the three stages.

While all this was going on, Ophelia Grimm was still recovering from the worst flu she'd ever known. The fevers had been blinding and, coupled with a hacking cough and headaches that felt like someone was poking her in the eye with a knitting needle, she was finally beginning to feel better – a week and a half after being struck down. She was glad that Aldous and Aggie had managed to stay healthy, but their absence was doing nothing to improve her spirits. Thankfully, the doctor said that she was no longer contagious and they could return home on Saturday evening. Ophelia was dozing between episodes of her favourite crime drama when she suddenly realised there was a lot of noise coming from the oval. With all the shouting and hammering and roaring of engines, it sounded as if a carnival had come to town.

'Hello dear,' Mrs Smith called, gently tapping on Ophelia's bedroom door. A second later, she appeared with a pot of tea and plate of home-made shortbread on a tray. She put it down on the bedside table and walked over to open the curtains. 'You need some air in here.'

'What's all that racket?' Ophelia asked. She wondered what day it was.

'The festival preparations,' Mrs Smith answered with a smile. 'It's on tomorrow, and I must say that everything looks fantastic. Those girls have worked terribly hard and I think you'll be very proud of them.'

Ophelia sighed. 'I can't imagine why I was so opposed to the idea in the first place.'

'If I may be so bold, Miss Grimm,' Mrs Smith began.

'For goodness sake, Doreen, call me Ophelia. I'm not *that* woman any more.' The headmistress rolled her eyes and sat up against her pillows.

'All right. Well, *Ophelia*, I think perhaps you were *that* woman again for a moment there. I'd blame it on the hormones and the changes that having a child brings. I suspect you might have felt as if you were losing control because Miss Reedy *was* doing such a sterling job, so you asserted yourself. Yet you knew all along that our girls would be up to the task,' Doreen said. 'Anyway, drink your tea and focus on getting better. The staff and students need you and so does that husband and adorable little girl of yours. I've made dinner for them so Aldous doesn't have to worry. There's a fridge full of food, and I'll make sure to have dinners sent from the dining room.

'And just between you and me, I'm afraid that in the past few weeks Miss Reedy has undone all of her good work and completely lost the plot – not with the girls, as far as I can tell, but if she sends one more offensive note to a staff member, there will be an uprising with pitchforks and fiery torches. They'll run her off the premises and Mr Plumpton along with her.'

Ophelia's eyes widened. 'Goodness, is it really that bad?'

'Possibly worse,' Doreen said. She turned and walked out of the room, leaving Ophelia alone with her thoughts.

Chapter 38

Alice-Miranda pulled on her long white socks and slipped her feet into her leopard-print shoes. She jumped off the edge of the bed and grabbed her brush from the bedside table, then tied her hair into a high ponytail, adding a pink scarf around her head.

'I can't believe Britt pulled all this together and got it here for us in time,' Millie marvelled, swishing her tulle skirt.

Alice-Miranda shrugged on her black leather jacket. 'She is amazing.'

When the parcel had arrived for the girls mid-week, neither of them could believe it. Alice-Miranda had felt so awful about not having written to Britt for a month that she'd decided to call the girl instead and, during their telephone conversation, they'd talked about the festival. Britt had then surprised Alice-Miranda and Millie with what had to be the trendiest outfits they could have imagined and now they were about to give them their first public showing at breakfast. They were almost matching, except that Alice-Miranda's headscarf was pink and Millie's was green, which looked perfect against her red hair and matched the sparkly green heart on her white T-shirt.

'And we get to stay in these clothes all day instead of having to wear our stuffy, old Winchester-Fayle Singers outfits. Miss Crowley is cool with a capital "C",' Millie said, grinning at her room mate in the mirror. 'Ready?'

Alice-Miranda nodded and added a touch of lip gloss. 'It's been a lot of work for everyone, but I just know today is going to be incredible. The most important thing is we help the Abbouds get back in their house and rebuild Fattoush as quickly as possible.'

'I hate to admit it – and I probably won't to anyone other than you – but Caprice did a good thing,' Millie said.

'And after all is said and done, Millie, I think you should tell her that. It would go a long way to making things better between you two. I would almost guarantee it.' Alice-Miranda considered her friend's outfit and pinned one last badge onto her jacket.

'I hate it when you're right.' Millie smiled and gave Alice-Miranda a huge hug. 'Come on, let's get this show on the road!'

The girls hurried down the hall to the dining room, where the atmosphere was electric. Nick Waterford's 'Greatest Hits' was playing through the speakers and, interestingly, quite a few of the girls were singing along despite their previous protestations that he was ancient. Everyone had pulled together something fabulous to wear too, including the teachers. Miss Crowley was in skinny jeans, black ankle boots and a shimmery silver top. Mrs Clinch had gone for gothic revival and had kitted herself out in black from head to toe, while Miss Wall was barely recognisable without her tracksuit on.

'Have you ever seen Miss Wall with her hair out?' Sloane whispered to Jacinta. The girl shook her head, her fishbone plaits flying from side to side.

Benitha Wall's long, dark hair was blow-dried and the woman had on a full face of make-up too. She looked like a completely different person in a short skirt and peasant blouse. Percy Pratt also caused quite the stir when he walked into the room. Gone was his lab coat, replaced with stonewashed jeans and a denim jacket over a dark denim shirt.

'Wow.' Millie giggled into her hand. 'I thought double denim was dangerous, but Mr Pratt's taken it to the next level.'

But something wasn't right – and not just with his outfit. The man had a face like thunder as he marched over to his colleagues. He produced a piece of paper from his pocket and the group huddled together. At one point Miss Wall threw her hands into the air and declared that she was going to see Miss Grimm. She strode from the room, leaving the girls wondering what on earth Miss Reedy had done now. Come to think of it, none of the girls could recall the last time they'd seen the acting headmistress. She'd been holed up in Miss Grimm's office, conducting interviews for over a week, and hadn't come to dinner at Caledonia Stables at all. Mr Plumpton had been nigh on invisible too.

Millie nudged Alice-Miranda as they headed for the servery. 'That doesn't look good.'

Unsure what to do about the note she'd found in the garden, Alice-Miranda had safely tucked it away in her desk drawer, but the girl had resolved to see Miss Reedy tomorrow, after the festival. This wasn't the school she knew and loved and the last thing she wanted was a staff coup.

Millie heaped a pile of pancakes onto her plate and drizzled them with maple syrup.

Mrs Jennings leaned across the counter, clearly chuffed. 'Mrs Smith's recipe.'

'They look delicious,' Alice-Miranda said, smiling at the woman, although she'd seemed to have lost her appetite after witnessing the upset among the teachers.

'Wow, you two!' Chessie grinned at Alice-Miranda and Millie as they slid along the bench seats.

'Courtesy of our Norwegian friend, Britt Fox,' Millie said, striking a pose.

'She's awesome,' Sloane said. 'You both look fantastic.'

'You aren't too shabby yourselves,' Millie said, admiring the girls' cute maxi dresses paired with denim jackets. Chessie's mother had sent some outfits and so had September Sykes. Between the two of them, the girls had come up with looks they loved. Actually, September was so excited about the event that she'd gone to the trouble of putting together a portfolio with suggestions tagged. She'd talked the girls through it over the telephone, raving on about how much she missed going to festivals herself. She'd even popped a crimping iron in the post.

Jacinta looked incredible too, but that was to be expected given her mother's fashion experience. The girl was dressed in a floaty green boho dress with ankle boots and a flower crown nestled atop her blonde locks.

'Has anyone seen Caprice?' Alice-Miranda asked, glancing around the room.

She was met with shaking heads as the girls were heavily invested in their surprisingly delicious pancakes and had their mouths full. Alice-Miranda checked the time and hopped up to speak to the teachers before she walked over to the microphone. Mr Trout turned down the music.

'Good morning, everyone,' Alice-Miranda began. 'I hope you're as excited about the festival as I am. I just wanted to say a huge thank you for your hard work and for all that is still to come. I love that you've gone to so much trouble to dress up and get into the right mood for music.' There was a loud cheer from the girls. 'On to more mundane things, if anyone needs an extra running sheet, there's a pile at the front of the dining room. Most of all, have a great day and let's get out there and raise enough money to see the Abbouds back home.'

The dining room erupted again.

Shelby Shore raced into the room, huffing and puffing. 'There are cars outside for miles!' she announced, gasping for breath. 'Charlie says they're already queuing through the village and on the Downsfordvale road. He's going to open the gates early as we don't want any accidents.'

'I'd better get to the ticket booth,' Millie said, and quickly shovelled in another generous mouthful of pancake.

'Has anyone seen Caprice?' Alice-Miranda asked again. She was beginning to worry, as it wasn't like the girl to miss the action, especially when she'd been so excited about the festival. Not to mention the fact she was managing the program on the main stage while Chessie and Sloane were in charge of Stages Two and Three.

'Here I am,' a voice sang out from the doorway.

All eyes turned to see who it belonged to. Millie almost choked on her pancake while Sloane spat her milk across the table.

'What *is* she wearing?' Jacinta blurted.

That was just the reaction Caprice had been hoping for. She simpered in a sparkling pink floor-length gown with her copper-coloured hair piled high on top of her head. She had a face full of make-up too and looked decades older than her peers. 'Mummy had it sent from Italy.'

'No, I didn't,' a voice rang out from behind her. 'I had Mrs Evans make it for you, as usual, and why you're swanning about in it now I have no idea.' Venetia marched into the room, looking less than impressed. She had popped over to the boarding house to see if Mrs Jennings had some more mixing bowls as she seemed to be running short and had already scarpered Mrs Smith's stash. The woman was dressed for action in jeans and a white linen shirt with a *Sweet Things* apron over the top. 'That dress is for performances only and you're not scheduled to appear until early this evening. You're not wearing it all day while you're managing the main stage, and what is on your face? It's called stage make-up for a reason, Caprice, not running-around-doing-your-job make-up. I don't know if you realise, but you will be racing about like a scalded cat and you're not doing it in that dress, looking twenty-five years old.'

'I hate you, Mummy!' Caprice screeched. She turned on her high heels so fast that she almost lost her footing.

Venetia pushed up her sleeves and ignored the impending tantrum. 'No, you don't, sweetheart. But I'd suggest you change quick smart, wipe your face and get to work – today is a team effort and there's no "I" in "team".'

Millie chortled and took another bite of her pancake. 'Gosh, I love that woman,' she said, before scampering off to the ticket booth.

Chapter 39

Alice-Miranda wished she had wings as she visited each site, making sure that everything was running smoothly. She was constantly checking the time too as the Winchester-Fayle singers were due on the main stage in thirty minutes and she didn't want to miss out.

She passed Miss Reedy and Mr Plumpton, who were a little less rock-and-roll than their colleagues but had dressed more casually than usual for the day. Alice-Miranda couldn't remember seeing

Miss Reedy in jeans before and Mr Plumpton was baring his lily-white legs in long navy shorts and a white T-shirt with an unbuttoned checked shirt over the top. It was a pity he'd worn socks with his sandals as he looked quite trendy from the knees up. Livinia was beaming and, together with her husband, was greeting the locals and visitors alike, who were all praising the merits of the event.

'Fabulous day, Alice-Miranda,' Livinia called with a smile. 'Well done.'

Alice-Miranda smiled back and waved, then continued on her way. It seemed strange that Miss Reedy was so happy while the rest of the teachers were whispering in corners and pointing fingers. It was as if she was completely oblivious as to what she was doing – either that or she didn't care, which Alice-Miranda found hard to believe.

The oval was a sea of colour with people dotted everywhere on picnic rugs and lawn chairs. The three stages were working perfectly with the second and third areas far enough away that they weren't competing for an audience or interfering with each other's sound. Stage Two featured child-friendly acts, from singers dressed as fairies to magicians and a puppet show, while Stage Three had a roster of folk musicians and the amateur musical society belting out show tunes. As predicted, the main stage had been the most popular with the Downsfordvale Concert Band having just finished their set of movie scores with a resounding crash of cymbals.

On the western boundary there was face painting, craft tents, story time, a fire twirler and even a fortune teller. On the other side, the food trucks were doing a roaring trade, helped by a gentle breeze that was sending their tantalising smells wafting over the crowd. Ada Abboud couldn't believe her luck to be working alongside the famed Venetia Baldini, who had focused on a range of Middle Eastern sweet treats to complement Ada's cooking. Zahra was there too, making falafels. She was glad to be busy as that gave her less time to worry about what was to come. Hatice and Esma were in Mrs Howard's care, enjoying the festival while the twins were being looked after by a local lass called Claire, who had worked as a casual waitress in their restaurant.

Lucas Nixon had been wandering the grounds, searching for Jacinta all morning to no avail. He considered the slightly wilted bunch of daisies in his hand. If he didn't find her soon, he'd have to toss them and buy some more. Jacinta didn't deserve shabby flowers, just like she didn't deserve a deadbeat dad, but it wasn't up to him to tell her what to think. Neville was her father and parents were complicated. Lucas knew that as well as anyone. He just couldn't bear the thought of her being hurt yet that's exactly what he'd done when he'd interfered.

'Lucas!' he heard someone call out. Alice-Miranda ran towards the lad, dodging through the crowd. He was surprised to receive a hug.

'Hi,' he said glumly.

She nodded at the flowers and grinned. 'Jacinta will love them.'

'Do you think so? She's still not talking to me,' the boy replied. 'I shouldn't have told her what I overheard.'

Alice-Miranda frowned. 'What happened?'

Lucas sighed. 'I came to talk to you last Saturday, but you weren't around. Then I ran into Jacinta and froze. I didn't tell her anything. It was only when she came to the school on Sunday that I couldn't keep it a secret any longer and opened my big mouth. She's been mad at me ever since.'

Alice-Miranda guessed this must have been what he'd started to tell Millie the other day. 'What did you hear exactly?'

Lucas explained everything. 'I just don't understand why Neville would stand to get money if he and Ambrosia were back together. That bit doesn't make any sense at all.'

Alice-Miranda could only agree. 'Poor Jacinta. She's been talking about all the plans her father's been making and she's so excited. He did come through with the fire twirler, but now I know why she was in a strange mood with you.'

'Maybe I got it wrong,' Lucas said with a shrug.

Alice-Miranda reached out and touched the boy's arm. 'Let's hope so – for everyone's sake. Sorry to leave you like this, Lucas, but I've got to check on the fortune-teller tent. There have been a couple of complaints.'

'You do know why that is, don't you?' Lucas chuckled. 'It's Figgy – he's dressed up as a gypsy with a wig and make-up. Apparently, Professor Pluss had been rostered to do it but decided there was no way he was playing with people's futures. When Mr Winterbottom called for volunteers, Figgy jumped at the chance.'

Alice-Miranda giggled. 'Well, that all makes perfect sense now. Our fraudulent fortune teller told Mr Munz he was going to leave the shop and become a movie star. Then he told Mrs Munz she was going to lose her husband. The poor woman was in floods of tears.'

'Good luck,' Lucas said, and gave his cousin a wave.

Alice-Miranda smiled. 'You too.'

Ophelia Grimm was feeling vastly improved since her husband and daughter had arrived home the previous evening. The three of them were sprawled on a rug in front of Stage Two with Aggie swaying in time to the music and beating her hands on the ground.

'This is pretty amazing.' Aldous Grump was sitting next to his wife and kissed her on the forehead. 'And I am so glad you're better. You had me very worried, darling.'

Ophelia smiled. She had to admit he was right about the festival, though last night she'd spent some time reading through the litany of complaints the staff were making about Livinia and her unreasonable demands. She wasn't going to spoil the day for everyone, but tomorrow they would have a serious discussion about the woman's future. Doreen was right in saying she'd turned into a tyrant and then some. Perhaps it was time for Livinia to think about a career move. People got stale and, though she didn't like the thought of going anywhere herself, maybe Livinia needed her own school.

Alice-Miranda was on her way to the main stage, having just ejected Figgy from the fortune-telling tent, when she caught sight of Jacinta standing head and shoulders above the rest of the crowd. She was dressed as a butterfly on stilts and juggling three balls in the air. Alice-Miranda cupped a hand to her mouth and called to the girl, waving with her other hand.

Jacinta waved back. She was flanked by a young lad kitted out as a unicorn and a girl who was a bumblebee. 'I've been trying to find Mummy and Daddy,' Jacinta said, then immediately spotted them walking towards her. Her mother looked stunning in a white linen pants suit with a striking silk scarf wrapped around her neck while Neville was the epitome of rural chic in his jeans and checked shirt with a fedora on his head.

'Hello Ambrosia, Mr Headlington-Bear,' Alice-Miranda said. 'Are you having a good time?'

'Apart from the crowds and all those ghastly smells.' Neville grinned tightly. 'I had no idea it would be this busy.'

'But that's a good thing, Daddy,' Jacinta said. 'Remember? It's all for a very important cause.'

'Yes, of course. All for a good cause,' he echoed, and sighed when his phone rang.

Jacinta frowned. 'Are you still being hounded by work? Surely you can tell them to leave you alone. It's your company, after all, and it is Sunday.'

'I'm beginning to think that Jamie must have a crush on you, darling,' Ambrosia said.

'Don't be so silly,' Neville said. He muttered something about finding the loo, and stalked away.

Ambrosia looked at him in surprise. Despite his attentions the past couple of weeks, the man was still a mystery in so many ways. The woman turned back to the girls and smiled. 'I love your outfit. Did you put that together yourself?'

Alice-Miranda explained about Britt Fox, her fashionista friend, who Ambrosia remembered from the leadership camp.

'That gives me a great idea for a story,' Ambrosia said, tapping her chin with a perfectly manicured finger. 'Perhaps a trip to Norway is on the cards.'

Alice-Miranda grinned. 'I'm sure Britt would love that. Maybe Jacinta and I could join you – and Millie and Chessie. I think Mummy would be up for it too.'

Ambrosia nodded. She'd like that very much and had been wondering about her next assignments. Since Neville had returned, she'd been completely distracted. He'd been badgering her to spend time with him in the city, and whenever she told him she had work to do, he pouted like a three-year-old. To say she was feeling mixed up was the understatement of the century, especially when he began talking about all the parties and social events he was planning. That was her old life and, while she realised that she still had feelings for Neville in spite of what he'd done, there was no thought of going back to how things were before.

Tabitha Crowley was making her way through the field, looking for her singers who were due to assemble at the side of the stage in fifteen minutes. She'd spied Millie in the distance and was trying to get the girl's attention when she bumped into someone else. 'Oops, sorry,' she said, spinning around. 'Oh, hello Alice-Miranda.'

Ambrosia studied the woman curiously. 'You *must* be Miss Crowley,' she said, holding out her hand. 'I can see why Alice-Miranda thinks you and Jacinta could be sisters. You two have quite the uncanny resemblance.'

'Yes, I suppose we do,' Tabitha said as she shook the woman's outstretched hand and tried not to stare. 'Your ring. It's beautiful.'

Ambrosia smiled, covering it self-consciously. 'Yes, it's stunning, isn't it? It was a gift from my ex-husband.'

'May I have a closer look?' Tabitha asked. She was surprised when Ambrosia took it off and passed it to her. Tabitha turned it over in her hand and gasped when she read the inscription. 'Where did you say you got this?'

'Neville, Jacinta's father.' Ambrosia tilted her head to the side. 'Why do you ask?'

Tabitha's mind was racing. When she'd said Jacinta's star necklace reminded her of one her great-aunt used to wear, she'd thought nothing of it — but now this. It had to be more than a mere coincidence.

'Is everything all right, Miss Crowley?' Alice-Miranda noticed the peculiar look on the woman's face and that she was still holding Ambrosia's ring.

'My great-aunt used to have a ring just like this one,' the teacher replied, passing the jewel back to its owner. 'I wondered what had become of it. She wasn't wearing it the last time I saw her, which was strange given I hadn't ever seen her without it . . .' Tabitha frowned, lost deep in thought. A crash of the cymbals brought her back to reality. 'Sorry,' she said, shaking her head, 'I'd best get going. Girls, please don't be late.'

Alice-Miranda had solved enough mysteries in her short life to know that something was up and she had a sinking feeling it was to do with Neville Headlington-Bear's surprise return to the family fold. She said goodbye to the group and set off to find Millie, who, last time she'd checked, was with Mrs Clinch in the cashier's tent. She spotted Neville up ahead and decided that now was as good a time as any to have a quick word with him. Alice-Miranda was just about to say something when a statuesque brunette woman in skinny jeans and sky-high heels pushed in front of her and tapped the man on the shoulder.

Neville turned around and gasped. 'Jamie, what are you doing here?'

'I decided to come and find you, seeing that you've barely taken my calls for weeks. What's going on, Neville?' the woman spat. 'I thought we were engaged.'

Alice-Miranda's eyes widened.

The man gulped. 'You need to go, Jamie. *Now*. We'll talk soon – everything's fine. I just have some urgent business to attend to.'

'But, Neville, I'm so lonely back in the city,' the woman whined. 'And what's all this *business*, anyway? You come home for a night and then you're gone again. I can't live like this – and my credit card's maxed out and you said you'd fix it and you haven't.' The woman began to cry big, racking sobs. Neville guided her around the corner between two tents. He offered her his handker-chief, which she noisily blew her nose into.

Alice-Miranda followed him. This was worse than she'd imagined but she had to know for sure.

'Excuse me, Mr Crowley,' she said with a beaming smile.

'Ye–' Neville flinched and turned around. 'What did you just call me?'

'Your name is Gilbert Crowley, isn't it?' the child said. 'Or at least it was before you changed it to Neville Headlington-Bear.'

'Who do you work for?' he snapped. 'Is someone paying you to say this?'

'What's she talking about, Neville?' Jamie said. She was clinging to the man like a limpet while mascara ran down her cheeks.

Alice-Miranda shook her head. 'I don't work for anyone, but if I did I'd say that I was an advocate for your wife and daughter, who deserve *so* much better than what you're currently dishing up.'

'Wife? Daughter?' Jamie's blue eyes were huge.

The blood was rising to Neville's face and he was getting redder and redder by the second. 'You don't know anything about me,' he spat.

'I know a lot more than you think,' Alice-Miranda challenged. 'You won't get the money. You and Ambrosia are divorced.'

'Divorced?' Jamie squeaked.

'Actually, sweet pea, we're not.' Neville smiled smugly. 'You see, my lawyer never lodged the final paperwork. Ambrosia and I are still very much married.'

'Still married?' Jamie sobbed.

Alice-Miranda put her hands on her hips and drew herself up to her full height. 'Mr Headlington-Bear, or whoever you really are, I have a suggestion for you. If there is one shred of decency in your body, you would have your lawyer lodge those divorce papers first thing tomorrow. Leave town tonight and tell Jacinta and Ambrosia you realised you're not worthy of them, and please don't come back. Your daughter and ex-wife will be just fine without you and your lies.'

Neville's mouth gaped open as if he were catching flies.

Jamie pulled away. 'We're finished, Neville. You can have your ring back too.' She twisted the giant rock from her finger and threw it on the ground.

'Jamie, stop!' Neville shouted. 'Come back!' He turned to Alice-Miranda. 'I don't know who you think you are, young –'

'I'd do exactly as Alice-Miranda says,' Lucas said, striding towards them.

'Who on earth are *you*?' Neville demanded.

Lucas ignored the question. 'I know what you're planning – to take Ambrosia to the city and leave Jacinta here and then you're going to dump Ambrosia again too once you have your money.'

'You two are delusional,' Neville said, shaking his head. 'You have no proof.'

'Apart from your ex-fiancée there?' Lucas challenged.

Miss Crowley hadn't yet made it back to the main stage but was hoping her singers had when she caught sight of Alice-Miranda and Lucas. Honestly, getting these children together was like herding cats. At this rate, they were going to miss their slot in the program. She hurried over to them. 'Sorry to interrupt,' she said, 'but I need you two on stage in two minutes.'

'Perfect timing, Miss Crowley,' Alice-Miranda said. 'Mr Headlington-Bear, please meet your cousin Tabitha – the one your aunt left half her fortune to.'

'Alice-Miranda, what are you talking about?' Tabitha frowned.

'That's preposterous,' Neville protested. 'Her name's Tabitha Crowl . . .' The man stopped as the realisation set in. He'd heard his wife say the woman's name before but he hadn't been paying attention.

'Gilbert?' Tabitha asked, her brow crinkling.

Alice-Miranda noticed a sturdy silhouette on the other side of the tent right by where they were standing. It almost looked as if whoever it was had their ear pressed against the canvas. She turned to the man. 'There were conditions attached to your inheritance, and if you can't meet them, your half goes straight to Jacinta to be held in trust.'

'What rot,' Neville huffed.

For a few seconds Tabitha Crowley was too stunned to speak. 'No, it's the truth,' she said, finally finding her voice. 'I told Alice-Miranda that, but I had no idea *you* were my cousin.'

'Face it, Neville, it's over,' Lucas said, stepping towards the man. 'If you have an ounce of feeling for your daughter or her mother, you'll do exactly as we ask – unless you'd prefer we go public now? We can get to a microphone pretty quickly.'

'You wouldn't,' Neville rasped.

Lucas narrowed his eyes at the man. 'Try us.'

'Fine!' Neville stamped his foot like a five-year-old. 'I couldn't stand another second of that whining brat of a child, anyway. And Ambrosia all hoity-toity with her "career" – who knew she had a brain let alone one she might use?'

The flap on the tent burst open and Myrtle Parker quite literally flew out. Her curly hair was standing on end and her face was bright red. 'Leave!' the woman thundered. 'Now, before I tear you apart limb by limb! Your wife and daughter are two of my dearest friends in the world – actually, I consider them my family and you are not going to destroy that poor woman and child again. GO! And do not ever return to our village!' Fortunately, the Fayle Pipes and Drums were on the main stage and no one could differentiate Myrtle's shrieks with the screeching bagpipes. 'And I want a letter telling them exactly what you were up to so there can be no doubt that you are the scoundrel that I have always taken you for. If you don't,' Myrtle hissed, her nose almost touching Neville's, 'I will find you and it won't be pretty.'

Neville swallowed hard and pushed the woman out of the way before legging it to the gate.

Ambrosia thought she saw Neville run past but shook the notion from her mind. He'd been complaining so much since they'd arrived at the festival she hadn't been enjoying his company at all. If she was truly honest with herself, she knew Neville was up to something. Tonight, she would tell him there wasn't going to be a reconciliation. She was a better person without him.

Alice-Miranda, Lucas, Miss Crowley and Mrs Parker looked at one another in stunned silence. It took a minute to register exactly what had happened.

'Mrs Parker – you were, magnificent.' Alice-Miranda reached out and hugged the woman around the middle.

Myrtle hugged the tiny child back. 'Well, Jacinta's going to need us all, but don't worry, she and her mother have a whole village behind them, and a new cousin too.'

Alice-Miranda nodded but her heart stopped when she heard the emcee, Tilde McGilvray, introducing the Winchester-Fayle Singers.

'Oh dear, we'd better go,' Miss Crowley said.

Alice-Miranda grabbed Lucas's hand and the pair of them were about to run when a shout rang out from the cashier's tent.

'Thief! We've been robbed!'

Alice-Miranda, Lucas, Tabitha and Myrtle ran around the corner to find Millie standing with her hands clutched to her head.

'The money,' the girl gasped. 'It's all gone!'

Chapter 40

Moments later, Ms McGilvray announced there was a change of plans and the Winchester-Fayle Singers would be appearing later in the program. Given that Alice-Miranda, Millie, Lucas and Miss Crowley were currently missing, it didn't come as a surprise.

'Where's Mrs Clinch?' Alice-Miranda asked.

'She went to find Charlie,' Millie said, on the verge of tears. 'He was going to escort her to the office to put the money in the safe. It was in a red bag on the table there and I only turned away for a second. When I looked back, it was gone. The Abbouds are not going to have any money and it's all my fault.'

'No, it's not,' Alice-Miranda said, putting an arm around her friend. 'And we'll find it. The thief can't have gone too far.'

But Millie didn't share her friend's optimism. She wiped at the tears that were stinging her eyes.

'Has anyone seen Constable Derby?' Alice-Miranda asked.

'He was manning the sausage sizzle with his wife, but I don't think Mrs Derby was feeling well,' Mrs Parker said. 'Actually, the poor woman was a peaky shade of green last I saw her. If I didn't know better, I'd say she was –'

'Coming down with the flu,' Alice-Miranda jumped in, having realised exactly what Mrs Parker was about to say.

'I'll go,' Lucas offered. 'And Alice-Miranda's right, Millie. It's not your fault.'

'Maybe we should make an announcement over the PA?' Millie sniffled. 'If the thief is still among the crowd, that might flush them out if they make a run for it?'

'Or hide,' Miss Crowley said.

'I'll find Miss Reedy,' Alice-Miranda said.

An enthusiastic crooner had replaced the Winchester-Fayle Singers and was treating the crowd to some mid-century classics as Alice-Miranda scanned the grounds for the acting headmistress. She spotted Tilde McGilvray heading for the food tents and was surprised to see a large group of teachers standing to one side of the main stage. Alice-Miranda picked her way through the patrons to the edge of the oval and ran towards them. 'Miss Wall, something's happened,' she called. 'We need you.'

The teacher turned and it was then that the child realised Miss Reedy was right in the middle of the huddle. It was an awful scene with lots of finger-pointing and raised voices. Alice-Miranda gasped and scurried over.

'You're nothing short of a tyrant, Reedy,' Mr Trout yelled. 'My music is spectacular, and how dare you hobble me and make all those insidious remarks.'

'And I refuse to take the long-distance swimming squad and lead by example – you know I'm not a strong swimmer. It's outrageous!' Miss Tweedle huffed.

'I'm a casual employee, Miss Reedy,' Dervla said, her fists clenched. 'Expecting me to cover prep time for the junior girls for no pay is completely out of line.'

'Please stop shouting at one another,' Alice-Miranda said, squeezing her way into the huddle and holding up her hands. 'You're adults, not schoolchildren.'

Livinia Reedy was trembling. 'I have no idea what any of you are talking about,' she said in bewilderment.

'Of course you do,' Miss Wall spat. She pulled a wad of pages from her shoulder bag, thrusting them at Livinia. She'd been carrying them around for days in the hopes of confronting the woman. 'As for telling me that I had to ditch all my new clothes and go back to regulation school tracksuits, well, you can bite me!'

Livinia looked at the first page and scanned its contents. 'But . . . I-I didn't write this,' she said, shaking her head. 'I'd never make such outrageous demands. I've been so busy and I trusted you were all just going about your business as per usual.'

'Don't try to deny it,' Benitha scoffed. 'It's your handwriting and these are your letterheads.'

Livinia's face scrunched. 'Yes, it is, and they are. I don't understand any of this.'

Alice-Miranda spotted Millie and Lucas. Chessie was with them too. In fact, most of the Winchester-Fayle Singers were standing outside the tent that had been set up as a green room for the performers. She retreated to join them while the teachers continued to rant and rave.

'What's all that about?' Chessie said.

'The teachers have finally taken matters into their own hands,' Alice-Miranda said, her mouth a grim line.

'That's hardly surprising,' Jacinta said, who was now off her stilts. Lucas flashed her an awkward grin. Jacinta couldn't help herself – that smile of his always made her go weak at the knees. 'I'm sorry,' she whispered. 'I know you only want the best for me.'

'I'm sorry too,' he said, and squeezed her hand. He didn't know how she was going to react to the news about her father but now wasn't the time to get into it.

Aldous Grump had taken Aggie inside to have a sleep while Ophelia went for a wander. The sun on her face was therapeutic and she'd been having lots of lovely chats with parents and villagers. She also wanted to find Mrs Abboud to see how she and the children were faring. As Ophelia neared the main stage, she noticed there was something going on and it wasn't just the man serenading the audience with his Frank Sinatra tunes. All that was missing from the scene were fiery torches and pitchforks.

'Good heavens,' Ophelia muttered, 'that's the last thing we need people to see!' She hurried over and planted herself in the middle of group. 'Right, you lot, calm down,' she said, 'and move around to the back of the stage. There are families out there who are thinking of sending their girls to the school and they won't if they see this nonsense.'

'Thank goodness you're here,' Miss Tweedle said. 'Miss Reedy has to go. She's a tyrant of monumental proportions.'

'And check her bag – she's a thief too,' Mr Pratt accused.

With all the drama between the teachers, Alice-Miranda had momentarily forgotten about the money. She looked at Mr Pratt and had one of her strange feelings. The man seemed to be enjoying the drama, which was very concerning indeed. She quickly gathered Dervla and Millie, and the three of them formulated a plan.

'I'll stay here and keep watch,' Millie said.

'Come on.' Dervla grabbed Alice-Miranda's arm. They'd get to Caledonia Manor much faster with the aid of the school motorbike, which was parked inside the stables. The pair shot off through the school.

'I hope I'm right,' Alice-Miranda said, as Dervla kick-started the bike. She held tightly to the woman's middle.

Meanwhile, back at the festival, things were spinning out of control. Livinia clutched her handbag under her arm and refused to give in to Mr Pratt's demands for her to show everyone its contents. Josiah Plumpton had heard enough. All week he'd seen staff skulking in pairs and threes and fours, whispering about his wife, and he would not stand another second of it.

'Mr Pratt, your accusations are ridiculous,' Josiah exploded, his cheeks quivering. 'I can't believe you'd say such a thing.'

'*Your wife* is ridiculous!' Percy shouted. 'And bossy and mean and stupid – I mean, she must be because she married you and you're just about the most preposterous person I've ever known.'

Josiah lunged at the man, unable to control his outrage. After their collegial day out at the science lecture on the weekend, he couldn't understand the man's spiteful remarks.

Percy ducked to the left then to the right and, before anyone knew what was happening, the two men were on the stage. 'Open her handbag and prove her innocence then!' Percy yelled.

The poor man who was singing spun around at the sound of the commotion. He faltered for a split second, then kept on crooning, hoping the interlopers would be gone the next time he looked.

'Terrible back-up dancers,' an elderly woman in the audience muttered.

But the melee was about to get worse. Benitha Wall picked up her loudhailer and demanded the pair stop. When they didn't, she leapt onto the stage and seized Mr Plumpton, daring Livinia to charge after her.

'Her bag!' Percy shouted, flapping his arms. 'Get her bag!'

Benitha swiped at Livinia's handbag and the two of them tussled back and forth in a tug-of-war before the English teacher was overpowered by the PE teacher's brute strength. As Benitha wrenched the bag from Livinia's hand, it flew open, spewing bundles of money onto the floor and into the sky.

'Good heavens!' Livinia gasped, her face ashen. 'Where did that come from?'

Mrs Clinch had arrived with Charlie. 'Shame on you, Livinia! You supported the festival from the outset and now you're stealing from it.'

The children were as stunned as the staff by the shower of cash. Ophelia Grimm had seen enough. She signalled to Constable Derby, who ran to the stage and apprehended the woman. Meanwhile, Benitha and Caroline had scooped up all the money. Mr Pratt pulled a red plastic bag from his back pocket and passed it to them. Millie's eyes bulged.

'I can't believe it, Livinia,' Ophelia said, shaking her head. 'You're not only a tyrant, you're a thief. Did you really think you would get away with this?'

Despite the commotion, the singer had managed to keep entertaining the crowds and no one seemed to notice what was happening at the rear of the stage. The high-pitched whine of a motorbike could be heard like a buzzing mosquito above the music. Dervla stopped at the edge of the oval and Alice-Miranda leapt off the back. She ran through the crowd and over to the group of teachers and students, waving a sheaf of papers in front of her.

'It's a set-up,' she panted, then paused to catch her breath. 'The handwriting on all those letters *appears* to be Miss Reedy's, but it's not. It's Mr Pratt's!' She pointed at the man, who was standing on the edge of the group, looking very smug.

'That's outrageous!' Percy sputtered. 'The child is delusional.'

'And you stole the money too – it was in a red bag and you have the bag,' Millie accused.

Dervla Nichols reached the group, gasping for breath. 'Alice-Miranda is telling the truth,' she panted.

Alice-Miranda and Dervla had gone to Caledonia Manor after the girl had realised she'd found the scrunched-up letter in the patch of garden right under Mr Pratt's window. When the man had accused Miss Reedy of being a thief, Alice-Miranda knew there was more to it as Miss Crowley was still over by the cashier's tent and she hadn't mentioned the money was missing to any of the teachers.

Miss Hephzibah and Miss Henrietta were just setting off to watch the festival's afternoon entertainment when Alice-Miranda and Dervla arrived. Alice-Miranda had quickly explained her theory to the women and Hephzibah used their master key to open the man's flat. Sure enough, there were stacks of notes written on letterheads from Miss Grimm and Miss Reedy and even some from Miss Wall and other teachers too. They then checked Miss Reedy's office and found notes she'd written months before and compared the handwriting. It was clear that while Mr Pratt was an excellent counterfeiter, he had slipped up a few times on his loopy 'g's.

'You're a good forger, Mr Pratt, but a careless one,' Alice-Miranda said. 'I found this under your window last week.' She produced the page from her jacket pocket. 'At first I thought Miss Reedy must have made a mistake – this request was too cruel for words – but then I realised she wouldn't write anything so ridiculous or preposterous, which is one of your favourite words, Mr Pratt – yet I can't remember Miss Reedy saying it very often at all. You've used it in the letters quite a bit, I see, which is another reason we know it was you. Miss Tweedle can't swim and Miss Reedy knows that. She would never order her to take long-distance swim coaching on the lake and insist the woman lead by example.'

'Of course I wouldn't,' Livinia said.

Ophelia looked at Mr Pratt. 'You changed my letters too, didn't you? The reason Livinia thought I agreed to the television interview was because you switched my note with yours.'

The man shook his head adamantly but everyone could see he was lying.

'Why?' Millie said. 'Why would you do it?'

Percy was cornered. 'It was the only way I could get rid of *him*,' the man said, pointing at Josiah and drawing a gasp from the assembled crowd. 'No one can see his incompetence, his stupidity – he gives Science teachers the world over a bad name,' Percy said, his face contorting with indignation. 'I knew he wouldn't stay if his beloved Livinia was crucified.'

'Despicable,' Benitha murmured. 'I'm so sorry, Livinia – we've all behaved dreadfully.'

'I would have done the same,' Miss Reedy said graciously. 'I'm surprised you didn't come for me sooner.'

'Mr Pratt, you might be a good Science teacher, but you're a poor judge of character,' Alice-Miranda said. 'Mr Plumpton might not always get his experiments right, but his classes are fun and engaging, and we all know that one of the best ways to learn is from our mistakes. We adore him and he's not going anywhere. Unfortunately, I don't think the same could be said for you. And it was really mean of you to steal that money from the Abbouds. They've been through enough.'

Percy scowled. 'They were always going to get it back,' he retorted. He smoothed his hair and straightened his tie. 'If you'll excuse me, I'll go and pack my things.'

'That's a very good idea,' Ophelia said, before she rushed over to Livinia and the two women embraced.

Chapter 41

'Excuse me! Coming through!' Caprice bustled into the middle of the teachers and students. She had changed back into her sparkly dress and had hastily reapplied her full face of make-up with her hair somewhat styled on top of her head. 'Could you clear out? The talent quest is about to start and I've rescheduled the Winchester-Fayle Singers to a slot straight afterwards, then we have me followed by Nick Waterford. Is there really another special guest, Alice-Miranda, or has that fallen over, in which case I'll take the last spot?'

Alice-Miranda looked at Millie, and the two girls smiled. 'There sure is,' she said, but there was something else the girls had to do first.

Miss Grimm rounded up her staff and directed them away from the stage, where she gave a rousing pep talk about what a magnificent group they were and, now that the rat in the ranks was gone, they'd better get on with it too and support their girls. The mood of the festival lifted to new heights among a slew of apologies and tears.

'Right, the girls need our help,' Livinia said. 'So, hop to it, everyone!'

Tilde McGilvray had returned from her break none the wiser about the earlier fracas and was about to resume her duties when she was intercepted by Caprice. 'It's my show now,' the girl sneered and snatched the microphone. Ever the professional, Tilde handed it over, but not before making a mental note of the girl's name and vowing she would never appear as a guest on her show.

Zahra Abboud chewed on her lip. She'd been keeping a watch on the time, her stomach twisting with each passing minute.

'Hello Mrs Abboud,' Millie said, dancing into the food tent. 'I'm going to take over from Zahra for a while.' She winked at the girl. 'Alice-Miranda's waiting for you in the green room,' she whispered out of the side of her mouth.

'What are you doing, Zahra?' Ada called after her daughter.

'It's all right, Ada, let her go,' Venetia said. 'We'll be fine. You go too, Millie.'

Millie grinned and took off through the crowd.

They could hear Caprice announce the first contestant in the talent quest. It was a little girl playing the ukulele and singing. She was terribly sweet and as cute as a button.

The next act was an elderly couple dancing the tango. The performances varied between good and very good to downright tragic, but at least the crowd got a few laughs – especially at the expense of a poor fellow with a magic act where absolutely nothing went right. First his cards flew out of his hands, then his magic wand broke, and when the dove he was going to pull out of his hat escaped from his sleeve and flew away he stormed off stage red-faced and in tears.

The second-last act was a young girl with a breathy voice that clearly no one found as easy on the ear as her own parents, who cheered her on from the side of the stage.

Finally, the last contestant was announced. Word had spread about Ada Abboud's delicious baalbek and the line snaked down past several other vendors. She was busy serving a young couple when a girl began to sing.

'Wow – now *that's* a voice,' a young woman standing in front of Ada said. She turned to see if she could catch a glimpse of the stage.

There were nods all around.

'She must be a professional,' another man said. 'And if she's not, she should be.'

Ada Abboud swallowed her surprise.

Venetia nudged the woman. 'Go – you need to see this.'

Ada took off her apron and hung it on the hook inside the tent, then wove her way through the crowd until she could see the main stage. Her breath caught in her throat at the revelation that the owner of that beautiful voice was her daughter. A tear dropped onto the top of her cheek as she was swept away with the music.

Zahra finished and looked out into the audience. She could hardly believe her eyes when she realised that her mother was there cheering the loudest. The girl took a bow to a chorus of 'Encore!', but Caprice was having none of it.

'Right.' The girl bustled onto the stage in her shimmery dress and grabbed the microphone. 'Thank you, Zahra Abboud. That was . . . quite good.' With a flash of annoyance, the girl realised the dress Zahra was wearing had once been hers. Her mother must have donated it without her permission.

'Wow, such generous praise.' Millie rolled her eyes.

Caprice announced the end of the contest and a short recess for the judges to retire to make their decision, which would be revealed at the very end of the festival.

At the rear of the stage, Alice-Miranda and Millie hugged Zahra.

'You were incredible,' Alice-Miranda said.

'So much better than Caprice,' Millie added.

'I heard that,' Caprice snarked as she walked past with her clipboard. 'And I'll have my dress back later too.'

'I should go and see my mother,' Zahra said as Caprice took to the stage for her own set. Zahra walked around the corner, where Ada was waiting. 'I am sorry, Mama,' she murmured.

'Whatever for?' the woman asked. 'Being talented and brave and doing what I could never have done?'

'For sneaking out to singing lessons,' Zahra said. 'That's where I was when the fire broke out. With Mrs Goodman.'

Zahra looked up and realised that the woman herself was sitting on a lawn chair in the front row beside Hephzibah Fayle. She jutted out her chin and clasped her hands together. 'Wonderful,' Mrs Goodman mouthed.

Ada drew her daughter into her arms and hugged her fiercely. 'I am so proud of you – and I love you very much.'

Tears spilled onto Zahra's cheeks.

But the night was far from over and there were still more surprises in store.

Caprice's set was met with rousing applause, although there was a general consensus among the audience that five songs would have been ample. When a helicopter whizzed overhead and landed in the bottom field, the atmosphere took on an electric charge. Nick Waterford was here!

Minutes later, the man leapt on stage in one of his trademark fluorescent pink suits and the crowd went wild, dancing and singing for the next hour. He was incredibly energetic for a fellow of advancing years. But it was the final act that was the biggest surprise of all.

Alice-Miranda grabbed her drumsticks and Millie picked up her tambourine. They grinned at Zahra, who had quickly changed into an almost identical outfit.

'Are we really going to get up there on stage?' Reg Parker grimaced. The man was wearing a pinstriped suit and a fedora at a jaunty angle.

'Absolutely.' Stan Frost picked up his electric guitar. He looked every inch the seasoned rock star in black from head to toe, including a skinny black tie. 'Come on, Reg, we might be dead tomorrow – it's time to live a little.'

Following three hotly contested rounds of scissors, paper, rock, Tilde McGilvray graciously conceded her emcee duties to Miss Reedy for the last part of the event. Livinia knew the role would get her close to Nick Waterford and she was right. She took photographs with him backstage and he'd even given her a kiss on the cheek, which she wasn't planning to wash ever again.

'Now, before I introduce our final surprise guests, I just want to say one more time – wasn't Nick Waterford incredible?' the woman asked, and received a huge cheer. 'We also have to announce the winner of today's talent quest, and it was none other than –' she looked at the envelope Caprice handed her, her lip wrinkling in surprise – 'Puggles the Pooch and Mr Cornish, the dancing doggy and his master. Well . . . that's, lovely.'

She wondered who the judges were. No one had thought about that so Caprice had appointed herself.

'Sorry you didn't win,' Alice-Miranda said to Zahra as they waited in the green-room tent.

'Me too, but you were never in the race with Caprice in charge.' Millie grinned.

Zahra shrugged. 'I don't mind. That was the best moment of my life so far up on that stage.'

'Well, here comes another one,' Millie said.

Back on stage, Miss Reedy was going through a long list of thankyous. 'It's been the most wonderful day, and I hope I'm not speaking out of turn by saying that I think the Fields Festival might become an annual fixture on the Winchesterfield-Downsfordvale event calendar.' Livinia glanced to the side of the stage, where Ophelia gave her two thumbs up. 'Without further ado, I give you two of the original members plus three junior members of the world-famous band Hoot!'

The squealing was insane. Middle-aged men and women were practically fainting while anyone younger than thirty looked completely bemused.

Myrtle Parker crossed her hands over her chest and prayed. 'Just don't make a goose of yourself, Reginald,' she whispered.

Ambrosia nudged the woman. 'Lighten up, Myrtle. I loved these guys when I was a kid – I can't believe you've kept it a secret from me all this time.' Ambrosia suddenly realised that Neville had gone missing hours ago. The fact she hadn't noticed until now only confirmed her decision that they had no future together.

Tabitha, meanwhile, stood in the crowd feeling more at home than she had in years. It seemed she'd finally found her place in the world and she hoped that this was right where she would be for a very long time to come.

'What are you lot doing?' Caprice asked as she appeared in the doorway of the green room. 'Are you the surprise act?' She could hear the crowd cheering louder than they had all night. 'Do you need a singer? I can do it.'

'It's okay – we've got Zahra,' Millie said, cocking an eyebrow towards the girl, who hadn't stopped smiling since the talent quest.

Caprice pouted. 'But I'm better than she is.'

'Maybe one day we can do a duet,' Zahra said graciously, but Caprice had already stalked off.

'Okay, let's do this,' Alice-Miranda said, and skipped out of the tent and onto the stage to take her place at the drums. She wriggled into position and put her left foot on the pedal. Zahra headed straight for the microphone in the middle while Stan plugged his guitar into the amp and Reg sat down at the keyboard. Millie climbed onto a podium with her tambourine.

'Hey, is that Mr Parker and Mr Frost up there with Alice-Miranda and Millie and Zahra?' Jacinta said, squinting into the bright lights that had just come on. She was standing next to Lucas, holding his hand. They'd already kissed and made up properly behind the ice-cream van.

'Yup.' Lucas nodded. 'Mad, hey?'

Alice-Miranda clapped her drumsticks together above her head. 'And a one, two, three, hit it!'

And just in case you're wondering . . .

The festival was a huge success. In the end they raised far more money than anyone expected. With ticket sales, novelties, food and additional donations from several anonymous sources, there was more than enough to rebuild the Abbouds' home and restaurant. Everyone agreed that the Fields Festival should become an annual event and no one was more excited about the prospect than Miss Grimm.

Ada Abboud and the children visited Mehmet in hospital the next day and, to his surprise, Ada babbled for an hour about how proud she was of Zahra's performance. That daughter of hers was going to be the next big thing for sure. Mehmet had hugged his daughter tightly and whispered that he knew her mother would come around one day. They were more than happy for her to continue her singing lessons and Zahra had her sights set on a local eisteddfod or two in the coming months.

Tabitha Crowley decided to stay at Caledonia Manor for a while yet. In the meantime, the Abbouds moved into her cottage. They needed the space much more than she did, and it would give her time to think about her remodelling plans. Fattoush was getting the most extraordinary new facade, designed by none other than Myrtle Parker herself, in consultation with the Abbouds and a pile of Middle Eastern history books.

When she'd first learned of her father's betrayal, Jacinta had sobbed for one gut-wrenching hour, but she soon realised that it would never have worked and that she and her mother were far better off without him. Besides, in the process of uncovering the truth, she'd gained a cousin – one that she liked very much. Tabitha and Ambrosia had many things in common, especially their love of fashion, and it didn't take long for Tabitha to become an adored member of the family.

Needless to say, Lucas and Jacinta were more smitten than ever. It helped enormously that he invited her to be his date at his mother's wedding. Ambrosia was happy to chaperone them, and there were plenty of stories she could write while she was in New York.

Reg and Stan were back in business. Their performance had caused ripples throughout the industry and there was now talk of a tour. Myrtle couldn't have been prouder, although she did make Reg double-insulate the garage before there were any more rehearsals.

Percy Pratt moved to live with his mother. With his track record, there was no chance of another school position. Instead he turned his hand to wedding calligraphy – and the odd forged document – which proved far more lucrative than teaching.

The equilibrium was soon restored at Winchesterfield-Downsfordvale. Miss Grimm allowed Miss Reedy to finish up her proper term before making the woman deputy head of

Organisation, while Miss Wall took on the role of deputy head of Pastoral Care. Both women were thrilled and worked together without a hitch.

Louella Derby finally made it past the point that she could tell everyone the real reason for her constant rushing off to the bathroom. The woman was three months pregnant and the girls couldn't have been more thrilled.

Miss Reedy heaped praise on Caprice for her role in the success of the festival – right before she made it clear that she still had nine and a half hours of community service to complete. Alice-Miranda continued her drumming lessons and, together with Zahra, Millie, Chessie, Jacinta and Sloane, the girls formed their own garage band. Guess who else is desperate for an invitation to join in?

Cast of characters

Winchesterfield-Downsfordvale Academy for Proper Young Ladies staff

Miss Ophelia Grimm	Headmistress
Mrs Louella Derby	Personal secretary to the headmistress
Mr Josiah Plumpton	Science teacher
Mr Percy Pratt	Science teacher
Miss Benitha Wall	PE teacher
Mr Cornelius Trout	Music teacher
Miss Livinia Reedy	Acting headmistress and English teacher
Miss Tabitha Crowley	English teacher
Miss Verity Tweedle	Art teacher
Mrs Petunia Clarkson	Housemistress of Caledonia Manor
Mrs Caroline Clinch	Maths teacher
Charlie Weatherly (Mr Charles)	Gardener
Mrs Rachel Jennings	Cook at Caledonia Manor
Mr Gordy Winslade	Librarian

Mrs Doreen Smith	Cook at Winchesterfield-Downsfordvale
Ginny	Assistant cook to Mrs Smith
Dervla Nichols	Stablehand

Winchesterfield-Downsfordvale students

Alice-Miranda Highton-Smith-Kennington-Jones	Only child, ten years of age
Millicent Jane McLoughlin-McTavish-McNoughton-McGill	Alice-Miranda's best friend and room mate
Jacinta Headlington-Bear	Friend
Sloane Sykes	Friend
Francesca Compton-Halls	Friend
Caprice Radford	Friend of sorts
Ashima Divall, Susannah Dare, Ivory Hicks, Shelby Shore	Committee members

Fayle School for Boys students

Lucas Nixon	Alice-Miranda's cousin
Septimus Sykes	Lucas's best friend and brother of Sloane
George 'Figgy' Figworth	Mischief-maker
Rufus Pemberley	Figgy's frequent partner-in-crime

Others

Aldous Grump	Miss Grimm's husband
Agnes Grump	Miss Grimm's daughter
Myrtle Parker	Village busybody
Reginald Parker	Husband of Myrtle

Stanley Frost	Owner of Wood End
Hephzibah Fayle	Friend of Alice-Miranda's and owner of Caledonia Manor
Henrietta Sykes	Sister of Hephzibah and step-granny of Sloane and Sep Sykes
Ambrosia Headlington-Bear	Jacinta's mother
Neville Headlington-Bear	Jacinta's father
Herman Munz	Owner of the local shop
Constable Derby	Local policeman, married to Louella Derby
Mehmet Abboud	Owner of Fattoush
Ada Abboud	Mehmet's wife
Zahra, Esma, Hatice, Miray and Hamza Abboud	Mehmet and Ada's children
Sue Trelawny	Myrtle's friend
Tilde McGilvray	Television host
Mr Coburn	Real-estate agent
Jamie	Neville Headlington-Bear's 'colleague'

About the Author

Jacqueline Harvey taught for many years in girls' boarding schools. She is the author of the bestselling Alice-Miranda series and the Clementine Rose series, and was awarded Honour Book in the 2006 Australian CBC Awards for her picture book *The Sound of the Sea*. She now writes full-time and is working on more Alice-Miranda, Clementine Rose, and Kensy and Max adventures.

jacquelineharvey.com.au

Jacqueline Supports

Jacqueline Harvey is a passionate educator who enjoys sharing her love of reading and writing with children and adults alike. She is an ambassador for Dymocks Children's Charities and Room to Read. Find out more at dcc.gofundraise.com.au and roomtoread.org.

Enter a world of mystery and adventure in

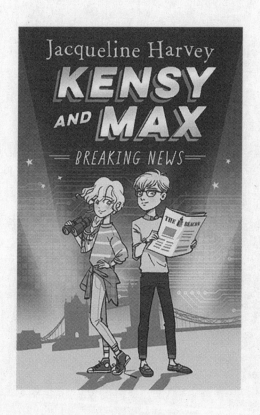

OUT NOW

Read on to see how it all began . . .

CHAPTER 1

BKDIXKA

Max woke with a start as the car crunched to a halt. He yawned and looked around at his sister, who was still asleep in the back seat. Her blanket had slipped down and she was drooling on the pillow that was wedged in the corner. She wouldn't thank him for noticing.

The boy peered out at the jewel box of stars in the clearing night sky. It had only stopped raining a little while ago. On the other side of the car, Max could see what looked to be a hotel. A dull glow shone from one of the windows high in the roofline. For a second, he glimpsed a face, but it was gone as soon as it had appeared. 'Where are we, Fitz?' Max asked.

Fitz turned and gave him a weary smile. 'This is Alexandria,' he replied, as if that was supposed to mean something. 'Be a good lad and take the daypacks with you, and mind the puddles. No one will thank you for tramping mud inside.'

Fitz opened the driver's door and hopped out of the Range Rover.

Max stretched, yawning again, then reached over and gently shook his sister's leg. 'Kensy,' he whispered, 'we're here.'

The girl groaned and flopped her head against the pillow but didn't wake up. It was to be expected given they'd just spent the past sixteen hours driving from Zermatt, near the Swiss–Italian border, across France and then to England.

Fitz reappeared at the open driver's window. 'Don't wake your sister unless you want your head bitten off,' he warned with a wink.

Kensy let out a grunty snore, as if to agree.

Max heard footsteps on the gravel and looked up to see a tall man approaching. The fellow was wearing a red dressing-gown and matching slippers. His dark hair had retreated to the middle of his head and he sported large rimless glasses. Fitz walked towards him and the two shook hands.

As the men spoke in hushed tones, the boy slipped out of the car. The stars had disappeared again and fat drops of rain began splattering the driveway. Max quickly collected the packs from the back seat while the man in the dressing-gown retrieved their suitcases from the boot. Fitz swept Kensy into his arms and carried her through a stone portico to an open doorway.

'Are we home?' she murmured, burrowing into the man's broad chest.

'Yes, sweetheart,' he replied. 'We're home.'

Max felt a shiver run down his spine. He wondered why Fitz would lie. This wasn't their home at all.

The four of them entered the building into a dimly lit hallway. Without hesitation or instruction, Fitz turned and continued up a staircase to the right.

That's strange, Max thought. Fitz must have been here before.

'Please go ahead, Master Maxim,' the tall man said.

Too tired to ask how the fellow knew his name, Max did as he was bid. The hypnotic thudding of their luggage being carried up the stairs made the boy feel as if he was almost sleepwalking. They followed Fitz down a long corridor and eventually came to a bedroom furnished with two queen-sized beds and a fireplace. Max's skin tingled from the warmth of the crackling fire. He deposited the daypacks neatly by the door and shrugged off his jacket as the tall man set down their bags and drew the curtains.

'Sweet dreams, Kens,' Fitz whispered, tucking the girl under the covers.

Without any urging at all, Max climbed into the other bed. He had so many questions, but right now he couldn't muster a single word. The soft sheets and the thrum of driving rain against the window panes made it hard to resist the pull of sleep. He closed his eyes as Fitz and the tall man began talking. Max roused at the mention of his parents' names followed by something rather alarming – something that couldn't possibly be true. He tried hard to fight off the sandman to hear more, but seconds later Max too was fast asleep.